THE NIGHT STALKER

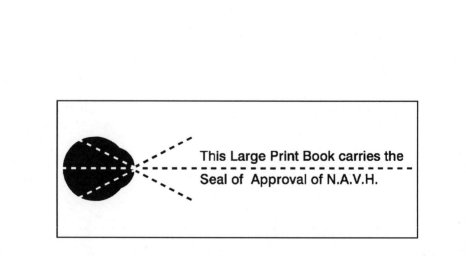

This Large Print Book carries the
Seal of Approval of N.A.V.H.

The Night Stalker

A NOVEL OF SUSPENSE

James Swain

THORNDIKE PRESS

A part of Gale, Cengage Learning

GALE
CENGAGE Learning

Detroit • New York • San Francisco • New Haven, Conn • Waterville, Maine • London

GALE
CENGAGE Learning™

LIBRARY OF CONGRESS CATALOGING-IN-PUBLICATION DATA

Swain, James.
    The night stalker : a novel of suspense / by James Swain.
        p. cm. — (Thorndike Press large print thriller)
    ISBN-13: 978-1-4104-1359-8 (alk. paper)
    ISBN-10: 1-4104-1359-4 (alk. paper)
    1. Serial murderers—Fiction. 2. Private investigators—Florida—Fiction. 3. Prisoners—Fiction. 4. Florida—Fiction. 5. Large type books. I. Title.
    PS3569.W225N54 2009
    813'.54—dc22   2008045173

Published in 2009 by arrangement with The Ballantine Publishing Group, a division of Random House, Inc.

Printed in the United States of America
1 2 3 4 5 6 7 13 12 11 10 09

For Laura

Just as a wise man keeps away from mad dogs, so one should not make friends with evil men.

— BUDDHA

■ ■ ■ ■

PART ONE:
A SHOT AT HEAVEN

■ ■ ■ ■

CHAPTER ONE

Noise was one of the few things that moved freely inside a prison.

The haunting echo of my own footsteps followed me down the long, windowless corridor inside the maximum security wing of Florida State Prison in Starke. I'd visited many prisons, and the smell was always the same: a choking mixture of piss, shit, fear, and desperation, wiped down by harsh antiseptics.

Walking through an electronically operated steel door, I was patted down by two stone-faced guards. Satisfied that I was not carrying weapons or contraband, they passed me off to a smirking inmate with a hideous purple birthmark on the side of his face. He took off at a brisk pace, and I followed him into the cellblock that housed death row inmates.

"What's your name?" I asked.

"Garvin," he replied, not breaking stride.

11

"What are you in for?"

"I shot up my family during Thanksgiving dinner."

I walked past the cells in death row with my eyes to the floor, feeling their occupants' presence like a fist pounding on my back. When we arrived at an empty cell, Garvin slid back the door, and stepped to one side. "Wait inside here," he said.

"What if no one comes?" I asked.

"Make some noise, and I'll come get you."

I entered the cell, a ten-by-ten concrete square with two wood benches anchored to the floor, and a small wood table. Garvin slammed the door behind me, making me jump. He chuckled as he walked away.

I took the bench nearest the door, and stuck a piece of gum into my mouth. I chewed so hard it made my jaw ache. I'd put scores of bad guys into Starke, and I didn't want to be here any longer than I had to.

I stared at the table. Inmates were not supposed to have anything sharp, but the table said otherwise. Names and dates and ugly epithets were carved into every inch of wood. One name stood out over the others.

Abb Grimes

I had been involved in Abb's case, and I knew his story. A Fort Lauderdale native, he'd quit high school at seventeen, done a stint in the navy, gotten married and had a kid, and gone to work driving a newspaper delivery truck — an ordinary guy, except that he liked to kill young women.

Abb's killings followed a pattern. Late at night, he left his house, and walked to the neighborhood grocery. There, he'd hidden behind the Dumpsters. When a young homeless woman would show up looking for food, he'd drag her into the woods, rape and strangle her, then stuff her body in a large garbage bag, tossing her into a Dumpster.

As mass murders went, it was nearly perfect. The victims were women no one cared about, and the bodies were disposed of for him. It might have gone on forever, only one night a surveillance camera filmed Abb with the body of a victim draped in his arms. As was his custom, the store manager viewed the tape the next morning. Seeing Abb, he called 911.

The police found the woman's body in the Dumpster. They got a search warrant for Abb's home and in his garage they found a cardboard box containing women's underpants. Each of the pairs was different.

Their next stop was the Pompano Beach landfill, where trash in Broward County was taken. Using earth movers and cadaver dogs, they'd moved several acres of trash, digging up the bodies of seventeen strangled women.

Eleven of the women were carrying ID. As head of the Broward County Sheriff's Department's Missing Persons unit, it had been my job to contact their families. It had been one of the hardest things I'd ever done.

The remaining six women were still Jane Does. I had hoped to identify them one day, and put their memories to rest. Only I'd lost my job after beating up a suspect, and never gotten it done.

It ate at me.

Hearing footsteps, I went to the cell door. Wearing leg irons and handcuffs and flanked by two guards, Abb shuffled down the hall. Tall and powerfully built, he had an angular jaw and dark, deeply set eyes. During his trial, the prosecution had called him "The Night Stalker," which had been a TV show that had lasted one season. It had scared the hell out of everyone who'd seen it. The nickname fit.

"Stand back," a guard ordered.

I retreated, and the three men entered. Abb dropped down on the opposing bench and looked at the floor, while the two guards remained standing.

An attractive brunette clutching a leather briefcase came in next. She was young and looked a little scared, and I found myself admiring her. It took guts for a woman to enter a prison filled with a thousand hardened criminals.

"I'm Piper Stone, Abb's attorney," she said.

"Jack Carpenter," I said.

"Thank you for coming."

We sat on the bench, and faced Abb. As strange as it sounded, he was my client, so I waited for him to start. Abb cleared his throat. He had a voice like gravel, and I guessed he didn't use it much.

"I'm going to die soon," Abb said. "Did my lawyer tell you that?"

"No, she didn't," I said.

"They're going to execute me in four days," Abb said. "Think you can find my grandson before then?"

Abb's grandson, three-year-old Sampson Grimes, had disappeared from his bedroom three nights ago. I'd read about it in the Fort Lauderdale newspapers, and knew that the police had been stymied in their efforts to locate him.

"I'm going to try," I said. "Now, why don't you tell me what happened."

"I get an hour each day to exercise in the

yard," Abb said. "Two days ago, a photo-graph of my grandson and a ransom note got slipped into my back pocket. I didn't see who did it."

"Do you still have the note and photo?" I asked.

"I gave them to Ms. Stone."

I looked at Stone. "I'd like to see them."

Stone unclasped her briefcase and handed me the items. The photo showed a tow-headed little boy with a face like the Gerber baby lying on a blanket. His clothes looked clean, as did his face and hands, and his eyes showed no sign of fear. I took these as a sign that his captor was not abusing him. Lying on the blanket was a copy of the *Fort Lauderdale Sun-Sentinel* with the date prominently displayed. It was a trick used by kidnappers to show that their victims were still alive.

I shifted my attention to the ransom note. Written in pencil, it said, *"Stop talking to the FBI or Sampson will die."* The handwriting surprised me. Most kidnappers used type-writers, or glued letters cut from a maga-zine. Whoever had kidnapped Sampson obviously didn't think he was going to get caught.

"What are you talking to the FBI about?" I asked.

"I'm in their VICAP program," Abb said. "I was supposed to go under hypnosis to help them identify those Jane Does. I still don't remember the things I did."

VICAP was the FBI's Violent Criminal Apprehension Program. Cops had an expression when criminals entered programs like VICAP, and agreed to help the police. They called it taking a shot at heaven.

"Does the FBI know you were contacted by your grandson's kidnapper?" I asked.

Abb shook his head.

"How about the police?" I asked.

Abb shook his head again.

"Why haven't you told them?"

"Because I want you to find him," Abb said.

"Why?" I asked.

"I've met six guys in Starke who are serving life for kidnapping little kids. You put them here. That's why."

I slipped the ransom note into my pocket.

"You're going to take the job?" Abb asked.

"Yes," I said.

"Good."

I stood and so did Stone. She went over and placed her hand on Abb's shoulder. Under her breath she said, "I'll call you tomorrow, and let you know how the appeals are going."

17

Abb gazed up at her and nodded.

One of the guards slid back the cell door. Stone and I started to leave. I saw Abb look directly at me. Something resembling hope flickered in his eyes. I decided to level with him.

"Your grandson's case is three days old," I said. "That's a long time when it comes to a kidnapping. I need to do a lot of ground-work, and talk to a lot of people."

"What are you trying to say?" Abb asked.

"I may not find Sampson before they execute you."

"Four days isn't enough?"

"I won't know until I start looking."

"I was hoping you —"

I cut him off. "I don't make promises."

"But —"

"That's the deal," I said.

Abb cast his eyes to the floor. He had asked me here because he did not want to go to his death knowing he'd caused an in-nocent child to suffer. I had to think it was one of the more decent things he'd done in his life.

"Okay," he muttered.

He was still staring at the floor when we left.

18

CHAPTER TWO

We walked back to the prison's main reception area. Stone had her personal items and cell phone returned, while I was given back my Colt 1908 Pocket Hammerless, which I slipped into the concealed holster in my pocket.

The parking lot was hot, the air still. Stone's sleek BMW sports car was parked beside my aging Acura Legend. From the glove compartment she removed my fee for finding Sampson, and had me sign a receipt for it.

"I'd like you to give me a progress report every day," she said.

"Of course," I said.

Stone made a call on her cell phone. I listened to her talk to another lawyer about filing an appeal asking the governor to halt Abb's execution. I didn't like lawyers, but I had to give her credit. She was going to fight until the bitter end. I said good-bye and she nodded.

I got into my car. I'd left the windows down, yet the interior was still warm. My dog, who was curled on the passenger seat, opened his eyes. He climbed into my lap, and we spent a few moments getting re-acquainted.

I've heard it said that bad things come in threes. The day I'd gotten thrown off the force, my wife walked out on me, and I'd gone to the Humane Society to find a new companion. I guess it said something about my luck that I'd come home with Buster, a chocolate Australian Shepherd who mis-trusted everyone but me and a few of my friends.

Buster was not an easy dog to be around. He had a temper, and some funny quirks. But he also had a nose like a bloodhound, and had saved my ass plenty of times on jobs. He was part of the team, and went where I did.

The two-lane road outside the prison was as straight as a shotgun blast. I pushed the Legend up to eighty, and kept it there. Taking the kidnapper's photo of Sampson Grimes from my pocket, I stuck it on the wheel, and stared at it as I drove.

I have spent much of my life looking for missing kids, and helping kids in trouble.

There's a reason for that. Back when my daughter, Jessie, was a little girl, a pervert exposed himself to her on the beach during a weekend outing. Luckily, I was able to rescue my daughter before the pervert did anything else.

What I remember most about that horrible day was my own fear. It replaced every other feeling in my body, and it flipped an invisible trigger inside my head that's never gone off. When I hear a baby crying, I run to the sound. When I happen upon a lost child in a mall or a parking lot, I help the child find her parents. And when I know that a kid needs help, I do everything in my power to help him. Sometimes that means breaking the rules and stepping on people's toes. I don't mean to cause trouble, but it happens. And like my dog, I don't see myself changing anytime soon.

I pulled into town. Although Starke was in north Florida, it was truly a Southern town, with a Wal-Mart-sized Baptist church on its main drag, and pickup trucks covered in NASCAR bumper stickers and Confederate flags. I drove around until I found a copy store, and went inside with my dog.

The owner was a possum-shaped man with straw-colored hair and blotchy skin —

21

what locals call a cracker. I asked if he had a computer that I could send an e-mail from, and a scanner.

"You came to the right place," the owner said.

He led me to the back room. His computer may have been the first one ever made, and was bigger than most TVs. He booted it up, and went into his Hotmail account. Then he showed me how to work the scanner, which sat on the desk beside it.

"I'd like to pay you for this," I said.

"Doesn't cost anything to send an e-mail," he replied. "That's a fine dog you've got. Does he hunt?"

"Just people," I said.

He smiled, thinking I was joking.

"I'll be out front if you need me," he said.

He walked out of the room. I sat down at the desk, and removed the kidnap photo and ransom note from my pocket. I placed both into the scanner, and scanned them into the computer. Then I composed a letter explaining how I'd come into their possession, and the things that Abb Grimes had told me.

When I was finished with my letter, I took out my cell phone, which, along with allowing me to take pictures and send e-mails, contained a memory bank of e-mail addresses important to me.

Opening the e-mail memory bank, I typed into the computer the e-mail address of every law enforcement agency in Florida that I worked with. This included the FBI, the Florida Department of Law Enforcement, the U.S. Marshals, and the National Center for Missing and Exploited Children. I also included Detective Ron Cheeks, who now ran the Broward County Sheriff's Department's Missing Persons unit. Rescuing kidnap victims wasn't easy, and I was going to need all the help I could get.

When I was done, I hit send, and everything on the computer screen disappeared. The store owner had been more than helpful, and I removed a ten-dollar bill from my wallet, and stuck it beneath the coffee cup on his desk.

I grabbed my dog, and went to the front of the store where the owner sat behind the counter reading a newspaper. I thanked him again.

"Come back anytime," he said.

Starke had every fast-food restaurant you could name. I bought two value meals at Burger King, and ate lunch with my dog. Buster had lousy table manners, but I put up with them. I didn't like eating alone.

We were splitting an oatmeal cookie when my cell phone rang. I pulled the phone off the Velcro patch on the dashboard hoping it was someone responding to my e-mail.

Caller ID said ANDY VITA. Vita was the Florida point man with the National Center for Missing and Exploited Children. I gave Buster the rest of my cookie, and answered the call.

"Carpenter here."

"Hey, Jack, it's Andy Vita. You busy?"

"Just finishing my lunch. What's up?"

"I just got off the phone with the principal of Oakwood Elementary School in Ocala. A four-year-old Honduran girl named Angelica Suarez disappeared from Oakwood this morning, and the cops are pulling their hair out trying to find her. The principal said you helped them with their abduction prevention program, and I was wondering if you remember the setup."

Back when I was a cop, I'd traveled around Florida and helped dozens of elementary schools establish procedures to protect them from child abductors.

"I remember Oakwood," I said. "It was tight as a drum."

"I think we're dealing with a pro," Vita said.

"Why do you think that?"

24

"Because the kid vanished without a trace. One minute she was sitting in the reception area of the principal's office, waiting to be assigned to a pre-kindergarten class, the next minute she's gone."

"She's new to the school?"

"Yeah. Mother brought her in at nine this morning. The kid doesn't speak any English, so the principal had to assign her to a teacher who was bilingual. The principal left the kid on a couch with a coloring book, and the kid disappeared."

"From the principal's office?"

"That's right."

"How long was she out of the principal's sight?"

"No more than a minute."

"If I remember correctly, the school had a full-time security guard. What's he saying?"

"He didn't see a thing."

"That's not good."

"It gets worse," Vita said. "The school doesn't even have a photograph of Angelica to use for an Amber Alert. We don't know anything about her except her name."

"Can't you get a photo from the mother?"

"The mother works as a chambermaid in one of the hotels. She gave the principal her number at work, only it's not right, so they're calling all the hotels, trying to track her down. I was wondering if you'd call the principal, and talk to her. Maybe she missed something."

I backed out of my spot in the Burger King lot with a squeal of rubber. The abduction prevention program I'd helped Oakwood establish included a photograph of every student along with their finger-prints. I didn't think it was a coincidence that the one child not in that database was now missing.

"How about I do it in person?" I said.

"Are you nearby?" Vita asked.

"I'm in Starke. Ocala is on my way home. I'll drive to the school, and see what's going on."

"Great. I'll call the principal and tell her you're coming. How soon can you be there?"

I needed to take Highway 301 to reach Ocala, and pass through three of the worst speed traps in the state. Vita had once run the Bureau of Alcohol, Tobacco, and Fire-arms, and still carried a lot of clout. I said, "That depends on what kind of police escort you can provide me."

Vita laughed under his breath.

"I'll see what I can do," he said.

CHAPTER THREE

I pulled into Oakwood Elementary's parking lot with my police escort in front of me. I'd made record time down 301, and wished I'd had a camera to record the faces of the different cops I'd passed on the way down. I leashed Buster and went inside.

In the lobby stood several nervous adults. With them was a small woman in her late forties wearing a black pants suit and a white brooch on her lapel. She introduced herself as Marge Heller, the school principal, and thanked me for coming. I smelled cigarettes on her breath and saw desperation in her eyes.

"Where are the local police?" I asked.

"Two deputies are in the back of the school, searching the grounds," Heller said. "The others are conducting a door-to-door search of the local neighborhood."

"They think the girl was taken off the property?" I said.

"Yes," Heller said.

Oakwood was a large school, and there were plenty of places within the building where a child could be hidden. The police shouldn't have left so quickly, but I saw no point in telling that to Heller or the others standing in the lobby.

"I need to speak with you in private," I said.

"Of course."

Heller led me down a hallway lined with classrooms. The school was locked down, meaning no children would be allowed to leave until Angelica Suarez was found. The classrooms were unusually quiet, and I wondered if the children knew that something was wrong.

We entered Heller's office. It had a waiting area, with a desk for a receptionist, a watercooler, and a pair of couches with matching blue cushions. Heller pointed at one of the couches. "That's where I left Angelica Suarez. I went into my office to call her new teacher. I wasn't gone more than sixty seconds. When I came back, the child was gone."

"Where was your receptionist?" I asked.

"Sally went to the cafeteria to get an orange juice for the child. I asked her to go."

"Your receptionist didn't see anything?"

"No. It happened when Sally was gone."

Her voice was trembling, and riddled with guilt. *If only I hadn't asked Sally to get that drink!* We went into Heller's office, which looked out upon a manicured ballfield behind the school. Heller sat down at her desk, while I remained standing. Her eyes fell upon my dog.

"He's beautiful," she said.

"Thank you."

"Does he help you find missing children?"

Hearing the hope in her voice, I nodded.

"I need to ask you some questions," I said.

"Of course."

"Is this the first time Angelica has been at the school?"

"Yes."

"What about her mother?"

"Her mother appeared in my office yesterday and told me she wanted to register her daughter for our pre-k program. I gave her the necessary forms to fill out, and told her to bring Angelica in this morning. This morning was the first time I actually saw the child."

I glanced at the wall beside her desk. It was covered with framed diplomas from various universities around the state. Heller was extremely well-educated, but none of her schooling had prepared her for this.

"I'm going to tell you what I think happened," I said. "It isn't pretty, but you need to hear it before we continue."

Heller placed her hands on her desk. "Go ahead."

"The person who abducted Angelica Suarez has been planning an abduction for a long time. He plans to sell Angelica to someone who's shopping for a little girl."

She put her hand over her mouth. "Oh, my Lord."

"I know this for several reasons," I said. "First, Angelica is a girl, and although I haven't seen a photo, I'm guessing she's pretty."

"She's a little angel," Heller said.

"Well, little angels fetch a lot of money, sometimes a hundred thousands dollars or more. They're prime targets for abductors."

Heller closed her eyes, then opened them.

"Second, Angelica doesn't speak English," I said. "That makes the abductor's job easier. If the child were to start screaming when she's out in public, most people won't understand what she's saying."

"A perfect victim," Heller said.

"That's right. The third factor is that Angelica is not in the school's abduction prevention computer database. She's new, and doesn't have a file."

"You think the abductor knew this?"

"Yes. Which leads me to my final conclusion. Someone on the inside, an employee of the school, was waiting for this kind of situation, and abducted this little girl."

Heller sat up in her chair like she'd been hit with a cattle prod. "But parents come into the school every day. Couldn't one of them have grabbed her?"

I shook my head.

"How can you know this for certain?"

"Your school has one entrance, and there's a security guard in a golf cart parked next to it," I said. "He would have seen them leave. One of your staff did this."

"Oh, God," she said.

"I'm guessing the girl was moved to an empty room inside the school, given a mild sedative, and then hidden."

"Hidden how?"

"She might be in a closet or a locker."

"But that's barbaric."

"The person who did this does not care about Angelica's well-being. He plans to sell her and collect his money."

"So you believe Angelica's still in the school."

"Yes. Once the police leave, her abductor will change Angelica's appearance, put her

31

into the trunk of his car, and go see the buyer."

Heller shut her eyes and took a deep breath. What I had just described to her was inconceivable. Adults did not do this to little children. I had to bring her back to earth, and I loudly cleared my throat. Her eyes snapped open.

"Is something wrong?" she asked.

"I'm not done," I said.

"I'm sorry."

"Who knew that Angelica was coming to school today?"

"Do you think one of them is responsible?"

"Please answer the question."

"Let me think. Her new teacher knew, and Sally, my receptionist. I also spoke to the school doctor, since all new children are required to have checkups."

"So four people knew," I said.

"That's only three," Heller said.

"I'm including you," I said.

Heller's mouth dropped open, but no words came out. An uncomfortable silence filled the office. I pointed at the phone on her desk.

"Please round up the other three," I said.

Heller called her receptionist, the school

doctor, and Angelica's new teacher, and asked them to meet us in the media room. Hanging up, she glared at me.

"Do you think that *I* might be implicated in this?" she asked indignantly.

"The four of you knew Angelica was coming to school today. That makes you all suspects until proven otherwise. It's how missing kids investigations work."

"Guilty until proven innocent."

"That's right."

"So I shouldn't take this personally."

I nodded. Heller stood up, and came around her desk. Her movements were brisk, and I could tell she was pissed off.

"After all," she said, "I'm the one who called the police."

I followed her into the hall. She shut the door behind her, took a key from her pocket, and locked it. Watching her, I noticed something that I hadn't seen before.

"You don't have a sign on your door," I said.

"I moved into the office last week. The sign's on order."

Heller started to walk down the hall. I remained behind, and stared at her blank door. She came back to where I stood.

"Are you coming?" she asked.

My mind was working hard now, seeing

33

what I hadn't seen before. I tore my eyes away from the door, and looked at her. "You said that Angelica's mother appeared in your office yesterday morning. How did she know where to find you?"

"Someone must have brought her to me."

"Any idea who?"

Heller shook her head.

I envisioned Angelica's mother coming to the school the day before, and getting lost. An employee had come to her aid, and escorted her to Heller's office. Along the way, they'd talked, and she'd talked about her daughter, while unwittingly passing along information — perhaps a nickname, or the name of a pet — that would let a stranger gain the child's confidence. That was why Angelica hadn't cried or kicked up a fuss when she'd left Heller's office.

"Where would she have parked?" I asked.

"In the visitor's lot in front," Heller said.

"Is that the only place?"

"Yes."

I thought about the security guard sitting outside in the golf cart. He would have seen Angelica's mother yesterday, and, hopefully, the employee who had befriended her.

"I'll be back in a minute," I said.

CHAPTER FOUR

Every public school in Florida employed a security guard. Oakwood's guard was a guy in his twenties with a bodybuilder's physique and a pistol strapped to his waist. His nametag said Ed Edwards.

Most security guards were guys who couldn't pass the test to become cops. Edwards was sucking on a Coke, and appeared overly caffeinated. I introduced myself, and told him I was looking for Angelica Suarez. I asked him if he minded answering a few questions.

"Not at all," he said. "Have a seat."

I slid into the empty seat of his golf cart. Buster hopped into the back, expecting a ride. It was funny, only Edwards didn't smile. If we didn't find Angelica Suarez, he would probably lose his job.

"Yesterday morning, Angelica Suarez's mother came to school to register her daughter," I said. "Someone helped her find the principal's office. I was wondering if you happened to see who helped her."

Edwards's eyes glazed over as he plumbed his memory. "Come to mention it, I did. She parked over by the fence. She looked confused, and started talking to a maintenance guy cutting the grass."

"Did he take her inside?"

"I'm not sure. I got pulled inside for a minute. When I came back out, she was gone, and so was the maintenance man, only his mower was still there."

"Had he finished cutting the grass?"

"I don't think so. There was a patch still left."

"What's his name?"

"Ray Hicks."

"Can you describe him for me?"

"Sure. Ray's my age, pretty tall, but out of shape. Tends to keep to himself. The first time I met him, he made my skin crawl. I called my brother who's a cop over in Jacksonville, and he had a records check pulled on him. Hicks was clean."

"But he bothered you?"

"Yeah."

Intuition was the messenger of fear. Edwards's intuition had told him that Ray Hicks was a bad character, even if there was no evidence to prove it. I thanked him for his help and went back inside.

The media room was directly off the main entrance, and was filled with computers, DVD players, and other electronic equipment that kids needed to learn how to use so they could teach their parents. I found Heller and three other people, who I assumed were the teacher, the receptionist, and the school doctor, sitting at a rectangular table in the room's center. I pulled Heller off to the side.

"What can you tell me about a maintenance man named Ray Hicks?" I asked.

"Do you think he's the one?" Heller asked.

"He's in the running."

"Ray works part-time cutting the grass and pruning. He's never been a problem, although I've caught him lurking around the halls a few times. I guess you could say he's a bit strange."

"Is there a reason you didn't mention him before?"

"All the maintenance men are strange."

"Does he have a place where he stores his things?"

"He has a locker."

"I'd like to see it."

Heller took me to the maintenance men's locker room, which was adjacent to the school cafeteria. Each locker had a piece of masking tape with its occupant's name printed on it. Hicks's locker was at the end of the row, and was padlocked.

"Is this locker school property?" I asked.

"Everything on the grounds is school property," she replied.

"We need to cut away this padlock. Where can I find some clippers?"

Heller led me to the tool room. Sixty seconds later, I cut away the padlock on Hicks's locker with a pair of steel clippers, and had a look inside. The locker contained a pair of work shoes, a change of clothes, and a can of Old Spice aftershave. Tucked in the back was a three-ring binder. I flipped through its pages, and found myself reading a series of e-mails between Hicks and someone who called himself Teen Angel. The e-mails discussed how to abduct a child from a public place, and included tips on how to gain the child's trust, and deal with things like temper tantrums and crying fits. I found myself shaking my head. Teen Angel had tutored Hicks over the Internet.

I came to the last e-mail in the binder. It was dated only a few short days ago. Teen Angel had wished Hicks good luck, and given him some parting advice. It read, *Remember, TWO HOURS MAX!*

I knew what that meant. Two hours was

the maximum amount of time that most abductors wanted to keep a child before turning them over to a buyer.

"How long has Angelica been gone?" I asked.

Heller looked at her watch. "One hour and fifty minutes."

We were running out of time. I tried to put myself in Hicks's shoes. This was the first time he'd done this. My guess was, he'd taken Angelica to a place where he felt safe.

"Where do the maintenance men hang out?" I asked.

"They have a shed behind the gymnasium," Heller said.

"Show me."

Heller led me outside behind the school, and pointed at a prefabricated shed nestled behind the gymnasium.

"For what it's worth, the police searched the shed earlier," she said.

Not very well, I nearly said.

"Call the police and tell them to get over here," I said.

With Buster by my side, I ran to the shed. The dog had tuned into my apprehension, and his hackles stood straight up. The shed had a single window, and I cleaned the glass with my fingers, and peered inside.

A lanky guy wearing a green uniform

covered in grass stains stood inside the shed. He had a pair of scissors in his hand, and he was giving a radiant, dark-skinned little girl sitting in a chair a haircut. The girl held a box of Milk Duds, and was squirming uncomfortably. I had found Ray Hicks and Angelica Suarez.

"Sit still," Hicks said in broken Spanish.

"I don't want my hair cut," Angelica replied in Spanish.

"Eat some more candy, and shut up," he said.

"I don't want candy," she said.

Angelica threw down the box of candy, and started to cry. Hicks looked nervously around the shed, then violently clamped his hand over her mouth.

"Shut up!" he said.

Drawing my gun, I found the door to the shed, and kicked it three inches above the knob. It came down, and I rushed inside. Buster flew past me, and went straight for Hicks's legs.

"Let her go," I said.

Hicks pulled Angelica out of her chair, and held the scissors against her throat. My dog had latched onto his pants, and was tearing the fabric.

"Get your dog off me," Hicks said.

I yelled to Buster, and he let Hicks go. He

came back to my side with a piece of pants in his mouth.

"You a cop?" Hicks asked.

I shook my head.

"Her daddy?"

My grandfather was a Seminole Indian, and my skin was dark enough to make me look Hispanic. I nodded.

"Okay, Daddy, here's the deal," Hicks said. "I want you to put your gun on the floor, and kick it over to me. If you don't, I'll slit her throat."

"Only if you promise to release her," I said.

Hicks dipped his chin. I took that as a yes, and I laid my Colt onto the concrete floor, and kicked it to him. Hicks knelt down and picked up my gun.

"How many bullets this thing got?" he asked.

"Seven," I replied.

"What kind?"

"Three-eighties."

"That should get us out of here," he said.

Hicks let Angelica go. For a moment, the little girl acted confused, and did not know what to do. I spoke to her in Spanish, and told her everything was going to be all right. She ran over to me, and I held her against my legs.

"You got a car?" Hicks asked.

"Yes," I said.

"We're going to take a ride. I've got a duffel bag over there. I want you to put your daughter in it, and carry her to your car. I'll follow you."

"Okay," I said.

"Pull any tricks and I'll shoot both of you."

"No tricks," I promised.

"You learn fast."

I saw movement in the window behind Hicks's head. Edwards the security guard was aiming his pistol through the glass at Hicks's back. He waved for me to get down. I grabbed Angelica and hit the floor.

The gunshot sounded like a cannon going off inside the enclosed space. Hicks lurched forward. A bloody hole the size of my fist appeared in the center of his chest. He touched it with his fingers, and stared at his own blood.

"Shit," he said.

Everyone dies differently. Hicks went down slowly, like he was sinking into the earth. We made eye contact, and I saw something resembling remorse cross his face. I only moved when I was sure he was dead, and that we were out of danger.

I carried Angelica outside into the blinding sunshine. She was crying, and I kissed the top of her head. This was the reward for the work I did, and it never got old.

Heller ran across the field toward me. One of her shoes flew off, then the other. That didn't slow her down. I passed Angelica to her, and she clutched the child to her bosom like she was her own.

"It's over," I said.

I went back inside the shed. Buster had parked himself next to Hicks, and was snapping at the flies buzzing around him. The security guard stood next to my dog, his face wet with fear.

"Is he dead?" the security guard asked.

I said yes, and pointed at the smoking pistol in his hand.

"I hope you have a license for that thing," I said.

CHAPTER FIVE

I stayed in Ocala long enough to give my statement to the police. Then I got onto 1-75, headed south to the Florida Turnpike, and went home.

I lived in Dania, a sleepy town south of Fort Lauderdale known for its dusty consignment shops that sold the world's best junk. It was pitch dark by the time I reached its deserted streets.

I drove east down Dania Beach Boulevard, then hung a left onto an unmarked road known only to locals. A minute later I pulled into Tugboat Louie's crowded parking lot. Loud music blared out of the speakers on the side of the building, and I tapped out the rhythm to the Rolling Stones' "Can't You Hear Me Knocking?" on my steering wheel.

Louie's was my idea of heaven. It had a good-time bar, dockside dining on a wide canal, and a small marina. It was also where

I kept my office. I wanted to see if anyone had written an e-mail back about Sampson Grimes, and I went inside.

Louie's owner — a hardworking Indian named Kumar — sat on a stool by the front door. Kumar came to work each day wearing black slacks, a white Egyptian cotton shirt, and an oversized black bow tie. Years ago I'd done him a favor, which he seemed intent on forever repaying.

"Jack, Jack, how are you?" Kumar asked.

"I'm fine. How about you?"

"Wonderful, fantastic, I can't complain. How is your dog?"

"He's chewing 'em up."

"Glad to hear it. Listen, there is a man here waiting to see you. I have to assume he's a policeman because he won't drink any liquor, just coffee. He's very unfriendly and keeps looking suspiciously around the room. He's making everyone very uncomfortable."

"Did he give you his name?"

"No."

I glanced into the bar. It was jumping the way only a Fort Lauderdale bar can: the music was deafening, the booze was flowing, and women were dancing in the aisles and on tabletops while letting their inhibitions fly out the door. I spotted Detective

45

Ron Cheeks sitting in the back, wearing a dark suit and shades, the proverbial turd in the punch bowl. I caught his eye, and waved. Within moments, Cheeks was on top of me.

"You and I need to talk," Cheeks said.

"Sure," I said. "Can I buy you a burger?"

"In private."

"It must be important," I said.

"Life-altering," he said.

I unhooked a chain to the stairwell, and we marched upstairs. Cheeks was your typical belligerent white male. Mid-forties, divorced, his head anchored on a dinner roll of a neck, his droopy handlebar mustache giving his face a permanent frown. He had taken over the Missing Persons unit after I'd left the sheriff's department. I didn't resent him for that, just the fact that he rarely gave me any jobs.

The second floor housed two offices: mine and Kumar's. My office was long and narrow, and contained a desk with a computer, two folding chairs, and a spectacular view of the canal. As I entered, Buster trotted to the corner and curled into a ball.

"You should get rid of that dog," Cheeks said.

"What's wrong with my dog?"

"He bites people."

46

"Only bad people."

"He's the anti-Lassie." Cheeks dropped into a chair and undid the knot in his necktie. He was wheezing from the climb, and took a moment to catch his breath. "If you were smart, you'd have him put to sleep."

"You need to get in shape," I said.

"Round is a shape."

I leaned against my desk, and waited him out.

"I got your e-mail about Sampson Grimes," Cheeks said. "I want to see what Abb gave you at the prison."

I handed Cheeks the kidnapper's photograph and ransom note. The detective removed his shades and gave them a cursory glance. His eyes were watery, ringed from lack of sleep. He stuffed both items into his jacket pocket.

"I know who kidnapped Sampson Grimes," he said.

"You do?" I asked.

"It was the kid's father, Jed Grimes. Unfortunately, I can't prove it."

"How can you be certain?"

Cheeks held up his outstretched hand, touching each of his fingers as he spoke. "Jed Grimes was the last person to see Sampson. Jed failed a polygraph test. Jed's fighting with the kid's mother over custody rights. Jed has a long history with the police. Is that enough circumstantial evidence for you?"

"Not really," I said. In most cases, that would have been enough to convince me. Only this situation was different. Abb Grimes had received a ransom note in which the kidnapper was threatening to kill the boy. It was far too important a lead to be swept under the rug.

"Look, Jack, I'm going to stop beating around the bush. I want you to drop this case. The last thing I need right now is you running around town, stirring up the pot. Jed Grimes is guilty. It's just going to take me awhile to prove it."

I bit my tongue in anger. I didn't care about Jed, just the boy.

"What about Sampson?" I asked.

"What about him?"

"He's been gone three days. We need to find him."

"We'll find him eventually."

"You're sure about that?"

"I'd bet my reputation on it."

I nearly laughed in his face. Years ago, Cheeks had fallen asleep on his desk, and woken up with the word *Homicide* printed backward on his forehead, the words picked up off an internal report. He'd walked around for hours without knowing it. He didn't have a reputation, at least not one worth betting on.

"I'm not dropping the case," I said.

"You're making a mistake."

I shrugged.

Cheeks retied the knot in his tie. "Okay, then I'm going to set some ground rules. One, no leaks to the press. Anything you learn, I hear about first. Two, no withholding information. If you find something out and don't tell me, I'll kill you. Three, no talking to suspects or visiting the crime scene without my permission. Four, no grand-standing. If you locate the kid, I don't want you rescuing him. That's my responsibility. You can stay in the shadows and collect your money. Understand?"

"Loud and clear."

Cheeks stood up, and put his shades back on. We'd been friends once, or so I'd thought. The man standing in front of me now was not my friend.

"You and I go back a long way, so I'm going to give you some advice," Cheeks said. "Drop this case, or it will be your last."

I had been threatened before, but never by a cop. The words carried a lot more menace coming out of Cheeks's mouth than

I would have liked.

"Sure I can't buy you a burger?" I asked.

"I'll ruin you," he said.

"They're really good. I'll even throw in a beer."

"You're not funny, Jack."

"How about some dessert? The chocolate cake is to die for."

Cheeks went to the door and jerked it open.

"Think it over," he said.

"I'll definitely do that," I said.

He gave me a parting look, then shook his head. I listened to his feet pound the stairs on the way down.

CHAPTER SIX

I sat at my desk and stared into space. Music from downstairs was making the whole building shake. I tuned it out and tried to think.

Before I'd left the police department, I'd written a turnover report. No one had asked me to, and it wasn't part of my job description, but I'd written one up anyway. It had been a hundred and fifteen pages long.

This turnover report contained every open missing persons case in Broward County, some dating back to my first day on the job. It included the case of a fourteen-year-old girl who'd gone into a department store and disappeared, and another about an elderly man suffering from dementia walking out of a nursing home, and never being seen again. If Cheeks had bothered to read any of what I'd written, he would have known that I had continued chasing leads on those cases long after they'd gone cold. Call it an obsession, but I'd refused to file them away.

I *never* quit a case.

My unwillingness to give up had defined my career as a detective, and later on, it had cost me my job and ruined my marriage. It was both my good side and my bad side, and I was past apologizing for it. Cheeks should have known better than to ask me to drop Sampson Grimes's case.

I booted up my computer. I had read about the Sampson Grimes case in the newspaper, but the news reports on the Internet tended to have more information than the paper did, and I now pored through them.

There were six different stories posted about Sampson's kidnapping. Each had been filed within twenty-four hours of the boy having gone missing. Reading them, I saw an unusual similarity. From the start of the case, the police had considered Jed Grimes their primary suspect, and had focused their investigation on him. Cheeks was quoted in two of the articles as saying that a break in the case was imminent.

I do my best thinking on my feet. I went to the window and parted the blinds. A conga line of drunken revelers had spilled from the bar and was winding its way down to the marina. I thought I knew what was going on. Cheeks didn't like Jed Grimes and had decided that he was guilty. As a result, Cheeks had not conducted a thorough investigation. Cops called this personalizing a case. It was the surest way to screw up an investigation that I knew of.

I needed to look at the crime scene. Unlike Cheeks, I wasn't wearing blinders, and I had a suspicion I might see things that Cheeks had missed. Cheeks had warned me not to go there, but I was going to ignore him.

I pulled the phone book out of my desk, and found Jed Grimes's address. He lived in Davie, about a twenty-minute drive. I clapped my hands, and Buster lifted his head.

"Let's go for a car ride," I said.

I got on 595 and headed west. Tourist season was in full swing, and the line of cars' headlights stretched in both directions as far as my eyes could see.

Fifteen minutes later, I exited into a middle-class neighborhood sandwiched between Davie and Cooper City, and found myself staring at poorly lit street signs as I searched for Jed Grimes's address. I had once known these streets like the back of my hand. Rampant development had changed that, and blurred the lines between where neighborhoods began and ended.

Five blocks later the scenery changed, and the streets turned mean. The houses were now made of cinder block, and many had iron security bars on their windows. Cars filled with angry young men roamed the streets, looking for trouble. Buster sat at stiff attention beside me, his lip turned up in a snarl.

Jed Grimes's street appeared in my headlights. It was called RichJo Lane, and was lined with falling-down bungalows built during the middle of the last century. I parked in front of a bungalow with yellow police tape surrounding the perimeter. Printed on the mailbox in black Magic Marker was the word *Grimes.*

I took a look around before getting out of my car. It was a rough-looking area. Had I still been a cop, I might have called for backup. I glanced at my dog.

"It's just you and me, pal," I told him.

Buster pawed his seat. He was ready to go. I liked that in a partner. I grabbed a flashlight from the glove compartment and opened my door. My dog climbed over me, and ran to the bushes surrounding Jed Grimes's house.

I got out of my car and stood on the

sidewalk. Jed's place was dark, and I shined my flashlight at it. Shingles were missing from the roof, the paint peeling like a bad sunburn. The carport was empty, and no one appeared to be at home.

I started to climb over the police tape. The articles I'd read on the Internet had said that Sampson had been abducted from his bedroom in the rear of the house. Stealing kids from their bedrooms was tricky, and I wanted to see how the kidnapper had pulled it off.

Hearing a woman's voice, I stopped what I was doing. Trespassing on a crime scene was a crime, and I didn't want to get caught in the act.

I looked up and down RichJo Lane, then heard the voice again. It had come from a white trailer parked on the street. I hadn't paid much attention to the trailer, thinking it belonged to a neighbor. Now I took a closer look.

It was the Broward County Sheriff's Department's Operations Center trailer, or what cops called the OC. When kids were abducted, the police parked the OC near the home, and conducted their investigation from it. This allowed the police to be near the crime scene, while giving the child's family some privacy.

A door on the trailer opened, and a young woman came outside and shut the door behind her. She was no more than twenty feet away from me, and stood beneath a streetlight. She started to cross the street, then halted, and looked directly at me.

"Mr. Carpenter? Is that you?"

She was a long-stemmed beauty with slender features and deeply troubled eyes. I couldn't place her, and I stepped forward to get a better look at her.

"Excuse me, but who are you?" I asked.

"Heather Rinker. I played basketball with your daughter in junior high school. You used to drive us to games."

Shock was the best word to describe my reaction. The last time I'd seen Heather, she'd been a skinny little girl in pigtails, and hardly resembled the stunning woman standing before me. I said, "It's been a long time. What are you doing here?"

"I was talking to the detective inside the trailer."

"About what?"

"You don't know?"

I shook my head.

"Sampson Grimes is my son."

I didn't know what to say. I put my hand on her shoulder. As a cop, I couldn't do that, but I wasn't a cop anymore.

"I'm sorry, Heather," I said.

Her eyes welled with tears, and she wiped them away. "I spoke to Jed earlier. He told me that his father's attorney hired you to find Sampson."

"That's right," I said.

"That's what you do, isn't it? You find missing kids."

I nodded. I sensed that Heather was dying inside, but I had to press her. "I need for you to tell me what happened to your son."

"Right now?"

"Now's a good time."

She took a deep breath. "Jed and I got divorced after Sampson was born, and I've been raising him myself. Last year Jed decided he wanted to help raise Sampson, and he sued me for custody rights. The judge said okay, and Sampson's been staying with Jed on weekends.

"It was going okay until this past Saturday. I was working, and Jed called me, and said that someone had come into his house through a window, and taken Sampson from his bedroom. Jed was freaking out, and didn't know what to do."

"Was anyone home when this happened?" I asked.

"Jed was, and his friend Ronnie."

"They didn't hear anything?"

Heather shook her head.

"What happened then?" I asked.

"I left work and raced over here. Jed and Ronnie were running around the neighborhood, looking for Sampson, and I joined in. We talked to all the neighbors. Nobody heard my son cry, or saw a car pull away. It was like . . ."

Her voice trailed off, and I touched her sleeve.

"Like what?" I asked.

"It was like Sampson disappeared off the face of the earth."

The memory was tearing her apart, and she covered her face with her hands. If I'd learned anything looking for missing kids, it was that children stolen from their bedrooms did not go quietly. They screamed and kicked and sometimes even bit their abductors. Something was not right with her story.

"I need to ask you a question," I said.

Heather lowered her hands.

"The detective handling the investigation thinks Jed did this," I said.

"He's wrong," Heather said.

"You're sure about that."

Heather nodded. "Jed had a rough time growing up. But he's changed. He was trying to do right by Sampson. He wouldn't do this to him. Or to me."

"Where is he?"

"Jed's staying at his mom's place. So am I. The police wanted us nearby, and I just couldn't stay here."

"Are you two back together?"

Heather smiled faintly. "We're trying."

I walked Heather to her car. She drove an aging Toyota Camry with a baby seat strapped in the backseat, and bumper stickers with Sampson's photograph and the word *MISSING!* plastered to the front and back bumpers of her car.

"I'd like a bumper sticker for my car," I said.

Heather opened the trunk. It contained a cardboard box filled with bumper stickers, and signs with Sampson's photo and a number to call that could be stuck in people's yards. She pulled a bumper sticker and a DVD from the box, and stuck them into my hands.

"I recorded this DVD at Sampson's third birthday party," she said. "I took it around to the TV stations, and asked them to show it on the news."

"That was very smart of you," I said.

I opened the driver's door for her. Heather started to climb in, then paused to look at me with her sad eyes. "Please find my baby,

Mr. Carpenter. I can't live without him."

I never made promises when I was looking for missing kids. They only filled people with false hope, and that was not the business I was in.

"I'll try, Heather."

She nodded woodenly, and left without saying good-bye.

CHAPTER SEVEN

Heather's taillights hung like an afterimage in the darkness. I stuck the bumper sticker to the trunk of my car, and tossed the DVD onto the passenger seat. Then I clapped my hands for my dog. Buster exploded out of the bushes around Jed's house.

"Time to go to work," I said.

I started to climb over the police tape, and glanced at the OC trailer. Normally, I would have told the detectives inside the trailer that I was here. But Cheek's threat had changed my mind. I wasn't going to talk to anyone with the sheriff's department unless it was absolutely necessary.

I walked around the side of Jed's house to the backyard. The backyard was like most in Broward County, and the size of a post-age stamp. Kids' toys were scattered around, including an expensive-looking tricycle and a plastic swimming pool. Jed had obviously indulged his son.

I shined my flashlight at the house. Three windows on the house faced the backyard, all of them screened. The screen on the corner window looked damaged, and was flapping in the breeze. I approached for a closer look.

The screen had been sliced horizontally, the cut about three feet wide. I shined my flashlight through the window, and found myself looking at Sampson's bedroom. A Spiderman mobile hung from the ceiling, and the walls were papered in cartoon characters. Like the backyard, there were toys everywhere. Throughout the room I could see traces of white powder from where a police technician had dusted for fingerprints.

I found the bed with my flashlight. It was built to resemble a miniature race car. The bed was unmade, and the impression of Sampson's body was still in the sheets.

A tiny light beside the bed caught my eye. It was faint, and difficult to see. I shut off my flashlight, and tried to determine what it was.

I realized it was a night-light. Then I saw the second one by the door. A lot of children slept with night-lights, but two was unusual.
Sampson was afraid of the dark.
That bothered me. Most children who

were afraid of the dark were also light sleepers. I wondered how Sampson's kidnapper had entered his bedroom without the boy hearing him, and yelling for help.

I was missing something. I stepped back, and started over.

The damaged screen: I had assumed that the kidnapper had popped it out, and stolen into Sampson's bedroom. But I didn't know that for a fact. I decided to see how difficult it would be, and I put my hands through the slice, and attempted to remove the screen. It refused to budge.

"What the hell," I said under my breath.

I inspected the screen's metal frame with my flashlight. It was held down by four screws covered in rust. This screen hadn't been removed for a long time.

I stepped back into the yard. The kidnapper hadn't gone into the bedroom. The boy had come to him and climbed through the slit. That was why no one had heard him leave. The boy had been an accomplice in his own kidnapping.

I turned off my flashlight. There was a picnic table in the backyard. I sat down on one of the benches. I had dealt with hundreds of child abductions and never encountered anything like this.

Little kids who were afraid of the dark didn't climb through windows at night, even if someone they knew was coaxing them. It was too scary. Yet that was exactly what Sampson had done. Whoever had stolen the boy had worked some special magic on him.

I looked around the yard. I had no witnesses to talk to, no clues to work with. Unless some piece of evidence fell out of the sky, I was in trouble.

Buster ran around in circles, sniffing the ground. It gave me an idea. If I could determine the escape route the kidnapper had taken, it might lead to new evidence like a tire track or a witness. I knew the police had already done this, but I would try it again.

I turned my flashlight back on. The fenced backyard had a small gate at the rear. I went to the gate and unlatched it.

The gate led onto a deeply rutted alley. One end of the alley was a dead end, the other end led to the street. I envisioned Sampson's kidnapper going that way during his escape.

Buster appeared by my side. I leashed him, and walked to the street. As I stepped out of the alley, I was bathed in bright streetlight. Cars were parked by the curb, and a dozen pedestrians lingered on the

64

sidewalk. It looked like a gathering spot.

I approached an older couple. They said hello, and inquired about my dog.

"He's an Australian Shepherd," I said.

"He's very unusual looking," the wife said.

"Do you walk here often?"

"Every night," the husband replied.

"Is it always this busy?"

"Usually," she said.

"Were you here three nights ago?"

"Is that when the little boy was kidnapped?" the husband asked.

"Yes."

"We were here," she said. "But like we told the police, we didn't see a thing."

The couple said good night. I walked back to Jed's house feeling stymied. People didn't vanish into thin air. How had Sampson's kidnapper gotten the boy away without being seen?

I came to Jed's property and halted. I hadn't paid much attention to the property directly across the alley from Jed's because it was so well-fortified. Now I gave it a closer look.

The property was several acres in size. There was no house, just an orange grove filled with ripening trees. The grove looked too small to turn a profit, and I guessed it was being maintained to give the owners a tax break.

The grove was surrounded by a seven-foot chain-link fence, with razor wire running across the top. I ran my flashlight over the chain link and looked for an opening. There wasn't one. Another dead end. I started to leave, but Buster remained by the fence, pawing feverishly at the ground. He wanted to go through. I knelt beside him.

"Is that where they went, boy? In there?"

His tail wagged furiously, and his tongue hung out of his mouth. Of course they did, you idiot, he seemed to be saying. I put my hands on the chain link and pushed. To my surprise, it gave several inches. Someone had tampered with it.

I ran my flashlight up the metal poles the fence was attached to. On the pole to my right, a piece of wire caught my eye.

I pressed my face to the pole. So did my dog.

It was a twist tie, attached to the pole at waist height. There was another at the bottom, a third near the top. The twist ties held the fence together, which had been cut the length of the pole. It was a masterful job, right down to the ends being snipped to avoid detection.

I have carried a pocketknife since I was a kid. Pulling it out, I cut away the twist ties, and started to pull back the fence. I stopped myself. The grove was part of the crime scene, and had not yet been searched by the police. I needed to alert Cheeks, and tell him what I'd found. If I didn't, he could have me arrested for tampering with evidence.

I took out my cell phone, and dialed the sheriff's department's main number. The call went through, and an operator picked up.

"Broward County Sheriff's Department."

I killed the call.

Cheeks had botched this investigation from the start. He had locked onto Jed Grimes, and had refused to broaden his investigation. As a result, Sampson had spent three days with his kidnapper when he might have been safely at home with his mother.

I slipped my cell phone into my pocket. I needed to search the grove and draw my own conclusions. *Then* I'd call Cheeks and tell him what I'd found.

And not a moment before.

CHAPTER EIGHT

Leashing my dog, I pulled back the cut fence and entered the grove.

The trees had been planted in rows approximately fifteen feet apart. I shined my flashlight on the ground covered in sugar sand. Two sets of footprints appeared before my eyes. One belonged to a man, the other to a small, barefoot boy. I followed the footprints into the grove, careful not to disturb them.

I heard rustling. There were animals nesting in those trees, snakes and raccoons and birds. I imagined the sounds scaring the daylights out of Sampson three nights ago, and I wondered what his kidnapper had said to keep him quiet. Maybe he'd told Sampson to cover his ears, or perhaps he'd briefly picked the boy up in his arms.

Fifty feet into the grove, I came to a clearing. Orange trees have a short life span, and the clearing was filled with dead trees, their brittle trunks piled up to be burned. Buster stiffened by my leg, and began to whine.

"What's wrong, boy?"

Then I smelled it. Strong, like a skunk.

Something dead.

I let my flashlight roam. In the center of the clearing was a campfire ringed with blackened stones, in its center several empty cans. Next to the campfire, a sleeping bag lay on the ground, behind it a shopping cart filled with old clothes and plastic bags.

A vagrant had set up house in the grove. Perhaps he'd done it on the sly. Maybe he had an agreement with the grove's owner to keep the orange trees maintained in exchange for squatter's rights. That wasn't uncommon.

Buster continued to whine, and I made him lie down. Then I heard something that I hadn't heard before: a sharp buzzing sound, like an electric saw.

Flies.

I found the swarm with my flashlight. Several hundred hovered around a tree on the other side of the clearing, their fluttering wings making them look almost supernatural in the darkness.

I searched the tree with my flashlight's beam. A pair of brown men's shoes were the first thing I saw, toes pointed straight down. They were a homeless person's shoes, and were falling apart.

I slowly lifted the flashlight's beam. Their owner was still in them. My flashlight settled on his face, and I heard myself gasp.

I have seen the dead more times than is healthy. What I saw hanging from the branches was shocking even to my jaded sensibilities: a white male, no more than five-two, dressed in tattered blue jeans and a torn flannel shirt, his wrists tied to the branches so he appeared to be crucified. His skull had been smashed with a blunt instrument, his face so lopsided that it looked melted. He had been dead for several days; whatever spirit had inhabited his body was long gone.

I drew several deep breaths, then moved closer. Lying on the ground beneath the dead man's feet was a cheap plastic wallet. I tore a branch off a tree, and used the branch to flip the wallet open. It contained a few wrinkled dollar bills, and a welfare card. His name was Clifford Gaylord.

I tried to imagine what had happened. Sampson's kidnapper had come into the grove three nights ago, and happened upon Gaylord. Not wanting a witness, he'd knocked Gaylord unconscious and tied him to a tree. Then he'd murdered him.

It made sense, only there were holes. Tying Gaylord would have taken both hands, as would killing him. That would have forced the kidnapper to put Sampson down. He might have tied Sampson to a tree to keep him from running away, or simply put him nearby, where he could keep an eye on the boy.

I searched the ground with my flashlight to see if I was correct. On the other side of the clearing, I found the impression of Sampson's body in the sugar sand. It was beneath a tree, and faced away from where Gaylord had died.

Buster pawed at a spot next to the boy's impression. I started to pull him away, then saw something appear in the sand. It was a small cardboard box.

"Good boy," I said.

I grabbed the box's lid, and gently pulled it free. It was an empty candy box, covered with ants. Flipping it over, I stared at the label.

Milk Duds.

An alarm went off inside my head. Angelica Suarez had been eating Milk Duds when I'd rescued her from Ray Hicks. It could have been a coincidence, only I didn't believe in those. I left the box in the sand where I'd found it, and dragged my dog into

71

the clearing. The moon had crept out from behind the clouds, and I shut off my flashlight.

I thought about the three-ring binder I'd found in Ray Hicks's locker. Hicks had been corresponding on the Internet with someone who called himself Teen Angel. Teen Angel had helped Hicks abduct Angelica Suarez, and Hicks had nearly succeeded. Teen Angel knew what he was doing.

I compared that case to this one. Sampson's kidnapper had covered his tracks as well as Ray Hicks had. He'd taken Sampson from his bedroom, and had fooled the police so badly that they were pointing the finger at the boy's father. He'd also used Milk Duds to keep the boy quiet, just as Ray Hicks had.

The cases were connected. Teen Angel had helped Ray Hicks, and I was willing to bet money he'd helped Sampson's kidnapper as well.

Teen Angel was the link, and I needed to find him.

I called the sheriff's department's main number, and identified myself to the operator. I asked her to call Ron Cheeks, and have him call me.

"It's an emergency," I said.

Cheeks called me back a minute later.

"What do you want?" he asked.

"I'm across the alley from Jed Grimes's house," I said.

"Goddamn it, Carpenter, I told you not to go there!"

I looked at Clifford Gaylord hanging dead in the orange tree. I didn't know what his story was, but I felt certain that he deserved a better ending than the one he'd gotten. Had I not happened along, he might have hung there for a long time.

"You missed something," I said.

Cheeks appeared in the grove fifteen minutes later looking like he'd just rolled out of bed. Clutched in his hand was a large Mag-Lite. I showed him Gaylord's body, and explained what had happened. He pointed across the clearing.

"Stand over there, and tie your dog to a tree," Cheeks said.

I went to the spot, and wrapped Buster's leash around the base of a tree. I watched Cheeks inspect the crime scene. Gaylord's ravaged corpse had a similar effect on him, and Cheeks crossed himself. When he was done, Cheeks came over to me.

"I should throw your ass in jail, but I'm going to give you a break," Cheeks said. "Get out of here, and don't stick your nose in this investigation again."

"Don't you want to get a statement from me?" I asked.

"No."

"You want to pretend like I was never here?"

"That's right. You were never here."

Cheeks tapped the heavy Mag-Lite on my shoulder, and let me feel its weight. There was a strange look in his eyes, and I wondered if he'd been drinking. In the distance I heard the sound of sirens, followed by the mournful bay of every dog in the neighborhood. I crossed my arms in front of my chest.

"I called 911, and alerted the Broward news media," I said.

Cheeks's mouth dropped open.

"Why?" he gasped.

"Because you're screwing up, and it's putting Sampson Grimes's life in danger. I'm not going to let it continue."

"You're going to talk to the press?"

"Only if you don't play ball."

His eyes narrowed. "What do you want me to do?"

"Sampson's kidnapper was helped by a guy who calls himself Teen Angel," I said. "I want you to talk to every pervert in the lockup and county jail, and tell them we're

74

looking for this guy. Chances are someone knows who he is."

"What if I don't?"

I had not forgotten Cheeks's threat in my office.

"I'll ruin you," I said.

Cheeks nodded solemnly. For a moment I thought he was agreeing to my request. He lifted the Mag-Lite off my shoulder, and held it directly above my head. The strange look returned to his eyes.

"Fuck you," he said.

I raised my arms as he brought the Mag-Lite down. The flashlight hit my forearm, and sent a shock wave through my body. I threw my shoulder into Cheeks's chest, and sent him staggering backward. Leaping up, Buster grabbed the sleeve of Cheeks's shirt, and shredded the fabric. Cheeks pulled his arm free, then stuck his hand into his pants pocket. I instinctively went for my Colt.

A deafening sound made us both look skyward. A police chopper had dropped out of the sky, and was shining a spotlight into the grove. Moments later, dozens of birds and other small animals exploded out of the trees.

The chopper hovered directly above us, and lit up the clearing. Cheeks glanced upward, as if willing the chopper to leave.

He had lost his chance to hurt me, and brought his hand out of his pocket. I lowered my arm as well.

"I want an answer!" I shouted over the chopper's din.

Cheeks tossed his Mag-Lite to the ground. The strange look left his eyes, and he was acting normal again. I untied Buster.

"Now," I said. "Before everyone gets here."

"All right," he said.

CHAPTER NINE

A half hour later, I pulled into the Sunset Bar and Grill on the northern tip of Dania Beach, parking my car so it faced the ocean.

I pulled back my shirt sleeve, and inspected my arm. Cheeks's Mag-Lite had left a purple welt the size of a golf ball. It also hurt like hell. Fighting with Cheeks had been a mistake. Cheeks was a cop, and in the long run, he could hurt me a lot more than I could hurt him.

I walked down to the shoreline with Buster. The tide was coming in, and I pulled off my sandals and stuck my feet into the tepid water. I had tasted despair many times in my life, and the ocean always restored my spirits. It wasn't long before I was feeling better, and I went inside.

The Sunset was a rough-hewn building, half of it sitting on the beach, the other half on wood stilts over the ocean. I rented a small studio above the bar, which was what four hundred and fifty bucks a month got you these days. It wasn't much, but the ocean view made it feel special.

I was greeted with a chorus of boozy hellos. Sitting at the bar were the same seven sun-burned rummies who'd been drinking there since I'd started renting my room. I called them the Seven Dwarfs because it was rare to see any of them standing upright. I took a stool at the end of the bar, and stared at the TV.

Sonny served me a cold draft and I ordered a burger with french fries. He asked how my day had gone.

"Couldn't have been better," I said.

"I taped your daughter's basketball game," Sonny said. "Want to see it?"

"You don't think the Dwarfs will revolt?"

"They're too drunk to notice."

"Sure."

Sonny tossed me the remote, and I made the screaming mutants on Jerry Springer vanish from the screen. Soon my daughter's basketball game was playing. It was between the Lady Seminoles of Florida State and the Lady Bulldogs of Mississippi State. The opening tip-off fell into my daughter's hands, and she dribbled downcourt, and scored an easy layup. I pounded the bar.

Jessie and I hadn't done much together

when she was growing up. Then in junior high school she'd taken a serious interest in basketball, and I'd nailed a hoop to the garage, and spent countless hours feeding her balls. Her prowess had earned her a full athletic scholarship to Florida State, making me the proudest father on the planet.

Five minutes into the game, Sonny served me dinner on a tray. Two cheeseburgers, two servings of french fries, and two glasses of wine.

"What's this?" I asked.

"You've got a visitor," Sonny said.

I sat up straight on my stool. "I do?"

"She's upstairs. Came in a couple hours ago, just dying to see you."

The Dwarfs got quiet. They weren't the kind of guys who could keep a secret very long, and I glanced down the bar at them. To a man, they were grinning their fool heads off.

"She's a real beauty," one said.

Sonny handed me the tray with a smile on his face.

"You're not going to tell me who's upstairs in my room, are you?" I said.

"That's for us to know and for you to find out," Sonny said.

I took the tray. The stairwell to my room was in the hallway, and I climbed up the stairs with Buster trailing behind. I hadn't had many lady visitors since my wife had left me nine months ago. In fact, I hadn't had any, and I was clueless as to what beautiful woman might be waiting for me.

My father died a long time ago. Before he did, he drummed a bunch of things into my head. One was the importance of manners.

I knocked on the door to my room. Whoever was in there waiting for me, I didn't want to startle her.

No answer. I kept my door unlocked because there was nothing in my room worth stealing. I twisted the knob, and poked my head inside. The sight of the woman lying on my bed took my breath away.

It was Rose, my wife.

She lay on the bed in her nurse's uniform, sound asleep. An open magazine lay on her chest, and her glasses were perched low on her nose. My wife was Mexican, small-boned and perfectly proportioned, with round, soulful, expressive eyes that never failed to light up my heart. I'd fallen for her the first time we'd met, and I'd hit the earth hard the day she'd walked out on me.

I put the tray on the night table and lay down beside her. She was in a deep sleep, and I kissed her on the cheek, and saw the beginnings of a smile.

"Hey, beautiful, wake up," I whispered.

Rose opened her eyes. The look on her face was one I was never going to forget. It was filled with longing and forgiveness. I held her in my arms and we kissed. A minute later, we came up for air.

"You smell like perfume," she said. "Is there someone I should know about?"

There was a twinkle in her eye and I grinned.

"I was just in an orange grove," I said. "What are you doing here?"

"The hospital sent its nurses to a special training seminar in Fort Lauderdale," she said. "I drove down this morning and thought I'd surprise you. What were you doing in an orange grove?"

"Fighting with a cop."

She thought I was kidding until I showed her the bruise on my arm.

"He must have been trying to hurt you," my wife said.

"Let's talk about it later."

"Okay."

We climbed off the bed, and went through our ritual of slowly undressing each other. It never failed to get us both aroused, and soon we were standing naked in the center of the room, holding hands and kissing.

Rose pulled me into bed, and we began to make love. My wife stands five feet tall, while I'm an inch over six feet, and it took us a few minutes to get our rhythm back. When we did, the walls began to vibrate and the room started to shake, and I don't think a full-blown nuclear attack would have stopped us.

We climaxed at the same time, the horn of a passing yacht outside my window masking both our yells. Rose fell on top of me, and I held her overheated body against mine, and tried to catch my breath. The bedspread and pillows were scattered around the room, and I had no idea how they'd gotten there.

"Oh, wow," she said.

Rose lay her head on my chest. For a while I listened to her breathing. Then I closed my eyes, and started to doze off. Her hand touched my face.

"Tell me why you were fighting in an orange grove with a policeman."

I opened my eyes, and stared at my room's cheap popcorn ceiling.

"We had a slight disagreement."

"How bad?"

"Remember Heather Rinker?"

"Sure. She was one of Jessie's friends in

junior high. She was kind of wild, but I liked her."

"Heather has a three-year-old son. He was kidnapped three nights ago, and I've been hired to find him. I'm certain his life is in danger. The detective working the case doesn't want me involved, and he's threatening me. So I threatened him back."

"Why would he threaten you?"

"I don't know. He's got my old job running Missing Persons. Maybe he's afraid I'll show him up. Or maybe he's trying to hide something."

"Can he hurt you?"

I turned and stared into her eyes. "Yes."

"How?"

"He could blackball me with other police departments and law enforcement agencies. All he has to do is send out an e-mail saying bad things about me, and I'm finished."

"You mean it would destroy your business."

"Yes."

We didn't talk for a while. The last time we'd been together, Rose had said that she'd be willing to leave her nursing job and come back to me, provided I could get my business going. If I kept warring with Ron Cheeks, that wasn't going to happen.

"You hungry?" I asked.

"Starving," my wife said.

"The food's probably cold."

"It will still taste good."

I opened the window and we sat in bed eating our burgers and watching the cruise ships and pleasure boats pass by. A stiff breeze off the ocean cooled us down. Buster showed his face when we were done, and Rose fed him the rest of our french fries.

"Are you mad at me?" I asked.

Rose took my head in her hands. "Should I be?"

"I may have really screwed myself this time."

"But you did it anyway."

"I couldn't help it. The kid's life is in danger."

"Let me ask you a question. Can this detective find him without your help?"

"Not at the rate they're going."

"Then you did the right thing. If you dropped this case and something terrible happened to Heather's son, you'd never be able to live with yourself."

Rose pulled my face to hers, eyes right next to mine. I felt like she was looking into my soul.

"Do you want to know something else, Jack?"

"What's that?"
"Neither would I."

CHAPTER TEN

I awoke at sunrise the next morning entwined in my wife's arms. While she showered, I went for a run on the beach with Buster. Then I came back, took a shower, and we made love again. At eight o'clock, I walked her downstairs to her car.

"How soon are you heading back to Tampa?" I asked.

"I'm leaving right now. I'm scheduled to work the afternoon shift, and need to be there by noon."

I didn't know what to say. My life had been complete with Rose. Now it wasn't. It was as simple as that, and at the moment there was nothing I could do to change it. I wrapped my arms around her tiny waist, and held her close.

"I miss you so much," I said.

"I miss you, too. Now promise me you'll stay out of trouble."

"I'll try."

"And try not to fight with any more cops."

"Okay."

I opened her car door. Rose started to get in, then stopped.

"I almost forgot something," she said.

Buster was sitting beside me, and Rose bent down and kissed the top of his head. Buster had taken a shine to Rose the first day they'd met. My dog was funny that way: he liked the people I liked, and tried to take a piece out of those I didn't.

"You take good care of my husband," she told him.

We kissed again, then she got into her car and drove away. I had never understood what it meant to have a heavy heart. Now I understood it all too well.

Going inside, I heard Sonny call my name from the bar. I stuck my head in to see what he wanted. Sonny had dressed up for work. He wore a Black Sabbath T-shirt with gaping holes in the armpits, and had several silver rings stuck through his eyebrows.

"You just got a phone call," Sonny said.

"Friend or foe?" I asked.

"Some asshole detective wants to talk to you. Said it was important."

"Did he leave a number?"

"Yeah."

At the bar, Sonny handed me the cordless phone and a bowl of table scraps, which I placed on the floor for Buster. In exchange for part of my rent, Sonny saved leftover food for my dog, and I watched Buster noisily chow down.

I felt a pair of eyes staring at me. Sitting at the bar was a perfectly proper British couple eating breakfast. Tourists occasionally ventured into the Sunset, thinking it was a respectable place. Seeing the Dwarfs or my dog usually changed their minds.

"Top of the morning," I said.

The couple settled their check and left. I filched a piece of toast off a plate.

"Where's the number?" I asked.

Sonny opened his hand. The number was written on his palm in red ink. I dialed it, and Cheeks answered.

"What's up?" I asked.

"I just found a guy in the county lockup who's willing to talk to us about Teen Angel," Cheeks said.

"What's his name?"

"Vonell Cook. He said he'll roll on Teen Angel if we put it in writing that he helped us. He's facing ten years to life for molesting a teenage girl."

"Did you agree?" I asked.

"Yeah, I agreed. You need to get your ass

over here."

"I'll be there in twenty minutes."

"I'll be waiting. And, Jack? If you bring that goddamn dog, I'll take him into the parking lot and shoot him."

"You're all heart," I said.

I made it to sheriff's department headquarters on Military Trail in good time. I didn't have much of a wardrobe, but I'd taken care to put on my cleanest pair of cargo pants and newest Tommy Bahama shirt. People I had once worked with were going to see me, and I wanted to make a decent impression.

Cheeks met me at the reception area wearing a rumpled suit and a hangdog expression. He pulled me to the side, and lowered his voice. "I'm sorry about last night. I was drinking before you called. I shouldn't have gone after you like that."

He was trying to make nice. I didn't see any good reason not to play along.

"How's your arm?" I asked.

Cheeks showed me where Buster had bitten him. The skin was hardly broken. I showed him the bruise on my arm where he'd hit me with his flashlight.

"I guess that makes us even," he said.

"I guess so," I said.

We went downstairs to the interrogation

cell where Vonell Cook was being held. Before entering the cell, Cheeks sounded a cautionary note. "Be careful what you say around Vonell's lawyer. He's a tricky son-of-a-bitch."

Broward County had a thousand registered sexual predators, and a small group of lawyers in town made a nice living representing them. These lawyers were scum, and loathed by everyone but their clients.

We entered the interrogation cell. Vonell Cook sat in a plastic chair, staring at the wall. In his late forties and shaped like a bowling ball, he wore a bright orange jumpsuit and flip-flops that had seen a thousand pairs of feet before his. Beside him stood his lawyer, a bottom-feeder with crooked teeth and shiny hair plastered to his head. I'd heard his name a few times around the courthouse, but had never bothered to remember it.

"Who are you?" the lawyer asked.

"Jack Carpenter."

"I've heard of you," he said.

"Everyone's heard of Jack," Vonell said.

I took that as a compliment. Grabbing the other chair in the room, I sat in it facing Vonell. As I started to speak, his lawyer interrupted me.

"Here's the deal. My client is being

90

charged with having sexual indiscretions with an underage girl. I want those charges dropped to indecent exposure so he won't go to prison with a sexual predator tag on his head. In return, my client will tell you what he knows about Teen Angel."

Vonell's lawyer was playing us like a fiddle, and was going to extract every favor he could on his client's behalf. I glanced at Cheeks.

"You have a deal," Cheeks said.

The lawyer dropped his hand on his client's shoulder.

"I'm glad we've come to this understanding," Vonell said.

"Start talking," I said.

Vonell smiled, more than happy to tell his secret. "You gentlemen are familiar with Internet chat rooms?"

Cheeks and I nodded.

"There are chat rooms for people with different sexual orientations whose members trade information," Vonell said. "Things like how to stay out of jail, what to do if your phones are being tapped, that sort of thing. There is one group that I regularly chat with. We call ourselves the Conspiracy Club and have six members. One member is engaged in frotteurism, another in zoophilia, a third in scatologia, one is into klismaphilia, another in coprophilia, and the last member is a pedophile."

"Hold on," Cheeks said. "Translate the Latin for me. What are these guys doing?"

"Why don't you tell him, Jack?" Vonell suggested.

Like so many sexual predators, Vonell didn't believe the things he did were wrong. Rather, he believed that society was wrong in the way it viewed his behavior. Vonell wanted me to translate to show that he wasn't the only person in the room who knew what these sick obsessions were. For Sampson Grimes's sake, I obliged him.

"Frotteurism is an obsession with rubbing," I explained. "Zoophilia is having sex at the zoo, but not with your girlfriend. Scatologia is a sexual fantasy stimulated by talking or loud belching. Klismaphilia is an obsession with giving and taking enemas — not something you want to put on a job résumé. Coprophilia is an obsession with feces. And we all know what a pedophile is."

"Very good," Vonell said.

"And you guys all get on the Internet each night and swap secrets," Cheeks said.

"That's correct," Vonell said. "Several nights ago, the pedophile in our group — a man who calls himself Teen Angel — was discussing the Sampson Grimes kidnapping. He had insider information about what had happened."

Vonell licked his lips and smiled. It was all I could do not to slug him.

"Go on," I said.

"Teen Angel said the police were focusing their investigation on the boy's family, which is common in most child abductions. Teen Angel said the evidence showed the boy had been abducted by a nonfamily member."

I glanced over my shoulder at Cheeks. His face had gone white.

"What evidence was that?" I asked.

"The torn window screen in the child's bedroom, which was mentioned in the newspaper," Vonell said. "Teen Angel said the torn screen showed that the abduction was a game Sampson was seduced into playing."

"A game?" I said.

"That's correct. Teen Angel called the game 'Hide from the Parents.' He said it was a common game for abductors to play when stealing children from their homes."

"Did he explain how the game worked?"

"Oh, yes. The abductor gave Sampson candy to entice him into playing, and a toy as a reward *for* playing. Teen Angel was certain about this."

"Candy and a toy," I said.

"Correct. Teen Angel said a specific brand of candy had been used, and was instrumental in keeping the boy quiet."

"Which brand?" I asked.

"Milk Duds."

"Why that brand and not some other?"

"I don't know. Teen Angel also said that he thought Sampson was a precocious child. He believed the boy had an agile mind, which allowed his abductor to trick him into thinking his kidnapping was a game. Teen Angel said it was harder to trick a stupid child than a smart one."

Vonell leaned back. I could see the dampness where his hands had rested on his jumpsuit. I said, "Anything else?"

"Yes, there was one other thing. Rather important, I think."

"What's that?"

Vonell started to answer, then began to violently cough. "I need some water. My throat is bone dry."

Cheeks went into the hallway to fetch Vonell some water. I leaned forward in my chair, and gave Vonell a harsh look. I had seen predators pull this nonsense before. During an interrogation they would stop the action, and make another demand. I had come to the conclusion that it was a subconscious need to be in control, or feel like they were in control, even when they weren't.

Cheeks returned with a paper cup filled with water. Vonell sipped the water, then spoke. "Teen Angel said the child had a special relationship with his abductor. He called it a bond of trust. He said that without that bond, the abduction could not have taken place."

"You mean a prior relationship?" I said.

"Yes. He said the abductor was someone the boy had contact with on a regular basis."

"A friend," I said.

"That's correct. I believe that's everything," Vonell said.

"If I wanted to contact Teen Angel, how would I find him?" I asked.

Vonell glanced over his shoulder at his attorney. The attorney gave him a nod that said it was okay to rat out his chat room buddy. Vonell resumed looking at me.

"Teen Angel works at a local theme park in security," he said.

I rose from my chair and acted like I was done. I had one more question, and I knew that it had to be said at exactly the right time. I waited until Vonell had let his guard down, then pounced.

"Was Teen Angel involved in Sampson

Grimes's kidnapping?" I asked.

Vonell started to answer, then clamped his mouth shut.

"Yes or no?" I asked.

Vonell dropped his eyes to the floor.

"Answer me or the deal's off," I said.

His head snapped up. "But Detective Cheeks said —"

"To hell with what Detective Cheeks said. Yes or no?"

Sexual predators had a code of silence they rarely broke. But Vonell knew I'd make good on my threat. He let a moment pass, then replied.

"I believe he was," he said.

CHAPTER ELEVEN

"Do you believe me now?" I asked.

Cheeks stood over the sink in the men's washroom, dousing his face with cold water. Lifting his gaze, he looked at me in the mirror. "Teen Angel might have helped kidnap the Grimes kid. Or he might be a closet pedophile who sits at his computer and fantasizes with other pedophiles about stealing kids. There are a lot of guys around who do that, you know."

"Not Teen Angel," I said. "He's helped with abductions before."

"You know that for a fact?"

"Yes. Teen Angel helped a guy named Ray Hicks abduct a little girl from an elementary school in Ocala. It was as clean as anything I've ever seen. I saw the e-mails Teen Angel sent Hicks. They spelled the whole thing out."

"You're saying this guy is a pro."

"A pro's pro."

Cheeks patted his face with a paper towel. He was one of the few guys I knew who could clean himself up and not look any better. "How do we find him?"

"Vonell said he works in security for a local theme park," I said. "Call the parks, and tell them you have evidence that a pervert is working for them. They'll cooperate once they hear that."

"You think so?"

"It always worked for me," I said.

Vonell's lawyer was waiting for us in the hallway. He'd written up an agreement on a legal pad that he shoved into Cheeks's face along with a pen.

"My client is being arraigned this afternoon," he said. "I need you to sign this statement stating that the charges against Vonell are being dropped from molestation with a minor to indecent exposure. You said you'd do this. It was part of our agreement."

Cheeks took the pen and scribbled his name on the bottom. The lawyer stuck the pen in his pocket, and started to walk away.

"Can I see that?" I asked.

The lawyer handed me the agreement. I read it quickly, and saw how he'd painted Vonell into some harmless middle-aged guy who occasionally showed off his dick in public. Vonell had been arrested for molesting a teenager, a crime that would leave a deep psychological scar on his victim for the rest of her life. Somehow he'd forgotten to mention that, and I shredded the agreement before his disbelieving eyes.

"Get lost," I said.

The lawyer followed us up the stairs, cursing his head off. When he didn't stop, the sergeant on duty in the reception area escorted him out of the building.

I followed Cheeks to his office on the third floor. Case files covered the desk and floor, and the room's shelving units sagged beneath the weight of missing person reports. Visible above the sea of paper was a phone, and a family photograph with Cheeks's ex-wife razored out.

Cheeks got on the horn and called Broward's three major theme parks. He spoke with their human resources departments, and using a threatening tone, obtained the names of each employee in security and their Social Security numbers, which he passed on to me.

"This is too easy," he said.

"No one wants a pervert working for them," I said.

Sitting at his computer, I accessed the sheriff's department's sexual predator website, which contained files of every known sexual predator in the United States. Entering each name and Social Security number into the search engine, I looked for a match.

On the twentieth name, I got a hit.

"Busted!" I said.

Cheeks came around to where I was sitting, and stared at the screen. The pervert's name was Lonnie Lowman, and he had surfer-white blond hair and bedroom eyes. His charming good looks had no doubt attracted a sixteen-year-old girl in Seattle, who'd willingly gone to his home one weekend, before being held captive and molested. In the mug shot, Lowman was still glowing from his conquest.

I went through his file. Lowman had done three years in prison, and been paroled for good behavior. Part of his release had required him to register himself as a sexual predator at his new address. Lowman hadn't done that. Instead, he'd traveled three thousand miles across the country and set up shop in Fort Lauderdale.

"Where does Lowman work?" I asked.

"Wet and Wonderful," Cheeks said.

"That figures," I said.

"How do you mean?"

"All of the kids are in bathing suits."

Florida hadn't invented theme parks, but it

had certainly made them popular. There were theme parks devoted to cartoon mice, old movie studios, the Bible, and underwater dancing mermaids. The theme park where Lowman worked was called Wet & Wonderful, and featured hair-raising water rides for kids and the world's largest swimming pool.

It was a gorgeous day and the park was jammed. As we crossed the parking lot, I tried to determine which was louder — the deafening roar of traffic on nearby I-95, or the high-pitched screams of kids riding the wave machines.

The park's business office was attached to the ticket office. Cheeks showed his badge to a cashier, and we were ushered into a reception area. We declined coffee and did not take the chairs we were offered.

Soon the park's female general manager appeared. She had a bluetooth stuck in her ear, a cell phone in one hand, and a walkie-talkie in the other. I wanted to ask her if she juggled, but didn't think it was the right time for a joke.

"How can I help you gentlemen?" she asked.

"We need to speak to an employee named Lonnie Lowman," Cheeks said. "I believe he works in your security department."

"May I ask what this is about?"

"We'd like to question him in regard to an ongoing criminal investigation," Cheeks said, making it as vague as possible.

The GM lifted the walkie-talkie to her face. Before she could radio Lowman, I stopped her.

"Please don't do that," I said.

"Excuse me?" the GM replied.

"Tell us where Lowman works, and we'll go talk with him."

A wall of resolution rose in the GM's face. "I'd prefer to bring Lowman here, and have you question him in my office. I have the park's reputation to think of, not to mention the traumatizing effect an arrest might have on the children in the park."

"Lonnie Lowman is a convicted sexual predator," Cheeks said. "Had your human resources department done a proper background check, you'd never have hired him. Tell us where he is, or I'll drag your ass down to the station as well."

Broward cops were required to take annual sensitivity training. It was obvious Cheeks had been sleeping through the classes. The GM led us outside, and pointed at an aqua blue trailer sitting behind a water slide on the opposite side of the park.

"He's in there," she said.

Back when I was a cop, I'd helped Wet & Wonderful beef up its security to prevent child abductions. I knew exactly what was in that trailer.

"Lowman works surveillance?" I asked.

"He runs it," she said quietly.

"For the love of Christ!" Cheeks said.

"He might be watching us on a surveillance camera right now," I said.

Smart people can see into the future. The GM's wasn't looking terribly bright, and she said, "That's right, although he's probably watching the pool or the water slide."

"Where the kids are," I said.

She nodded. I looked at the trailer. Lowman had done time for child molestation in Seattle. Even though I had never stepped foot in Washington State, I guessed the treatment he'd received in prison had been the same as it was for child molesters everywhere, and that he'd been routinely bullied and tortured by the other inmates, who'd made his life a living hell. More than likely, he'd taken steps to ensure he never went back to prison, including carrying an illegal handgun, planning an escape route in case of arrest, and having his passport handy.

"Where does Lowman park his car?" I asked.

"In the company lot," the GM said.

"Would you be able to identify his car from the other employees' vehicles?"

"Yes. Every employee has a parking pass that they leave on their dashboards. The pass has their name and photograph attached to it."

"Your security people need to block Lowman's car from leaving," I said.

The GM called park security on her walkie-talkie, and told them what she wanted done. Hanging up, she said, "Lowman's car is being blocked. What else can I do?"

I continued to look at the surveillance trailer. Two grown males walking through a sea of kids would be easy for Lowman to spot. If Cheeks and I weren't careful, we might end up looking down the barrel of a loaded gun.

"I want you to call Lowman, and divert him until we enter the trailer," I said. "Think you can do that without tipping him off?"

"Of course," the GM said.

"Then do it," Cheeks snapped.

The GM called Lowman as Cheeks and I entered the park.

CHAPTER TWELVE

Wet & Wonderful was a slab of concrete filled with water-themed attractions and concession stands. We shouldered our way through a sea of kids in wet bathing suits, and soon were wet as well. Cheeks was breathing heavily by the time we reached the trailer.

"You really should start exercising," I said.

"Shut up," Cheeks said.

Cheeks clipped his silver detective's badge to his lapel and rapped loudly on the trailer door. A voice from within told us to enter.

"Remember to go slow," I said.

"Right," Cheeks said.

The trailer's interior was dark and chilly, the walls lined with high-definition digital monitors showing the action outside. Lonnie Lowman sat at a desk with his back to the monitors, talking to the GM on a walkie-talkie. He said, "Let me call you back," and hung up, his eyes frozen on

Cheeks's badge.

"Lonnie Lowman?" Cheeks asked.

Lowman nodded stiffly. He'd done a makeover since his mug shot, and now sported a short, conservative haircut, drug-store reading glasses, and a cosmetically altered nose. What hadn't changed were his eyes; green and almost pretty, they darted back and forth between us like a caged animal's. The hunter had become the hunted.

"We'd like to talk to you," I said.

"Am I under arrest?" Lowman asked.

"No," Cheeks said. "Your name came up during an investigation, that's all."

Cheeks leaned against the wall, while I stood across from Lowman's chair. When I was a cop, I'd carried a pack of gum to break the ice during interrogations. It was a tradition I'd continued, and I offered Lowman a stick. He declined, and I stuck one into my mouth while staring at the monitors. There were twelve in all, displayed in a matrix. Six monitored the deep end of the swimming pool, where a giant slide deposited screaming kids into the water. On one of the monitors a girl came down the slide, and hit the swimming pool. The force of the water pulled the top of her bikini off. She came out of the water laughing, and with her mother's help, got redressed. It was as innocent as eating a hot dog, but not meant to be seen by the eyes of a predator.

"My boss knows about this, doesn't she?" Lowman asked.

"Afraid so," I said, trying to control my temper. "If you cooperate, we'll tell her you're square, and there will be no harm done."

I felt Lowman sizing me up. It was like being watched by an untrustworthy dog. I continued to work my gum.

"All right, ask your questions," Lowman said.

"Do you go by the name Teen Angel on the Internet?" Cheeks began.

Lowman's face turned so red it looked like he had hives. "Who told you that?"

"Vonell Cook," Cheeks said.

"Never heard of him."

"He's into molesting underage girls. You talk to him on a chat room called the Conspiracy Club," Cheeks said.

Lowman stared at Cheeks, and said nothing.

"We had a chat with Vonell this morning at police department headquarters," Cheeks went on. "Vonell shared with us your insights into the Sampson Grimes kidnapping. They were so interesting, we decided we wanted to meet you."

Lowman twisted uncomfortably in his chair. "I had nothing to do with that. I'll take a polygraph if you want me to. I didn't steal that little boy."

"Any idea who did?" I asked.

Lowman violently shook his head.

"You didn't talk to him, and give him tips?" I said.

"No!"

"You don't expect us to believe that, do you?"

"Look. I did a bad thing a few years ago in Seattle," Lowman said. "But I did my time and paid my debt to society. I've changed. What I told Vonell and the other members of the Conspiracy Club were idle ramblings, nothing more."

Sexual predators *didn't* change. They could be scared straight or sent into hiding, but you couldn't change them. Lowman was lying.

"You called Sampson's abduction a game," I said. "What did you mean by that?"

Lowman took off his glasses and shoved them into his shirt pocket. It was a bad move, for it showed how scared he was. "The boy was persuaded to leave his bedroom during the night, and to climb through a slit screen. He wasn't taken. He was removed."

"Meaning what?" I asked.

"Sampson was playing a game with his abductor," Lowman said.

"Do you think it might have been one of Sampson's parents?" I asked.

"No. Parents enforce the law. This game was an act of defiance. That was where the cut in the screen came in."

I glanced at Cheeks out of the corner of my eye. He had gone white.

"But it was someone who knew Sampson," I said.

"Knew him well," Lowman said.

"You told Vonell that Milk Duds were involved in Sampson's abduction," I said. "How did you know that?"

Lowman looked furtively at the floor. I heard the uptick in his breathing, the air moving rapidly through his nostrils and pouring from his mouth. He almost sounded like he was running.

"I just guessed," he said.

I grabbed the arms of his chair and shook it. Lowman's head snapped up.

"Quit lying," I said.

"I'm not lying," he protested.

"Yes, you are. Keep it up, and Detective Cheeks will arrest you."

Many criminals scoff at being arrested.

Sexual predators do not. Going to jail is often the equivalent of a death sentence, and they will do anything to avoid it.

"Milk Duds are a favorite enticement among child abductors," he said quietly. "Children like them, and they're larger than most candy."

"So?"

"A child can't yell for help with a Milk Dud in his mouth. He has to spit it out first. That gives the abductor time to clamp his hand around the child's mouth, and subdue him. It's an old trick."

"Did you tell Sampson Grimes's abductor that?" I asked.

"I told you, I don't know who abducted the Grimes boy."

"How about Ray Hicks?"

Lowman jerked up in his chair.

"You know Ray?" he squeaked.

"We met yesterday," I said.

The blood drained from Lowman's face. Before my eyes, a metamorphosis took place, and the respectable citizen that Lowman was pretending to be disappeared, while the monster lurking below surfaced. His pretty eyes shrunk into slits, and his nostrils flared. A guttural sound came out of his throat that reminded me of a dog choking on a bone. He shoved me, and spun around in his chair.

A laptop computer sat next to the console. Lowman began to type a command into the laptop's keyboard, his fingers a blur.

"No, you don't," I said.

I came around Lowman's chair, and tried to pin his arms to his sides. He wrestled with me while cursing under his breath. I looked to Cheeks for help.

"You want to participate?" I asked.

Cheeks was moving in slow motion, looking like he was going to be sick. I thought I knew what was wrong. His theory about the Grimes abduction had just gone up in flames, and he didn't know what to do.

"Come on," I urged him.

Cheeks drew his gun from his shoulder harness, and pointed it at Lowman.

"You're under arrest," he said.

Lowman's fingers continued to pound the keyboard. I dragged him out of his chair, and shoved him into the wall.

"Calm down," I said.

Finally, Lowman settled down. I made him put his hands against the wall, and frisked him. He was clean, and I looked at Cheeks.

"I want to see what's on his computer," I said. "You need to watch him."

"Okay," Cheeks said.

I sat in Lowman's chair. His laptop computer was plugged into the console, and I clicked the mouse and accessed his e-mail. He'd sent over a hundred e-mails out today. I clicked on one, expecting the worst.

A film of a young girl losing her bathing suit in the swimming pool appeared on the laptop's screen. It was set to raunchy music, the film slowing down as her suit came off. Lowman was editing surveillance tapes, then e-mailing them to other perverts. The children he was supposed to be protecting, he was instead exploiting.

I stood. "There's enough evidence on this computer to put you in jail for the rest of your life. Do you want that?"

Slumped against the console, Lowman shook his head.

"Then help us find Sampson Grimes," I said.

"What will I get in return?"

"We'll tell the judge you cooperated."

"Like you did with Vonell Cook this morning?" he asked.

The question caught me off guard.

"Who told you about Vonell?" I asked.

"His lawyer."

I looked at Cheeks and saw him shake his head. Lowman seized the moment, and stuck his hand beneath the console. There was a loud ripping sound. His hand re-appeared clutching a dark object.

"Gun!" I shouted.

CHAPTER THIRTEEN

I lunged across the trailer as Lowman fired his weapon.

The bullet whistled by my head, and ricocheted inside the trailer. More cops die from ricochets than by criminals shooting at them. I dove to the floor, as did Cheeks. Lowman kicked open the trailer door.

"Screw your deal!" he said, and ran out.

Cheeks was lying on top of me, and I had to shove him to get up. The trailer door had shut itself, and I stared at the monitors covering the wall. Instead of running toward the park's entrance, Lowman was running toward the rear. He'd had his escape route all planned out.

Cheeks was having a hard time getting up. I offered my hand and he refused it.

"You okay?" I asked.

"Get the bastard," he wheezed.

I ran outside. Lowman was tall, and easy to spot in the crowd. He had circled the swimming pool, and was now headed toward a gate with an "Employees Only" sign hanging on it. I wasn't going to catch him unless I did something drastic.

Cheeks staggered out of the trailer. I took out my Colt, and tossed it to him.

"Hold this," I said.

My sandals came off next, and I leaped into the pool. The water was highly chlorinated and stung my eyes. I swam competitively as a kid, and might have broken a couple of records had I not discovered girls. Flying across the water, I lifted my head. Lowman waited for me on the other side.

I dove straight down as he fired. A bullet whizzed silently past, and went right between a little boy's legs in the shallow end. Some people will tell you there is no God, but I've seen enough things like this to tell you there is.

My head broke the water's surface, and I swam to the pool's edge. Lowman had given up trying to kill me, and was running toward the gate. He was going to escape.

I stared into the faces of the crowd. Several guys my age were giving me curious looks. They knew something wasn't right; they just didn't know what. Cupping my hands over my mouth, I yelled, "Stop that guy! He molested my daughter!"

"Him?" a guy yelled back.

The guy was huge, and had two kids with him. He was standing a few feet from Lowman. I yelled, "Yes. Watch out, he's got a gun."

The guy let go of his kids, and brought his forearm down on Lowman's shoulder. Lowman's knees buckled, and his gun fell out of his hand.

"Pervert," the guy said.

Several other guys in the crowd began to pummel Lowman as well. Lowman twisted like an animal caught in a trap, but could not break free. Cops had a special name for when crowds got angry enough to tear someone apart. They called it a feeding frenzy.

I pushed my way through the mob with Cheeks behind me. In a loud voice, Cheeks announced that he was a cop, and Lowman's attackers backed away.

Lowman lay sprawled on the ground. His shirt was a memory and blood poured from his nose and mouth.

"Don't let them kill me," he begged.

I don't like being shot at. I dragged Lowman to the edge of the pool, and dunked his head into the water. The crowd erupted in cheers.

"Drown him!" someone yelled.

"I'll help you hold him down," another offered.

I waited a few moments before pulling Lowman's head out of the pool. He spit out a mouthful of water, and looked fearfully at me. "Tell me what you know about Sampson Grimes's kidnapping, or I'll let them have you," I said.

The words hit Lowman harder than any punch. He grabbed my shirt with both his hands, and held me like he was never going to let go.

"I'll do whatever you want," he said.

Cheeks drove us to Lowman's house in his Suburban. I sat in the backseat beside Lowman and watched his hands, which were handcuffed behind his back. He had closed his eyes, and was breathing heavily. Lowman lived in a subdivision in Pembroke Pines on the curve of a cul-de-sac, an attractive one-story with a terra-cotta roof. As Cheeks parked in the driveway, I spied a hammock in the side yard moving back and forth in the wind.

At the front door Lowman offered up his house keys, which were resting in his pocket. Cheeks unlocked the front door, and we entered the chilly interior. The shades were drawn on every window, and the place felt

117

like a tomb.

I flipped on the lights. The furnishings were sparse. Hanging from the walls were blowups of young girls with their swimming suits falling off. They were everywhere I looked. Cheeks had Lowman sit in a leather chair in the living room.

"Do not move," Cheeks ordered.

I pulled Cheeks aside. He was breathing hard, and looked like hell.

"Do you want me to search the place?" I asked.

"I'll do it," Cheeks said.

"You sure you're up for it?"

Searching a predator's house meant banging on every ceiling and wall, and checking every loose floorboard. If you didn't, you might miss a hidden crawl space where a child could be held prisoner.

"Just watch him," Cheeks said, going into the back of the house.

I stood in front of Lowman's chair. His face was caked with dried blood and covered with ugly purple bruises.

"Start talking," I said.

Lowman stared at the floor. A long moment passed.

"I changed my mind," he said.

Behind where I stood was a wall unit lined

with DVDs. In anger, I started pulling the DVDs out, and throwing them at Lowman's head. One DVD caught my eye, and I stopped long enough to read what was written on the box.

CONFESSION

I waved the DVD in front of Lowman's face. "What's this?"

"You have no right to look at that!" he protested.

A computer sat in the corner of the living room. I powered it up, and popped the DVD in. The computer's screen flickered to life, and a film of Lowman appeared. I listened to him recite every crime he'd ever committed in his life.

"Wow," I said. "You made a confession."

"I thought I was dying of colon cancer a few years ago," he said.

"Trying to cleanse your soul?"

"Something like that."

"Too bad it didn't work. What do you want me to do with it?"

Lowman's head snapped. "What did you say?"

"You heard me. Would you like me to destroy it?"

"Yes — yes!"

"Will you play ball then?"

"Yes!"

"How do I know you're not lying?"

"There's an e-mail stored in my computer that Sampson's kidnapper sent me," Lowman said. "I will explain what it is. It will help you find the boy."

Lowman gave me the password to his e-mail account. Using the mouse on his computer, I entered his e-mail account, opened it using his password, and went into his Saved box. An e-mail from someone calling himself Big Daddy jumped out at me. I clicked on it, and found myself staring at a photograph of a little boy sitting in a dog crate. It was Sampson. I ejected the DVD of Lowman's confession from the computer, and broke it in half.

"Start talking," I said.

"Burn it," Lowman said.

"Excuse me?"

"A broken DVD can be restored and played. Burn it."

You learn something new every day. I put the DVD into an ashtray on the coffee table. Lowman directed me to a drawer containing a collection of restaurant matchbooks. I lit a book, and dropped it in. We watched the DVD catch fire and melt.

"Now tell me what this photo means," I said.

"Sampson is giving his kidnapper problems," Lowman said. "The boy fights and screams and tries to escape whenever he can. His kidnapper couldn't handle him, so he turned the boy over to a pair of drug enforcers. These men are used by drug dealers to collect money. Sometimes they take children into their possession as collateral."

"That's who has Sampson now?"

"Yes."

"And they're keeping him in a dog crate?"

"That's right."

Sampson's photo was still on the computer screen. Instead of being scared, the kid looked fighting mad. I didn't know this little boy, yet I admired the hell out of him.

"Did the kidnapper say where they were keeping him?" I asked.

"In a hotel in Fort Lauderdale," Lowman said.

"Is that where this photo was taken?"

"Yes."

I brought my face inches from the computer screen. The photo said a lot. Along with the dog crate, it contained a night table, a worn patch of carpet, and wallpaper with a logo embedded in the design. There were cops around the country who were experts in identifying hotel room interiors, and I felt certain one of them would be able to tell me in which chain Sampson was being held prisoner. Knowing that, and the fact that he was in Fort Lauderdale, would make it easy to track him down.

I printed the photograph on Lowman's laser printer. It was sharp and clear. I held it in my hand, and felt my heart race.

I was one step closer to finding him.

CHAPTER FOURTEEN

From another part of the house I heard a door open. Then Cheeks staggered into the living room. He'd pulled off his sports jacket, and his chest was heaving.

"What's wrong?" I asked.

Cheeks didn't reply, and fell heavily against the wall. I rushed to his side. The look in his eyes bordered on helpless, and it appeared that he couldn't breathe. I punched 911 into my cell phone without taking my eyes off Lowman.

"Tell me your address," I said.

Lowman gave me the address, which I relayed to the 911 dispatcher. Hanging up, I made Cheeks lie down on the living room floor, and elevated his legs with a pillow.

"Where's the aspirin?" I asked.

Lowman led me to the medicine cabinet in the master bathroom.

"Unlock these handcuffs, and I'll help you," he said.

If a snake could talk, I imagined it would have sounded like the reptile standing in front of me. I escorted Lowman back to the living room and fed two aspirin to Cheeks. I saw Lowman inching toward the front door.

"Sit down," I said.

Lowman returned to his chair.

"What do you want me to do?" I asked Cheeks.

"Take him in, and book him," he said.

"That will be a pleasure," I said.

Within minutes an ambulance came and two medics entered the house, tied Cheeks to a gurney, and loaded him into the back. I stood in the doorway and watched, while keeping one eye on Lowman. Cheeks was not my friend, but he was still a cop, and I did what I always did when a cop went down, and said a silent prayer.

The ambulance backed out of the driveway. I made Lowman get up and pulled him outside. Cheeks's car was in the driveway, the keys still in his pocket, while my Legend was parked at police headquarters.

"Do you have any money?" I asked.

"About forty dollars. Why?" Lowman asked.

"Because you're paying for the cab to take us to the police station."

■ ■ ■ ■

The fare to the Broward County Sheriff's Department headquarters came to $26. I pulled two crisp twenties out of Lowman's wallet and told the driver to keep the change.

The booking area was in the rear of the building. As I escorted Lowman through the front doors, I took a step back in time. The smells were the same — strong coffee, foul body odors, forbidden cigarettes — and so were the faces, including several silver-haired deputies I'd known since the day I'd started.

There was a long line at the intake booking area. For safety's sake, each perp had his wrists handcuffed behind his back, and stood three feet away from the suspect in front of him. I pushed Lowman to the front of the line, and rapped my knuckles on the desk. "I'd like to make a citizen's arrest," I announced.

Captain Mike lifted his eyes from a stack of forms. His job was to process perps and bag their personal belongings. A smile lit up his face.

"Jack Attack," he said.

"Hello, Captain Mike," I said. "How's the

family?"

"Everyone's well. Who's this clown?"

"A child molester who was running security at a local theme park. I helped Ron Cheeks bust him."

"Where's Cheeks? Dunkin' Donuts?"

"He went to the hospital. He wasn't feeling too well."

Captain Mike filled out a processing form for Lowman. I helped by removing Lowman's watch, wallet, belt, rings, and shoelaces, which Captain Mike bagged, tagged, and inventoried. When we were done, Lowman edged up beside me.

"You'll never find the Grimes boy," Lowman said.

"Is that a fact?" I said.

"I'd put money on it," he said.

Taking a Sharpie from Captain Mike's desk, I wrote PERVERT on the back of Lowman's shirt, then handed him off to a pair of deputies, who led him to a holding pen yelling his head off.

"Does the brass know Cheeks went to the hospital?" Captain Mike asked.

I shook my head. I hadn't bothered to call anyone, having assumed it would be taken care of when Cheeks was admitted to ER.

"I need to tell them," Captain Mike said. "Make yourself comfortable."

I took a chair in the waiting area. There was red tape on the floor to signify that the section was for visitors, and not people in custody. I had always found the tape comical, considering the crimes most of these guys were in for. A man dressed in a tailored suit materialized beside me.

"Your friend looks like he needs some help," the man said.

"Are you a lawyer?" I asked.

He said yes, and reached for his business card.

"Do you represent child molesters?" I asked.

"All the time," he said.

"Go fuck yourself."

Captain Mike called me back to his desk. "I just spoke with the chief. He wants to see you in his office."

"All hail the chief," I said.

Captain Mike cleared me through the booking area, and I walked down a long hall to a bank of elevators. A minute later, I was sitting across from Sheriff Lester Moody, the man who'd ousted me from my job nine months ago. Moody was a big man with a mane of silver hair and a face like a slab of granite. Since getting the top job, he'd started wearing ill-fitting suits and bright neckties, and looked like a used-car salesman.

"I spoke with Cheeks," Moody said. "The doctors are keeping him for a few days at Memorial Hospital. Giving him aspirin was a smart call."

"Cheeks needs to lose some weight. You, too," I said.

"Can't anyone have a civil conversation with you?"

"Want me to leave?"

"Not until I finish what I have to say."

"Then say it. I have a little boy to find."

Moody's cheeks burned. He drummed his desk while glaring at me. He was accustomed to talking down to people. I wasn't letting him do that.

"I want to find Sampson Grimes, too," Moody said. "Unfortunately, Cheeks didn't bring anyone into the loop regarding the investigation. From what I can gather, you know as much as he does."

"More," I said.

"All right, you know more. I'd like to offer you a deal."

"I'm listening."

"I'm putting another detective in charge of finding Sampson Grimes. I need you to bring that detective up to speed. In exchange, I'll pay you for your time."

128

"Put me in charge of the investigation."

"That's out of the question. I can't have you running things."

I'd fallen on hard times since leaving the force, yet I'd never regretted the decision. It had allowed me to listen to my conscience. I stood up.

"Have a nice day," I said.

"You're being unreasonable," Moody said.

"Cheeks put you in a tough spot. He botched the investigation, then ignored evidence that it was an abduction. How's that going to look when it hits the news?"

"Jack, sit down."

"It's going to look horrible. Only Cheeks is sick, so he won't get blamed. *You'll* get blamed. Your only salvation is finding Sampson Grimes. Put me in charge."

"I can't do that. But I will offer you a compromise."

"What's that?"

"Do you remember Candice Burrell?"

"Sure, I trained her."

"I'm putting Burrell in charge of the investigation."

Burrell was one of the smartest detectives on the force. So smart that she'd been passed over for countless promotions, while lesser lights had risen to the top. If anyone could clean up Ron Cheeks's mess, it was Candy.

"I'll work with Burrell on one condition," I said.

"Name it."

"I want access to the crime scene and the investigation's case file."

"Done. Now let's talk about your fee."

"I'm already being paid by the Grimes family."

Moody rose from his desk. "I'm glad we've reached this decision."

Sometimes bullshit gets in the way of what's important. I removed the photo of Sampson that I'd printed off Lowman's computer, and dropped it on Moody's desk.

"This photo was taken in a Fort Lauderdale hotel," I said. "The interior looks like it's a chain hotel. The guys need to examine it."

Moody's face lit up. "I'll put them right on it. Anything else?"

I started to say no, then remembered Lowman. I wrote his address on a slip of paper, and gave it to Moody. "There's a pervert in the lockup named Lonnie Lowman," I said. "I cut a deal with him, and destroyed a DVD of him confessing to a bunch of crimes. I ran the DVD on his computer, so there's a copy on the hard drive. You need to send someone over to Lowman's house to retrieve it."

Moody stared at the address and nodded. "I'll put an officer right on it," he said.

CHAPTER FIFTEEN

Redemption.

It was just a word until you experienced it; then it was like no other feeling in the world. I was working with the Broward cops again, and I was doing it on my terms. It didn't get any sweeter than that.

I was sitting in traffic on 595, listening to Boston's "More Than a Feeling" on the car stereo while smelling the salty ocean breeze through my open window. My wife believed that everything in the world happened for a reason, and I thought about all the good things that had happened to me since my fight with Cheeks in the grove. I decided to call her, and as I punched her number into my cell phone, it began to ring.

Not many people had my cell number. I stared at my cell phone's face. Caller ID said UNKNOWN.

"Carpenter here," I answered.

"Is this *the* Jack Carpenter, the ex-cop

who finds missing kids?" a man asked.

"You got him. Who's this?"

"Call me Pepe. One of your pals at the police station gave me your number. I've got someone here who wants to speak to you."

"Put him on," I said.

The cars in front of me started to move, and I goosed the accelerator.

"This is Sampson," a tiny voice said.

I lowered the volume on my tape deck. "Sampson Grimes?"

"Yeah," the boy said.

"Are you all right?"

"No!" Sampson began to wail.

I pressed the cell phone to my ear. It was broiling hot, along with everything else inside my car. "Please talk to me," I said.

Sampson continued to cry. I tried to determine what the background noises were, and thought I heard a plane passing overhead. Finally, Sampson stopped crying.

"I need to tell you something," the boy said.

"I'm listening," I said.

"Tell Grandpa . . ."

"Yes?"

". . . to stop talking to the FBI."

"You want me to tell your grandfather to stop talking to the FBI?" I repeated.

There was a pause, and I heard a man in the background mumble softly.

"Yeah," Sampson said.

"I want to talk to the man you're with," I said.

A car horn honked in the background, followed by the sound of another airplane. I guessed they were calling from a pay phone near the Hollywood/Fort Lauderdale airport. The airport was isolated, and did not have many retail stores nearby.

"I'm back," Pepe said.

"I want you to release the boy," I said.

"Fat chance, brother."

"You're getting paid to hold the boy by his kidnapper," I said. "Let him go, and I'll pay you more."

Pepe laughed derisively. "I've heard about your deals. No thanks."

Pepe dropped the phone, and I heard it bang against a wall. Then I heard a car pull away, its muffler rattling loudly. There was a convenience store on Griffin Road by the airport that had a bank of pay phones outside the store. It was only a minute away. I pulled onto the highway's shoulder and hit the gas. Pepe sounded smart, and I didn't think he'd speed away, arousing suspicion. With any luck, I'd catch him.

■ ■ ■ ■

I drove with my eyes peeled to the oncoming traffic, looking for a car with a dying muffler. At the convenience store on Griffin Road I slowed to stare at the pay phones on the side of the building. One was off the hook.

I raced down Griffin Road toward I-95. I've always been good at putting myself in a criminal's shoes, and anticipating how they were going to act. I decided that Pepe had gotten onto I-95, and headed north into Fort Lauderdale.

Traffic on I-95 was the usual mix of blue hairs doing thirty and crazy Cubans trying to break the sound barrier. I got into the left lane, and pushed the Legend up to ninety. Soon I saw a tail of black exhaust ahead of me. I stuck my head out my window, and heard Pepe's car.

I drew my Colt from my pocket, and laid it on my lap. The car was a few hundred yards ahead, a black Chevy Impala with no plates driving in the center lane. In most parts of the state, driving without license plates would get you pulled over. In South Florida, it was a way of life.

I got behind the car and slowed down.

Two men occupied the front seat. Lonnie Lowman had said that Sampson was being held by a pair of drug enforcers. I didn't see Sampson, and guessed he was either strapped down in the backseat or stowed in the trunk.

I dialed 911. My call was answered by an automated police operator. I saw the Chevy speed up, and I got back into the left lane. I needed to get a good look at the driver, and pass his description to the police.

As I got close to the Chevy, the driver jerked his head. Young, Hispanic, and missing several front teeth. His eyes grew wide, and I realized I'd been made.

The driver shouted to his partner. His partner grabbed a handgun off the floor, and climbed into the driver's lap. I wasn't going to get into a shooting match with him, and risk harming Sampson. I hit my brakes, and let the Chevy get ahead of me.

I stayed a hundred yards back. The guy with the gun lowered the passenger window, and stuck his weapon out. Overweight and in his forties, he was the opposite of his partner. I thought he was going to shoot at me, but that wasn't what he had in mind.

Instead, he aimed at the minivan in the lane next to him. It was filled with kids, the woman driver on her cell phone, oblivious to what was going on.

Then he looked at me.

I instantly understood. If I didn't back off, he was going to shoot the woman and kill her, and probably all the kids as well. I couldn't be responsible for so many innocent people dying, and flashed my brights while slowing my car. He grinned.

The Chevy speeded up, and was soon a memory. I heard a voice on my cell phone.

"Broward County police. Do you have an emergency?"

I told the operator what had happened while getting off the interstate.

I pulled into the convenience store on Griffin Road and went inside. It was a squat, one-story building, the windows plastered with ads for the Florida Lottery. A surveillance camera hung over the door. I asked the manager if it worked.

"Naw."

I inspected the bank of pay phones outside. The middle phone was off the hook. I knelt down, and looked at the plastic handle. Pepe's fingerprints were all over it.

Sirens wailed in the distance. I had asked the police operator to send a cruiser to the convenience store. I went to the sidewalk to meet the cruiser, and heard a car start up.

Across the street a souped-up Camaro was parked in the front of a storage facility. Two young white males were inside, shooting me mean looks. I crossed the road at a trot.

"I need to speak to you for a minute," I called to them.

The Camaro backed out with a squeal of rubber. I drew my Colt and pointed it at his windshield.

"Get out," I said.

They got out. Low-slung pants, lots of jewelry and tattoos. I made them for gang members, and had them stand with their hands on the roof and their legs spread wide, and patted them down. Both were carrying heat, and I slipped their pieces into my pants pockets. Then I popped the trunk. It was loaded with stereo equipment.

"You boys work for Circuit City?" I asked.

Neither replied.

"I want you to help me," I said. "There were two guys standing outside the convenience store making a phone call. They had a little boy with them. Did you see them?"

The driver glanced at me. He had a tattoo on his neck that said Born Loser. "What if we did?"

"What can you tell me about them?"

"Couple of spics."

138

"Did you hear anything they said to each other?"

The driver shook his head.

"Tell me about the boy who was with them," I said.

"He was a little guy with blond hair," the driver said. "One of the spics was holding him up to the pay phone, and the kid was going nuts."

"Was the man hurting him?"

"He slapped him a couple of times," the driver said.

"Why didn't you do something?" I asked.

"What do you mean?"

"Why didn't you stop him from hurting the boy?"

The driver and his partner looked at each other, and started laughing.

A wailing police cruiser braked in front of the convenience store, and a pair of uniformed cops jumped out with their weapons drawn. As they crossed the street, I grabbed the gang members' heads, and banged them together.

■ ■ ■ ■

PART TWO:
THE OLD
NEIGHBORHOOD

■ ■ ■ ■

CHAPTER SIXTEEN

Buster was lying beneath a table as I entered the Sunset. He refused to make eye contact, no doubt still angry that I'd left him. Australian Shepherds were great dogs until you left them alone. Then they destroyed furniture and caused all sorts of problems.

"How's he been?" I asked Sonny.

"He tried to bite the mailman and pissed on the floor," Sonny said. "Outside of that, he's been fine."

I crawled under the table and scratched Buster's head. Soon his tiny tail started to wag, and we were friends again. Then my cell phone rang. I was not normally this popular. I took it out of my pocket, and saw the caller ID — CANDY.

"Hello, Detective Burrell," I answered.

"Hello, Jack," Burrell said.

"I hear you've been given the Grimes case."

"Good news sure travels fast. I just got off

the phone with Chief Moody. He said you were involved in a car chase on I-95, and nearly rescued the boy."

"I got close."

"I want to hear more. I'm in the orange grove across the street from Jed Grimes's house. How soon can you get over here and give me an update?"

"I'm leaving right now," I said.

RichJo Lane looked different in the harsh daylight, the yards down-trodden, the houses dirty and small. It was easy to call the owners lazy, but I'd been broke long enough to recognize when people were just getting by.

The street was blocked by TV news vans. I parked on a side street, and walked to Jed Grimes's house with my dog. A mob of reporters stood on the lawn, hurling questions at four uniformed cops standing behind a police barricade with their arms crossed. When children went missing, the media cheered law enforcement at the start of the investigation, then jeered them if the case stalled. If this scene was any indication, the police department's honeymoon with the Broward media was over.

I pushed my way through the crowd, and showed my driver's license to the uniforms.

"Detective Burrell is expecting me."

One of the uniforms took my license, and made a call on his cell. I felt someone bump me from behind, but I didn't turn around.

"Isn't that Jack Carpenter?" a male voice asked.

"I think it is," a female voice said.

"Jack, it's Chip Wells, with Action Eleven Eyewitness News," the first voice said. "Can you tell us why you're here? Are the police using you to find Sampson Grimes?"

Chip Wells was not a friend. He'd done a series of pieces about me when I'd been kicked off the force that had been less than flattering. Something about his tone of voice told me I was being recorded.

"I'm selling Girl Scout cookies," I said, not turning around.

"Be straight with us," Wells said. "People want to know what's going on."

"Screw 'em," I said.

The uniform confirmed that I was expected. He led me around the house, and across the alley to the grove.

"Detective Burrell's in there," the uniform said.

The grove had undergone a dramatic transformation. Twelve-foot-high metal poles had been stuck around the perimeter and translucent plastic sheeting spread between them, covering everything inside. As I lifted a flap, a black guy wearing a U.S. Marshals cap came out. His shirt had a dark butterfly of sweat, and ringlets fell from his scalp.

"Who let you back here?" he demanded.

I told him Burrell was expecting me, and he told me not to move.

Soon Burrell appeared. Her cheeks were windburned, making her slate blue eyes look electrified in the ruddy glow of her pretty face. She came from a family of cops; her father, two brothers, and uncle had all worn a badge. She was a tough young woman, and stubborn to a fault. In that regard, we couldn't have been more alike.

"That was fast," she said.

"Cheeks left you a real mess, didn't he?" I said.

"That's an understatement. What's with the dog?"

"He's my partner. He's good at finding things."

"Is he friendly?"

"Not really."

Burrell bravely stuck her hand beneath Buster's snout, and to my surprise, got licked in return. "I like him," she said.

We entered the tentlike structure. The air was hot and sticky. As we walked, I stopped

146

to look at eight-by-ten glossies attached to tree branches. Each glossy showed a piece of evidence that had been discovered at that spot, and taken away for examination. It was a clever way to preserve a crime scene, and typical of Burrell's thinking.

We came to the clearing. In its center was a fireplace ringed with darkened stones. Sitting among the stones were several charred cans, including a thirty-two-ounce can of Dinty Moore stew. The can of stew had bothered me the night before, and I used a stick to fish it out of the fireplace. Burrell edged up beside me.

"What are you thinking?" she asked.

"I'm thinking that thirty-two ounces of stew is more than one person can eat," I said.

"Do you think Sampson's kidnapper fed the vagrant before killing him?"

"Yes."

"I think the other detectives need to hear this."

The other detectives were my old unit. It was going to feel strange talking to them, but I didn't see how I had any other choice.

Burrell clapped her hands. "Listen up, everybody. Stop what you're doing, and come into the clearing. We have a guest."

Six detectives drifted into the clearing.

They were all sweaty and looked drained. I shook their hands and said hello. Their collective reaction to my presence was one of shock. I'd left the force under a dark cloud, and they were surprised to see me back.

"Jack has signed on to help with the Grimes case," Burrell announced. "He has some insights he'd like to share with us."

Burrell gave me the floor. I gazed into the detectives' faces before speaking. Several were trying not to smile, and it made me feel good.

"I've been working this case for two days, and here's what I can tell you," I said. "Our kidnapper knew the boy and had built a relationship with him. Four nights ago, he came into this grove, had dinner with a vagrant, and killed him. Then he crossed the alley, and coaxed Sampson to climb out of his bedroom window using candy and a toy. He brought the boy back here, and altered his appearance, then left. I'm guessing some things got left behind. Did any of you find a child's toy during your search?"

Detective Jillian Webster spoke up. "I found a fake light-up cell phone. Still has the price sticker on it."

"Where was it?" I asked.

"Beneath an orange tree on the west side of the property. I assumed it was tossed there. I bagged it, and put it in the evidence box."

"Was it *directly* beneath the tree?" I asked.

"Yes," Webster said. "Is that significant?"

"Sampson wouldn't have tossed a toy away, but his kidnapper might have. And his kidnapper wouldn't have tossed a toy out in the open. He's way too smart for that."

Webster's head rocked back. "He tossed it *up* in the tree, and it fell to earth."

"That's right. I suggest you search every tree in this grove."

"What else will we find?" Webster asked.

"The boy's pajamas," I said. "Sampson's kidnapper changed the boy's appearance before leaving the grove. He did a good job, because no one spotted him."

I paused and let my words sink in. Then I asked if there were any questions. There were none, and Burrell spoke up.

"Let's start looking for the boy's PJs," she said.

My old unit dispersed. The heat had sucked the life out of them, and they were moving in slow motion. I pointed at Buster.

"Let my dog help," I said.

"Is he good at tracking scents?" Burrell asked.

"The best."

Burrell made a call on her cell. A few minutes later, a uniform brought a paper bag containing the sheets from Sampson's bed into the grove. I shoved Buster's face into the bag. Human beings shed dead skin cells constantly, and each flake carries a microscopic trace of bacteria called an aromatic signature. My dog lived for those odors.

"Find the boy," I told him.

Buster darted down a row of trees with his nose vacuuming the ground. At the property's edge, he stopped beneath the last tree in the row, and pawed its trunk. Burrell got beneath the tree, and shook the limbs. A plastic bag came tumbling down, and Buster brought it to Burrell in his mouth. I wanted a camera.

The bag had come from a local grocery store, and was tied with rabbit ears. Burrell slipped on a pair of rubber gloves, and untied the knot. Out came a little boy's pajamas.

"Now we're getting somewhere," she said.

CHAPTER SEVENTEEN

The pajamas were taken for an evaluation to a police forensics lab on the other side of the county. Very soon, we were going to know if the DNA samples on the pajamas matched Sampson's, and if my assumptions about the kidnapping were accurate.

I stood with Burrell by the campfire drinking bottled water. I could tell that she was upset with herself. It was natural for cops to miss clues while conducting searches, only telling her that wouldn't change how she felt. Twenty minutes later her cell phone rang, and we learned that a match had been made. The pajamas were indeed Sampson's.

"You're batting a thousand so far," she said.

"Don't forget Buster," I said.

She glanced at my dog, then tossed her empty bottle into the campfire. "You and I need to be clear about something. You think an outsider did this. I don't, and neither

151

does the FBI. One thing Cheeks got right: Jed Grimes is responsible, and I'm going to arrest him."

I tossed my bottle next to hers. "When did the FBI get involved?"

"This morning. I called a special agent in Quantico that I know. He reviewed the evidence, and thinks Jed is guilty as sin. So do I."

I had worked with the FBI many times. They had an approach that I didn't agree with. They would come up with a theory, then try to shoehorn all the evidence to make that theory work. It was great, except for the times when they got it wrong.

"What evidence are you talking about?" I asked.

"Jed failed a polygraph that was taken after Sampson was abducted. He also has a history with the police, and has been hauled in fifty times. One of those times was for arson when he was a teenager. He tried to torch the garage behind his mother's house, which was the same garage where the police found the underpants of his father's victims."

"What happened?"

"There was a trial in juvenile court. Jed claimed that curiosity seekers were going into the backyard and photographing the garage, so he decided to burn it down. The judge felt sorry for him, and gave him probation."

"How old was he?"

"Fifteen."

I gazed across the clearing at the tree where the dead vagrant had been tied. His killing had been committed by someone practiced in deception and cold-blooded murder. It was an unusual mix of skills that were usually honed over time. Jed, who was the same age as my daughter, didn't seem old enough.

"I want to talk to Jed before you arrest him," I said. "I've known his ex-wife since she was a kid, and I also met with his father yesterday."

"You think he'll open up to you?" Burrell asked.

"He might."

"All right. But I want you to wear a wire."

I had worn wires before, and had discovered that they often telegraphed themselves through body language and other subliminal signs. I also didn't like the idea of having cops lurking nearby in a van.

"No wire," I said.

Burrell shot me a disapproving look. "What if Jed confesses to you, and we don't record it? What then, Jack?"

"We get him to confess again," I said.

"I need to hear what he says to you."

"I'll tell you what he says, word for word."

"Why are you being so stubborn?"

"I need Jed to trust me. I can't do that if I'm sweating through my underwear because there's a mike taped to my stomach and a bunch of cops sitting outside."

Burrell considered what I was saying. Then she called Jed's mother on her cell phone, and arranged for me to meet with Jed at his mother's house in thirty minutes. She ended the call and gave me his mother's address.

"I hope you're right about this," she said.

There are times when it's good to own a mean dog. Walking back to my car, I was accosted by Chip Wells and his camera crew, who wanted to interview me for the evening news. Buster was on a leash, and my dog lunged at them so viciously that Wells and his crew ran for cover.

The interior of my car felt like an oven. I rolled my windows down, then took my cell phone off the dash, and punched in my daughter's cell number. I knew Jessie's class schedule by heart, and she was on break right now.

"Hey, Daddy," she answered.

"Is this the best women's college basket-ball player in the country?" I asked.

"Did you see the game?"

"I sure did. You were a star."

"I was voted most valuable player, and got interviewed on cable TV after the game. Believe it or not, he asked me out on a date."

"Who did?"

"The announcer who interviewed me."

My daughter's games were shown on a lo-cal cable station, the announcer a blow-dried ex-jock who never stopped talking.

"I'll kill him," I said.

"Daddy, please!"

"I need to talk to you about something."

"Sure."

"I saw an old friend of yours last night."

"Really? Who was that?"

"Heather Rinker."

"God, I haven't spoken to Heather in months. How's she doing?"

"Not so good. Her son was abducted, and I've been hired by the family to find him. What can you tell me about Heather's ex-husband, Jed Grimes?"

"Oh, God."

"Is he a bad guy?"

"No, he's just messed up. Jed and Heather were sweethearts in junior high. When they were sixteen Jed got Heather pregnant, then refused to help raise her little boy, so Heather quit school to work at Blockbuster. She finally got her life together, then Jed reappeared and filed for joint custody and won. I spoke with Heather over the holidays, and she told me Jed was actually trying to be a good father."

"Have you ever met him?"

"I met him at a party once. He couldn't stop talking about his father's crimes. He was sort of obsessed. I think it had something to do with the old neighborhood."

"The old neighborhood?"

"Jed's mother never moved."

"Maybe she couldn't afford to."

"I know, but she didn't change the house, either. Inside, it's exactly the same as it was when her husband was arrested. Same furniture, same paint, same everything."

"Do you think it warped Jed?"

"Yes. I've got to go. I've got a math test in an hour that I haven't studied for."

I started my car. I was getting a clearer picture of Jed, while beginning to understand why he was the main suspect. He sounded like a disturbed young man, but I still didn't think he was guilty.

"Good luck," I said. "Oh, and Jessie?"

"Yes, Daddy?"

"I was serious what I said about that announcer. He's nearly my age."

"Good-bye, Daddy."

CHAPTER EIGHTEEN

Jed's mother's name was LeAnn Grimes. I'd seen her on the news and still remembered her story. She came from a family of citrus farmers, and was a small woman with a pretty face and nervous hands. She'd sat dutifully behind Abb during his trial, and when the guilty verdict was read, had sobbed uncontrollably.

She lived on Magnolia Lane in west Davie. The house was made of cinder blocks and was rather small, with dark shades covering the windows, and several "No Trespassing" signs displayed prominently on the lawn. I parked across the street. A group of six tourists stood on the sidewalk snapping pictures. They had accents that I couldn't place, and had come in a van. They were dressed alike, and wore black pants and black T-shirts that featured the infamous picture of Abb Grimes holding his last victim in his arms. I couldn't understand what they were saying, except they mentioned the Night Stalker over and over, their voices hushed and reverential. Abb had gone to prison over a dozen years ago, yet it was obvious his infamy lived on.

I waited until the tourists were gone before knocking on LeAnn Grimes's front door. It cracked open, and a white-haired woman with sunken eyes stared at me. It was LeAnn. The years had taken their toll, and robbed her face of its natural beauty.

"Don't tell me you want your picture taken," LeAnn said.

"I'm Jack Carpenter," I said. "Your husband hired me to find your grandson. I'm here to speak with Jed."

She looked me up and down. "What's with the mutt?"

"He's my partner."

LeAnn opened the front door and ushered me inside. Her movements were slow, as if an invisible weight rested on her shoulders. She led me to the living room, which was dark save for the TV playing in the corner, and dropped onto a couch that had seen better days. I stood in front of the couch, Buster by my side.

"Is Jed here?" I asked.

"He's taking a shower. Do you have any news about my grandson?"

"Not yet," I said.

She shut her eyes and placed her hands in her lap. She looked like she was going into a trance, and a long moment passed. I let my eyes wander the room. Most of the furniture was tagged for sale, and I glanced at a lamp on a table. The price was $2,000. It seemed an outrageous amount, and I checked the tags on several other items. They were also in the stratosphere.

"See anything you like?" LeAnn asked, her eyes now open.

"A little expensive for my taste," I replied.

"The tagged items were my husband's things," she explained. "Jed plans to auction them on eBay after the execution. I think I hear him now."

Jed Grimes entered the living room a few moments later. Boyish and handsome, he stood about six feet and was blessed with a lean, muscular body. He didn't look old enough to be shaving, much less have a three-year-old son. Seeing me, his eyes narrowed, and I felt him sizing me up.

"This is Jack Carpenter, the man your father hired to find Sampson," his mother said. "That's his dog."

Jed nodded woodenly at me.

"Glad to meet you," I said.

"I heard you were a cop," Jed said.

"I was. Not anymore."

"You bring any cops with you?"

I pointed at Buster. "He's one. That's his disguise."

LeAnn let out a throaty laugh. It brought Jed's guard down, and I crossed the living room and stuck out my hand. He smiled thinly and shook it.

"We need to talk about Sampson," I said.

"Let's go outside," he said. "My mom's favorite program is on."

Jed led me outside to the garage. Buster caught a scent as we entered, and vanished into the back. Square and high-ceilinged, the rafters were adorned with stolen street signs and old license plates. Thumbtacked to the walls were a collection of old *Playboy* calendars, including a centerfold of Anna Nicole Smith from 1993. The workbench, which took up the back wall, was filled with rusty tools. A thin layer of dust had settled over the floor, and lifted mysteriously each time we moved.

In the center of the garage sat a vintage Harley-Davidson motorcycle with chrome so shiny that I could see my reflection in it. It was the only thing in the place that was clean and looked well-maintained. Jed leaned against the seat, and faced me.

"You going to sell the bike?" I asked.

"My father wanted me to keep it," Jed replied. "He's going to die soon. Did he tell you that?"

"Yes. Did your father tell you to sell the stuff in the house?"

"Yeah. Called it his life insurance policy."

Jed's voice was flat, but there was pain in it. I stepped in front of the bike, and looked him in the eye. Most people hate when I do this, but Jed didn't flinch.

"I have a pretty good idea who kidnapped your son," I said.

Jed nearly fell down. "You do? Who?"

"Someone in the neighborhood who had a score to settle with your father."

"Okay."

"But I'm having a problem moving my investigation forward."

"Why?"

"Because the police think you're guilty. Until I can convince them that you didn't kidnap your son, I'm stuck."

"The *police*." Jed said the word like it was a curse. He lowered his gaze, and stared at the concrete floor. "What do you want me to do?"

"You could start by answering some questions for me."

"Go ahead."

"You tried to burn this garage down four years ago. Why did you do that?"

He swallowed hard. "What's that got —"

"Just answer me."

"A kid at school told me my daddy was worse than Ed Gein. I didn't know who he was, so I looked him up. Ed Gein was a serial killer who made furniture from women's body parts. They based the movies *Psycho* and *Silence of the Lambs* on him. The article said that after Gein was arrested, the local townspeople burned his house to the ground."

"So you decided to burn your father's garage," I said.

Jed nodded. "I was kind of crazy back then."

"Next question. You failed a polygraph test. Why did you lie to the police?"

"I only lied about one thing."

I crossed my arms and waited for him to continue.

"I told the police I was at home when Sampson was taken," Jed explained. "I was actually next door, bumming a joint from my neighbor."

"You smoke dope?" I asked.

"I quit a year ago," Jed said. "It was for my friend Ronnie, who was in the house with me. He still gets high."

"Why didn't you tell the police that?"

"I didn't want to get anyone in trouble."

"It was just a joint."

"My neighbor does a little selling on the side."

Jed had lied to protect someone else. That happened all the time during criminal investigations, and the police were used to it. I needed to get Jed back to the station house and have him take another polygraph.

"If I told you that taking another polygraph would help rescue your son, would you do it?" I asked him.

Jed lifted his gaze. "Not if Detective Cheeks was there."

"You have a problem with Cheeks?"

"Yeah. He hates me."

"Cheeks is in the hospital. I'll go with you to the police department and be there when they administer the polygraph. I'll also tell them ahead of time what you did, and ask them not to ask you to finger your neighbor."

"You can do that?"

"Yes, sir," I said.

Jed pushed himself off his father's motorcycle and slapped me on the shoulder.

"I'm with you, man," he said.

Jed walked me to my car. I had expected

him to be an emotionally twisted young man, and was pleasantly surprised by what I'd found. He was surprisingly well adjusted, considering the circumstances. How Cheeks or anyone else at the police department could consider him their prime suspect was a mystery.

"I'll need a few hours to get things set up with the police," I said.

"I'll be here waiting," he said.

I got into my car with my dog. As I started the engine, a car pulled in behind me, and four Asian tourists got out. Like the group I'd seen before, they were dressed in black, and began to photograph the house. I motioned to Jed, and he came to my window.

"How long has this been going on?" I asked.

"Years. Ever since my father was put in prison," he replied. "We usually get six or seven groups a day. They come here, then go to the Smart Buy supermarket."

"What's at the Smart Buy?"

Jed's face turned sad, and I realized I'd struck a nerve.

"The Dumpsters," he said quietly.

I didn't know what to say. Jed banged his hand on my roof, and went back inside.

I watched the Asians for a while. For them, Abb's house was a tourist attraction, and it bothered me how much they seemed to be enjoying themselves.

Finally, they got back into their rental car, and drove away. One of them had a map, and was giving directions to the driver. I decided to follow.

They drove three blocks down Magnolia, then turned into the parking lot of a grocery store. As I followed them into the lot, I saw that it was a Smart Buy. Jed had been right: the Asians were going to finish their tour by seeing the Dumpsters where Abb had killed and disposed of his victims.

I followed them around to the rear of the store. The building had a flat roof and peeling orange stucco, and sat on a low parcel of land. In back was a loading dock where trucks brought deliveries. Next to it, the infamous Dumpsters.

The Asian tourists parked next to the Dumpsters and got out of their car. Then they started taking pictures. I parked well behind them, and had a look around.

The old neighborhood. I hadn't understood what Jessie had meant earlier, but now I did. Abb's house hadn't changed in twelve years, and neither had the site of his killings. The place was a time warp.

One of the tourists approached my car. He was smiling and holding an expensive camera. I stared at his T-shirt. On it was a picture of Abb Grimes holding his last victim. The picture had been enhanced, and showed bright red blood dripping out of the victim's mouth. It triggered a lot of painful memories, and I thought of the seven Jane Does I'd never identified. Those women had suffered and died, and this guy was wearing a T-shirt that exploited them.

"Excuse me," the man said in broken English.

"You're excused," I said.

"Would you take a photograph of me and my friends?"

I shook my head.

"I will pay you," he offered.

"Not interested," I said.

The man pulled out his wallet, and dangled a twenty-dollar bill in front of my face. His friends were standing in front of the Dumpsters, smiling and waiting to have their group picture taken. Something inside of me snapped.

"You need to leave," I said.

"But we are not done," the man said.

"Yes, you are."

I opened my door, and hopped out of my car. The man stepped back.

"Is something wrong?" he asked.

I drew my Colt, and tucked its barrel down behind my belt buckle. Then I crossed my arms, and gave the guy a menacing look. Cops called this getting western on someone. He got the message and quickly gathered up his friends. They left in a cloud of dust.

CHAPTER NINETEEN

I waited until the tourists were gone before getting back in my car. Then I called Burrell on my cell. She answered on the first ring.

"Jed Grimes didn't kidnap his son," I said.

"You're sure about that," Burrell said.

"Yes."

"I'm inside the Operations Center trailer next to Jed Grimes's house. Why don't you come over here? I want to show you something."

I drove to Jed's house and parked next to the OC trailer. Buster was snoozing on the passenger seat, and I rolled down the windows before getting out.

I found Burrell sitting at a desk inside the trailer, sucking down a Gatorade. Her clothes were drenched in sweat, and she looked miserable. The trailer was jammed with equipment, including a dozen phone lines, two computers, and three TV sets that stayed on 24/7. I grabbed the only other chair, and sat down across from her.

"Jed's guilty," Burrell said.

"What did you find?" I asked.

Four photographs were lying facedown on the desk. Burrell flipped the first one over, revealing a surfer dude with shoulder-length blond hair. "This is Ronnie Wild, Jed's best friend. Ronnie was in the house with Jed the night Sampson was kidnapped. Every time we interview Ronnie, he tells us something new. This morning, Ronnie told us that Jed left the house when his son was kidnapped, and went next door to see a neighbor."

"I know," I said.

Burrell looked surprised. "Jed told you?"

"Yes."

"Did Jed tell you who his neighbor was?"

"He said his neighbor peddled drugs, and he wanted to score a joint from him."

Burrell flipped over the second photograph. "This is Jed's neighbor, a drug-pushing lowlife named Cody Barnes. Barnes has been peddling drugs since he was fifteen years old. Mostly weed, but also coke. Now, here's where it gets interesting."

Burrell flipped over the last two photographs. They were both aerial shots, and showed two Hispanic guys, one skinny and missing several teeth, the other older and overweight. It was the same pair I'd chased on I-95 that morning.

"Where did you get these?" I asked.

"They're from the DEA, courtesy of my friend with the FBI. The skinny one's named Pepito Suarez, and his partner just goes by Oscar. They're Colombian hit men. They worked for the Cali drug cartel, then got involved in a shootout down in Miami and killed two DEA agents. They've been on the run ever since. Word is, they hire themselves out to drug dealers, and help them collect their money."

"These are the guys I saw this morning," I said.

"That's what I figured. Guess who they're friends with?"

"I have no idea."

Burrell tapped the photograph of Cody Barnes. "Jed's neighbor, that's who."

"And you think Jed asked Cody Barnes to hire these goons to watch his son," I said.

"That's exactly what I think."

I pushed myself away from the desk. The scenario Burrell was suggesting looked great on paper, and that's the only place it looked good. It had FBI written all over it, and I sensed that Burrell's friend at the Bureau was behind it.

"You're wrong, and so's your friend at the FBI," I said.

Burrell threw her Gatorade at my head. I ducked, and heard the bottle hit the wall.

"Prove it," she said angrily.

Scotch-taped to the wall were several photographs of Sampson, and I pulled down the one that showed him riding a bright blue tricycle.

"See this tricycle?" I said. "I saw it in the backyard of Jed's house, along with a dozen toys and a plastic swimming pool. I also saw a bedroom filled with toys, and cute wallpaper with cartoon characters. Do you know how much that stuff costs?"

Burrell shook her head. The look on her face said she wanted to kill me.

"Try hundreds and hundreds of dollars," I said.

"So what?"

"Jed Grimes was trying to be a good father."

"What does that have to do with this?"

"Everything. What kind of father hires a pair of professional killers to guard his son?"

Burrell swallowed hard. "A bad one."

"That's right, a bad one. Bad fathers feed their kids cold SpaghettiOs and let them watch X-rated movies. They don't buy them tricycles and expensive toys."

I picked up her bottle of Gatorade from the floor, and put it on the desk. Then I headed for the door. "You're going down the wrong road. Jed Grimes is a victim. If you arrest him, you'll end up ruining your career. I'd be willing to put money on it."

Burrell sank down into her chair. "What should I do?"

"You need to refocus your investigation. Yesterday I gave the chief a photograph of Sampson sitting in a dog crate in a hotel room. Has anyone tried to figure out which hotel chain the photo was taken in?"

"The techs examined it. They couldn't tell which hotel it was."

"Then call Sally Haskell. She should be able to help us."

"I thought Sally was running security for Disney," Burrell said.

"She is. A guy on her staff is an expert at identifying hotel interiors. He helped me find a man who'd abducted his daughter, and was sending his ex-wife photos. Sally's guy identified the hotel chain they were staying in, and where it was located."

"I'll call her right now."

I opened the door while continuing to stare at Burrell. I had trained her the same way I'd trained every detective who'd ever worked for me. It was all about following

173

your instincts. She was losing sight of that, and letting outsiders cloud her judgment.

"How long did you work for me?" I asked.

"Six and a half years," she said.

"What was the first thing I ever taught you?"

"It's all about the kid."

"I'll talk to you later," I said.

I drove to a convenience store a few blocks away, buying a package of cupcakes and a Dr Pepper for myself, some beef jerky for Buster. I had stopped eating junk food years ago, except when I was working a case. Then it was the only thing I ate.

As I paid up, I saw a stack of local newspapers by the register. The headline read NIGHT STALKER TO DIE. I bought a copy, and read the article in my car.

The article didn't say anything new. Abb would be executed by lethal injection in three days. The governor wasn't going to stop it, and none of the organizations against capital punishment were voicing a protest. His time had run out.

The article had a sidebar that talked about the seven Jane Does. Forensic imaging had been performed on each victim using pictures of their skulls in the hope that someone might recognize them. I looked at their faces long and hard. Maybe someday we'd know who they were. But I had a feeling that someday was a long way off.

My cell phone rang as I was pulling out of the lot. I pulled the phone off the Velcro on the dash, and flipped it open.

"Carpenter here."

"My name is Charles Crippen," a man with a deep voice said. "You may have heard of me. I own a law firm in town."

I had heard of Charles Crippen. He was considered one of the better lawyers in south Florida. "What can I do for you, Mr. Crippen?" I replied.

"One of my employees has gone missing. I need you to find her."

"I'm sorry, but I'm working a case."

"Her name is Piper Stone. She was in the process of filing an appeal for a stay of execution for Abb Grimes, and now no one can find her."

An icy finger ran down the length of my spine. I turned my wheels so my vehicle was pointed at the street.

"Give me your address," I said.

CHAPTER TWENTY

Crippen & Howe had been advertising on billboards throughout the county since I was a kid. The ads showed two men. Charles Crippen, the firm's elder statesman, wore a neatly trimmed goatee and a yachtsman's deep tan, while his partner, Bernie Howe, was a bulldog with a bad hair replacement job. Their law firm occupied a two-story Spanish colonial on Broward Boulevard surrounded by an imposing wrought-iron fence.

I parked in the private lot behind the building, grabbed my dog, and walked down a sidewalk to the front entrance. The gate was locked, and I pressed the buzzer while looking into the lens of a boxy security camera.

"May I help you?" a woman's voice said over the intercom.

"Jack Carpenter for Charles Crippen."

"Is he *expecting* you?"

"I'm here about Piper Stone."

"Stay right there."

I waited. The sun was shining and sweat poured down my back. Finally, the receptionist returned. "Mr. Crippen will see you now."

She buzzed me in, and I walked up the brick path and entered the building. The reception area was no more than an alcove. Behind a desk sat a woman with a hairdo that looked like a Macy's Thanksgiving Day Parade float. She came out of her chair like she'd been hit with a cattle prod. "Sir, no dogs are allowed in the building."

"You let criminals in here every day," I said. "Drug dealers, murderers, rapists. But you're telling me dogs aren't allowed. How does that work?"

Before she could respond, Charles Crippen entered the alcove. He was tall, and wore a dark pin-striped suit and blazing red tie. He asked me to follow him.

Crippen's office was on the second floor of the building. It was enormous, with furnishings befitting a king. Once the door was closed, he sat at his desk and undid his necktie. He started to speak, then noticed Buster standing by my side.

"Is he with you?" Crippen asked.

"Never seen him before," I replied.

"I heard you were a character. Please have a seat."

I pulled up a chair and sat down while Buster lay dutifully beside me.

"It all started last night," Crippen said. "I came back from a client meeting, and found Piper in her office. It was about nine-thirty. I assumed she was preparing for her murder trial today. Then I glanced at the pages on her desk, and saw the transcript from Abb Grimes's murder trial. I asked her what she was doing, and Piper told me she'd found something very disturbing.

"I left shortly after that. Piper's a bright lady, and I knew she was on to something. When I came in this morning, she was still here, and was all fired up. She said she'd found a basis for a new appeal, and was going to investigate it further."

"Did she say what it was?" I asked.

"It was something to do with slippers."

"Men's or women's?"

"She didn't say. Piper was supposed to be at the courthouse at eleven o'clock for the opening arguments in another trial. She told me she was going to stop at Memorial Hospital first, and talk to someone regarding these slippers."

"Did she say who?"

"Some detective who's been ill."

"Was it Ron Cheeks?"

Crippen plumbed his memory. "Yes, that was the name. Piper left after we spoke, and hasn't been seen since. She was a no-show at the courthouse, and hasn't called in. That's when I called the police."

"What have the police done?"

"They went to Piper's apartment and got the superintendent to let them in. There was no evidence of foul play. They also put out an APB on her car. As you know, that's about all they can do."

"Did they search her office?"

Crippen lowered his hands. "They wanted to, but I was fearful that they'd see her files. She's working on several important cases right now, and they're spread across her office."

"Can I take a look?"

"Certainly."

Crippen led me down a hallway lined with polished wooden doors. Stone's office sat next to the copy room, and screamed new hire. Metal desk, a laptop, a couple of old chairs, and a diploma from the University of Miami Law School hanging on the wall. There were no personal items, save for a framed photo of Stone cuddling a Lab puppy.

"May I?" I asked.

"Of course," Crippen replied.

I sat at Stone's desk. It was covered with the transcript from Abb Grimes's trial along with a number of police reports. Stone had brightened the lines on several pages with a yellow highlighter, and I read those sections first. What I saw made my eyes pop.

Ron Cheeks's name was everywhere. He'd been the first detective to arrive at the Smart Buy, and had also handled the subsequent investigation. While it was his partner who'd arrested Abb and testified at his trial, it was Cheeks who'd run the show.

I pored through the transcript. Toward the back was an evidence log showing the various items that were taken from Abb's home after his arrest. Stone had highlighted the word *slippers,* and written something in cryptic scrawl beside it. I showed the writing to Crippen.

"This make any sense to you?" I asked.

Crippen slipped on a pair of bifocals and studied the writing. "It says, 'Where did they go?' I assume she's referring to the slippers."

"That's what she went to see Cheeks about. Abb Grimes's slippers."

"That would be a fair assumption."

"And no one's heard from her since."

"That's correct."

The phone on Stone's desk rang. Crippen snatched it up and said hello. Then he looked at me and shook his head. He hung up.

"Has anyone bothered to check Stone's voice mail?" I asked.

"I did," Crippen replied.

"Recently?"

"Several hours ago."

"Let's check it again."

Crippen punched a code into the phone, and put it on speaker. There were six messages stored in Stone's voice mail. We listened to several seconds of each before Crippen saved them. Each was from a client, until the very last. The last message sounded like a crank call, with music by Gloria Estefan and the Miami Sound Machine pouring out of the speaker. It lasted for about ten seconds, then abruptly stopped.

"Did you hear that sound in the background?" I asked.

Crippen had brought his ear a few inches from the speaker. "No, but I'm half deaf. What did you hear?"

"It sounded like a voice. Play it again."

Crippen replayed the message. The sound was too faint to be discernible. Crippen said, "Let me get a better phone," and went to the office next door to get a newer phone, which he put on the desk. Over this phone, the message was much clearer.

"It *is* a voice," Crippen said.

"I think it's a woman."

"What is she saying?"

"I'm not sure. We need more volume."

Crippen cranked up the phone's volume and replayed the message. We both leaned in to listen. The voice was a woman's, and she sounded as if she was at the bottom of a deep hole.

"Somebody help me!"

"Is that her?" I asked.

Crippen opened his mouth, but no words came out. It was all the answer I needed.

CHAPTER
TWENTY-ONE

"Call the police," I said.

Crippen was visibly shaken. He picked up the phone on Stone's desk, and mechanically dialed 911. Taking the transcript and police reports, I went into the hall and copied the pages that Stone had highlighted, then returned the originals to the office. I clicked my fingers, and Buster rose from the floor.

"Where are you going?" Crippen asked.

I stopped in the doorway. I was going to Memorial Hospital to visit Ron Cheeks, and talk to him before the police did. I wanted to know why Cheeks hadn't leveled with me about his involvement with Abb Grimes's case. Only Crippen didn't need to hear that.

"I'm going to look for Stone," I said.

"Please call me immediately if you learn anything."

"I will. I'd appreciate it if you did the same."

Crippen nodded absently and I left.

The hospital lot was full. I parked on a residential side street and rolled down the windows. Buster got the hint, and curled up on the passenger seat. I went inside.

The lobby was filled with pregnant women and half-dead retirees. I got Cheeks's room number from the receptionist, and took a stairwell to the fourth floor. Cheeks was in a single at the end of the hall. I peeked into his room to make sure he had no visitors. Cheeks sat upright in bed watching *Divorce Court* with the volume jacked up and a big smile on his face. The room was devoid of flowers or balloons or even a single Get Well card. As I entered, he jumped.

"What the hell are *you* doing here?" Cheeks asked.

"Bedpan check," I said.

"I'm recuperating. Get out."

"Not before we have a little chat."

"I don't have anything to say to you."

I tossed the copied pages onto his lap and pulled up a chair, the metal legs scraping harshly across the floor. Cheeks grabbed the phone from the nightstand.

"I'm calling security," he said.

"I'm working with the police," I said. "Call Chief Moody if you don't believe me."

"I don't care who you're working for. I'm having you tossed."

"Do that, and I'll tell Moody about you and Piper Stone."

Cheeks's face twisted in a frown. "The bitchy little lawyer? What about her?"

"She disappeared this morning. Left her office and came over here to talk to you about Abb Grimes's trial. That was the last anyone saw of her. She left a message on the voice mail at her office. You can hear her screaming. Where did you put her, Ron?"

Cheeks dropped the phone into the receiver with a horrified expression on his face. "Are you accusing me of abducting her? You're flipping nuts. I'm sick."

A clipboard hung on the edge of his bed. I picked it up, and read through Cheeks's medical condition as recorded by his doctor at nine o'clock this morning.

"According to this, you're perfectly normal," I said, dropping the clipboard. "My guess is, you faked that heart attack, giving you a convenient way to get taken off the case. But Stone figured out you've been hiding something, and she confronted you."

"Crazy talk," Cheeks said.

185

"Did you speak with Stone this morning?"

His face reddened. "What if I did?"

"What time?"

"You don't have any right to grill me."

"I'm on the case, dickhead. What time did she come in?"

"Around eight. It was cordial. I got the orderly to get her coffee. We talked for about twenty minutes, then she split."

Cheeks was softening up, trying to placate me. I pointed at the copied pages lying in his lap. "You were actively involved in Abb Grimes's murder investigation. Is that what you and Stone talked about?"

Cheeks hesitated. He blinked several times.

"She wanted to go over some things," he muttered.

"What things?"

"I don't remember."

"She was only here a few hours ago."

"I took a nap after she left."

I picked up the pages and found the evidence log. I showed Cheeks the word *slippers* and saw him squint to read what Stone had written beside it. His face got even redder and I pounced. "There were a pair of slippers in the evidence log that somehow disappeared. Were they Abb's slippers?"

"I guess so."

"Is that a yes or a no?"

Cheeks pulled himself up and killed the TV with the remote at the same time. I could feel him retrenching, readying for a fight. He cleared his throat. "We took over a hundred pieces of evidence out of Abb's house, cataloged them, and stored them in the police warehouse. We separated the clothes and took them to a forensics lab, where they were checked for DNA, hairs, and fibers. We were hoping to use the evidence to identify the victims we found at the landfill."

"Find anything?"

"No. The clothes were clean, and we didn't turn up anything. During the transfer from the lab back to the warehouse, the box containing the slippers got misplaced. I don't know what happened to them, and I'm never going to know. If you tell me that never happened to you during an investigation, you're a fucking liar."

"It never happened to me," I said.

Cheeks shook his fist a few inches beneath my chin. The strange look in his eyes that I'd seen in the orange grove returned. I touched the automatic control on the side of his bed, and sent him backwards.

"Cut it out," he said angrily.

"I don't like being threatened."

"I'm not threatening you, for Christ's sake."

I decided to take him at his word, and returned the bed to its original position.

"Why did Stone think the slippers were significant?" I asked.

"She didn't say."

"Then what did she want?"

"She wanted to know what had happened to them. I told her exactly what I just told you. The slippers got lost."

"Did she buy it?"

Cheeks shot me a hard look. "There was nothing to *buy.* The slippers never came up during the trial. They were meaningless. End of story."

I took the pages from him, stuck them beneath my arm, and got to my feet. Cheeks was lying through his teeth. He hadn't taken a nap earlier; he'd rehearsed this little speech, knowing that his encounter with Stone was going to come back to haunt him. I needed to hunt Stone down, and get to the truth.

"Did Stone say where she was going?" I asked.

Cheeks rubbed his chin thoughtfully, then folded his hands on his chest, and shook his head. I was getting nothing more out of him. He had won this round, but he hadn't won the fight.

"When are they letting you out?" I asked.

"Soon," he replied.

"I may have a few more questions. Where's the best place to reach you?"

"I'll be at home getting my strength back."

"You still live in Plantation?"

"Yeah. I got the house in the divorce."

"How did you pull that off?"

"My wife decided to leave the state."

"Where did she go? Antarctica?"

Cheeks smiled at my joke, then realized it was aimed at him. He looked for something to throw at me, but by then I was out the door.

CHAPTER
TWENTY-TWO

Tucked beneath the windshield wiper of my car was a parking ticket. I had parked in a fifteen-minute zone, and owed the county a hundred and eighty bucks. I'd pay it after I won the lottery. Buster feigned sleep as I started the ignition.

"Some watchdog you are," I said.

My cell phone chimed. I pulled it off the dash and retrieved a voice message that had come in. It was Charles Crippen, and he had a lead on Piper Stone. I called his number and he picked up.

"Have you talked with the police?" I asked.

"They just left my office," Crippen replied. "They're driving to Memorial to interview Cheeks. I wanted to warn you."

I didn't like lawyers, just the way they thought. "I just left Cheeks. Stone visited him this morning, and they discussed the missing slippers."

"Is Cheeks hiding something?"

That was a good question. I'd fallen pretty low since losing my job, but I wasn't going to rag on another cop unless I could prove that he'd broken the law.

"I don't know," I answered.

"I've been doing some digging of my own," Crippen said. "I don't mean to sound egotistical, but I carry some weight in this town. Piper's credit cards and cell phone are both paid for by the firm. I called the credit card companies and the cell phone company, and put them to work."

"Any luck?"

"Piper made two cell phone calls this morning. The first was to a cell phone owned by Jed Grimes. The second was the message you and I heard. The cell company tracked her phone's location using tower pings. Piper's somewhere in Davie."

"You mean her cell phone's in Davie," I said.

"Trust me. Piper and her phone rarely part."

Cell towers worked in grids. Crippen gave me the names of four streets in Davie that defined the portion of the grid where Stone's cell phone was sending its signal from. I took a map from the glove compartment, spread it on my lap, and located the four streets. Then I froze. Stone's cell phone was in LeAnn Grimes's neighborhood.

"Did you share this information with the police?" I asked.

"I wanted you to have it first," Crippen said. "Not being a cop, I figured you'd know what to do with it."

I understood what Crippen was saying. Not being a policeman allowed me to do a variety of questionable things without fear of jeopardizing the police's case. It was why people hired me, but the cop in me still had a hard time accepting it.

"I'll call you when I learn something," I said.

There was no quick way to Davie, and I wove in and out of traffic on 595 with my hand on the horn. Piper had called Jed Grimes after leaving Memorial, and now her cell phone was emitting a signal from the area where Jed's mother lived. I needed to talk to Jed, and find out what he and Stone had talked about. There was a chance that Stone had told him where she was going, and that I'd be able to track her down.

My tires rubbed the curb as I parked in front of LeAnn Grimes's place. A new gang of tourists was standing on the lawn, using their cell phones to snap digital photographs of the house. I was getting a sense of what life had been like for LeAnn and Jed for the past twelve years, and it was turning my stomach. They didn't deserve to be punished for the heinous things Abb had done.

With Buster on a leash, I walked up to the tourists, and told them they were trespassing. There were six of them, and they didn't move. One was posing for his friends while holding a photo of Abb taken at his trial. Abb was sitting at the defense table with a stony expression on his face that made him look like a zombie.

I unleashed my dog. Buster circled the tourists, barking viciously. They scurried into a minibus and drove away. My dog pressed up against my leg.

"That's more like it," I told him.

I walked up the front path and pressed the buzzer. Heather Rinker opened the door with a towel wrapped around her wet head. Seeing me, her face brightened.

"Mr. Carpenter. We were just talking about you."

"I don't have any news about your son," I said. "Is Jed here? I need to speak with him."

"He's in the living room with his mom."

Heather led me into the house. Jed and LeAnn shared the living room couch, their faces illuminated by an old Burt Reynolds movie playing on the TV. Jed had his shirt off, and the movie's images were interacting with the swirling tattoos of dragons and demons inked on his upper torso. His expression was filled with hope, as was his mother's.

"Any news about Sampson?" he asked.

I shook my head. "I need to ask you some more questions."

"About what?"

"Piper Stone, your father's defense attorney. She's disappeared."

Jed hesitated, and I swore his lips seemed to quiver.

"Didn't you just see Ms. Stone this morning?" LeAnn asked her son.

"Yes, Mama," Jed said quietly.

Jed muted the TV with the remote. I wanted to get him outside the house so we could talk in private, but he was glued to his mother's side. I pulled up a chair and sat across from him. Buster dropped by my feet and stared at Jed.

"Would you like something to drink, Mr. Carpenter?" Heather asked.

"Water would be fine," I said.

Heather disappeared into the kitchen. Jed took a shirt off the back of the couch, and put it on. He buttoned the shirt up to his neck so that his tattoos were hidden. I sensed that he was uncomfortable with how he looked, at least around me.

"Tell me about your meeting with Piper Stone," I said.

"She came over here around eight-thirty, and we went for a drive in her car. We talked about my father's execution. She told me she wanted to file another appeal."

"Did she mention your father's missing slippers?"

Jed hesitated. I sensed he was holding back.

"Who told you about the slippers?" he asked.

"I'm an investigator, remember?"

He laughed, but it was a hollow sound. "Yeah, she mentioned the slippers. She wanted to file an appeal because evidence was lost in the case that might have been destroyed. I told her it was a waste of time."

"Why is filing an appeal a waste of time?"

"Because my father's ready to die. He told me so the last time I went to Starke and saw him. He said he was ready to pay for the things he'd done. Those were his exact words."

"What did the missing slippers prove?"

Jed shut his eyes, and I thought he might break into tears. LeAnn placed a consoling hand on her son's knee. He took a deep breath and composed himself.

"My father wasn't sane when he killed those women," he said quietly.

Heather brought my glass of water, and I drank it while studying the young man sitting in front of me. He looked tortured, but I had to ask him.

"Was your father wearing the slippers when he killed his victims?" I asked.

Jed's eyes snapped open, and for a moment I thought he was going to come over the coffee table and pummel me. Instead, he slammed his fist onto the arm of the couch.

"I don't want to fucking talk about this anymore," he said angrily.

"Jed!" his mother said.

"Sorry, Mama."

"Did Stone tell you where she was going after she left?" I asked.

Jed hit the couch again. "You don't listen, do you?"

"Did she?"

"She said she had some more digging to do. Now can we stop talking about this?"

I had a habit of pushing people to the breaking point when I was working a case. I'd reached that point with Jed, and I saw no reason to ask him any more questions.

"Sure," I said.

"You've upset my son," LeAnn said. "I think it would be best if you left."

"Of course," I said. "I'll see myself out."

Buster followed me into the kitchen, where I placed my empty glass in the sink. The faint sound of music floated through the air, Sheryl Crow's "All I Wanna Do (Is Have Some Fun)." The music was tinny, and I realized it was the ring tone to a cell phone.

The window above the sink was cracked a few inches. I stuck my ear to the opening, and heard the music coming from outside the house.

I hurried down the hallway toward the back door that Jed had used earlier to take me to the garage. As I passed the doorway to the living room, Jed looked up from the couch.

"Where are you going?" he asked.

"I heard something in your backyard," I said.

"What?"

"I don't know, but I'm going to find out."

Jed came into the hallway with Heather right behind him. His body language wasn't friendly, and he put himself between me and the door. I nudged my dog, and Buster curled back his upper lip and emitted a menacing growl.

"Hey. Get him away from me," Jed said.

"Back off," I said.

"This is my house. You can't order me around like that."

"It's your mother's house. Now move."

Jed got out of my way. I threw back the deadbolt on the back door, and went outside. The ringing grew louder. The garbage pail by the back door seemed the likely culprit, and I pulled off the lid. Lying on a bag of garbage was a bright red cell phone. Caller ID said OFFICE. I flipped the phone open.

"Hello?" I said.

"Who is this?" a man's voice said.

"This is Jack Carpenter," I said.

"Jack, this is Charles Crippen. Did you find Piper?"

"Not yet. Is this her cell phone you called?"

"Yes. I was hoping she'd pick up."

"I'll call you right back."

I folded Piper Stone's cell phone. Jed and Heather had come outside, and were standing on the stoop behind me. When I showed Stone's phone to Jed, his face did not register any emotion.

"Recognize this?" I asked.

Jed shook his head.

"It's Piper Stone's cell phone," I said.

Jed's mouth dropped open. If he was acting, he was doing a hell of a job. Lying on the bag of garbage inside the pail was a piece of clothing. It was frilly and feminine, and I held it up by a single finger. It was a pair of women's black lace underwear.

"How about these?" I asked.

Jed said *"Shit"* under his breath. Heather clasped her hands over her mouth, and stared at her ex-husband.

"Oh, my God, Jed. Oh, my God," she said.

Jed looked at the underwear, then at me. His breathing had gone shallow, and for the first time, I saw how strongly he resembled his father.

"I don't know how those got there, either," he said.

"You need to tell that to the police," I said.

"I'm not talking to the police."

I started to tell him that was a bad idea, but before I could, Jed jumped off the stoop and ran around the side of the house.

CHAPTER
TWENTY-THREE

Coming around the front of the house, I yelled for Jed to stop. He was halfway across the front lawn, and he glanced at me over his shoulder, his face wild with fear.

"Fucking cop!" he screamed.

LeAnn Grimes stood just around the corner, holding a broom. Moments later, my legs were tripped out from beneath me, and I was lying on my back in the grass, staring at a formation of clouds. Buster began barking, and I heard fabric being torn.

"Get away from me!" LeAnn screamed.

I lifted my head. Buster had grabbed the hem of her dress and was shredding it.

"Make him stop!" LeAnn yelled to me.

I pulled myself to my feet, my head spinning. Jed sat in a beat-up Firebird parked at the curb in front of my Legend. He was desperately trying to get the car started, only the engine refused to turn over. Each time he twisted the key, he jerked his head in my direction and shot me a crazed look.

I walked toward the Firebird with my palms out in a neutral pose. Jed didn't appear to be armed, nor did I see any guns lying on the passenger seat. The tourists had returned, watching now with mouths agape.

When I was a few yards from the car, Jed got the engine started, and backed up into my Legend. I winced at the sounds of crunching steel and shattering headlights. Throwing the Firebird into drive, Jed plowed into the tourist's rental van, parked in front of him. The rental bucked into the air, but didn't move. Jed did another backward thrust and again smashed my car. It was enough to make me cry.

The Firebird's right front tire let out a mournful hiss and the car sank into the ground. Now we were both without wheels.

Reaching the curb, I grabbed the Firebird's passenger door with my free hand. If I could get Jed out of the car without hurting him, so much the better. Something heavy fell on my back, and I realized there was a person on top of me.

"Run, Jed, run!" Heather yelled.

Heather was holding on to me with all her might. My legs buckled and my body started to spin from her weight.

"Get off me," I said angrily.

"Leave my husband alone," Heather said.

"I said *off!*"

"Run, Jed!"

Reaching behind me, I grabbed one of Heather's ankles, and gave it a healthy pull. She came off my back and fell on her rump on the lawn.

I chased Jed down the street. I wasn't going to catch him — he was half my age, and probably twice as fast — but I wanted to see where he was going.

Two blocks later, I got my answer. Jed turned off the street and darted between two houses. I was ten seconds behind him, and as I ran between the houses, I saw that both had "For Sale" signs on the front lawn. No one was living in them.

I came to a tall fence with a latched gate. I unlatched it, and cautiously entered a backyard that led to a swamp thick with trees and dense vegetation. Jed's footprints ran into the middle of the swamp, then disappeared.

I stood perfectly still and listened. There was no sound coming from the swamp, save for a squirrel's frantic chirping. I sensed that Jed was close by, but that didn't mean I was going to blindly follow him. This was the neighborhood he'd grown up in, and I had no idea what he might have hidden back there.

"Jed? Are you there?" I called out.

I heard a swishing of leaves, followed by a branch being broken.

"You set me up!" Jed shouted back.

"I didn't set you up," I said. "I don't know how those things got there."

"Fucking liar! You're no better than the rest of them."

"The rest of who?"

"The cops!"

I started to reply, only my words were cut off by a loud *thwap!* A steel-tipped arrow was sticking in the fence three feet from my head, its colorful tail vibrating.

I walked backward through the gate opening and shut it behind me. I learned long ago that heroes were dead people who got buildings named after them, while smart people lived to fight another day. Buster appeared in the street, holding a large piece of LeAnn Grimes's yellow dress in his mouth.

The front door of LeAnn Grimes's house was locked, and I banged on it loudly with my fist.

"Let me in," I said.

"Go away," Heather said through the door.

"I'll kick it down."

The door opened, and I entered with Buster. Heather stood in the foyer, an ice pack on her neck, eyes red from crying. I followed her into the living room where LeAnn sat on the couch in a bathrobe. Seeing Buster, she cowered in fear.

"Keep that monster away from me!"

"Did he bite you?"

"No, but he destroyed my dress."

"You're lucky."

Buster still had her torn dress in his mouth. I clicked my fingers and my dog lay down. I took the shredded garment from him, and tossed it into LeAnn's lap. Then I pointed at the empty spot on the couch.

"Sit next to your mother-in-law," I told Heather.

Heather dutifully obeyed. The two women shifted their gazes to the floor, and said nothing. Women were the most logical creatures on the planet, except when it came to men. Then they acted as crazy as everyone else.

"Are either of you hurt?" I asked.

LeAnn shook her head.

Heather said, "I'm okay."

"What the two of you just did was really stupid," I said.

Neither woman replied.

"I'm here to help, in case you didn't know

it," I said.

Again, nothing.

"I think Jed is innocent, but I can't do much if you won't level with me."

They looked up in unison, the expression on their faces identical. They didn't trust me, but they *wanted* to.

"Tell me why Jed ran away," I said. "If he didn't know how that cell phone and pair of underwear got in the garbage, then he should be willing to talk to the police."

LeAnn laughed under her breath.

"Why is that funny?" I asked.

"The police are not our friends," LeAnn said. "That's why my husband hired you."

"I'm not above the law," I said. "I have to call the police, and tell them that I found Piper Stone's cell phone in your garbage pail. Before I do that, I want you to tell me what happened this morning when Jed met with Stone."

This request was met with silence. I crossed my arms and waited.

"I wasn't here," Heather finally said.

LeAnn redid the knot in her bathrobe before replying. "It was about nine. I was pulling weeds in the front when a black BMW drove up with Stone behind the wheel. Jed came out of the house, and they left in her car."

"Did you see her again?" I asked.

"No," LeAnn said. "Jed came back fifteen minutes later. He was very upset, and had been crying. I asked him what was wrong, and he shook his head, and went inside the house."

"Did Stone drop him off?"

"No, he was on foot."

"Do you remember anything else? Anything at all?"

LeAnn shook her head.

"Please stay here," I said.

I went into the kitchen and rifled the pantry. Finding a plastic Ziploc bag, I put it over my hand, went outside, and removed Stone's cell phone and the pair of underwear from the garbage can without contaminating them any further. My gut told me that Jed hadn't put them there, only the evidence was saying otherwise. It was one more piece to a puzzle that I still couldn't put together.

I called 911 on my cell phone.

CHAPTER
TWENTY-FOUR

Five minutes later, a cruiser pulled up in front of LeAnn Grimes's house with its bubble light flashing. It contained the classic mismatch of uniformed officers: a crusty male veteran, and an inexperienced young female. The pairing worked great on TV cop shows; in real life it created nothing but friction. Standing on the front lawn, the pair listened to my story.

When I was done, the male officer took me aside. His nameplate said J. Botters. On the plus side of fifty, with leathery skin and thinning hair, he exuded the casualness of someone ready to retire.

"Show me where Jed ran off to," Botters said.

I walked Botters down the street and showed him the route Jed had taken, and the arrow he'd shot at me. Botters pulled the arrow out of the fence.

"Think he was trying to kill you?" Botters asked.

"He was just trying to scare me off."

"Want to go look for him?"

I had told Botters and his partner that I was an ex-cop. Maybe Botters had misconstrued that to mean I was prone to taking risks.

"Only if you go first," I said.

Botters studied the arrow, then shook his head. We walked back to LeAnn's house. I was holding the Ziploc containing Stone's cell phone and underwear against my chest, and I handed Botters the bag. He studied the cell phone through the plastic.

"Most ladies won't part with their phone *and* their undies," Botters said. "Jed must have done something to her."

"Do you know Jed?" I asked.

"Oh, yeah," he said.

Botters's partner appeared in the doorway of the house, beckoning him to join her. "Yes, dear," Botters said.

His partner scowled and went inside.

"What can you tell me about him?" I asked.

"Jed's a strange kid," Botters said. "He's been down to the station house fifty times for doing stupid things like loitering and creating a disturbance. It was sort of a running joke. He liked to stand in the booking area, and call us a bunch of fucking liars."

"He called me that, too. Did he ever mention missing evidence from his father's trial?"

"All the time," Botters said.

Botters shoved the Ziploc into his pocket, and went into the house. A policeman who went strictly by the book, he couldn't charge Jed with any crimes, so he wasn't going to do anything.

I spent a few minutes mourning my car. Its headlights were smashed, the hood an accordion. The engine hissed as I drove it away, with wisps of steam escaping from beneath the hood. Even Buster seemed alarmed by the dire sounds it was making.

"I can make her pretty again, but it's gonna cost you," Big Al, owner of Big Al's body shop, told me a half hour later. We'd gone to high school together, and after Big Al had gotten out of prison for peddling marijuana, I'd looked him up, and renewed our friendship. He dropped a meaty hand on my shoulder. "You ready?"

We were standing in the dusty yard of his shop in Dania, our shadows looming large in the dirt. My Legend was parked a few yards away, her pretty exterior marred by a young man's rage. I braced myself.

"Ready," I said.

"Twenty-four hundred bucks, and that's just for parts."

"How much for the labor?"

"Nothing. I don't make a profit on my friends."

I removed my wallet and took out my last credit card. I kept the card for emergencies, and I dropped it into Big Al's hand, then gave him a bear hug. From the mechanic's sheds came a loud wolf whistle.

"Get back to work," Big Al yelled.

We retreated to his office, a disastrous affair with bills and invoices strewn across a desk and a radio that played nothing but Rush Limbaugh and Sean Hannity. I had spent many hours in this office talking to Al about getting my life back together, a subject on which he was an expert. For years I'd thought he was still selling dope on the side, the lure of easy money hard to get out of your system. But I'd discovered that wasn't the case. Big Al put in long days and made his money honestly, and I admired him for that.

Big Al got on the phone, and soon had a replacement hood, front lights, and a brand-new transmission. Hanging up, he said, "I'll have your baby fixed in a day or two."

"Thanks, man," I said.

I went outside with my dog. The days were heating up, and I stood in the shop's shade, and took stock of my situation. I was no closer to finding Sampson than when I'd taken the case, and now I was without wheels. Jessie was always telling me to look on the bright side of things, which was quite a challenge in this situation. I leashed Buster and headed down the road toward Tugboat Louie's.

Distances were deceptive in south Florida. The land was as flat as a pancake, so it was easy to mistake a long trip for a short one. By the time I got to Louie's, my feet were aching and I was drenched in sweat. I could almost taste an ice-cold drink as I opened the front door. Then I heard a car door slam, and I turned to see Candy Burrell barreling across the lot toward me.

"What the hell has gotten into you?" she asked.

Her tone said I was in trouble. The question was how much?

"What did I do?" I asked.

"Get in my car," she said.

Burrell drove a sexy red Mustang with racing stripes painted down the side, the kind of car I'd drive if I had the money. I made

Buster lie down on the pavement, then got in. Burrell got behind the wheel and glared at me. "Let's see. You grilled Ron Cheeks without clearing it with me. Then you grilled Jed Grimes, also without clearing it with me. You also let Jed Grimes get away without explaining how that cell phone and pair of panties got in his mother's garbage pail, knocked his ex-wife to the ground, and had your dog attack LeAnn Grimes. That's got to be some kind of record."

"Not for me," I said.

"Don't push it, Jack."

"Do you want to hear my side of it?"

"I'd love to, only I'm meeting with the mayor in fifteen minutes. He wants an update on the Sampson Grimes investigation."

The mayor of Fort Lauderdale was an egotistical blowhard, and having a meeting with him usually meant getting yelled at. I felt bad for Burrell. She'd stepped in shit with this case, and the slide was getting progressively worse.

"I want to ask you a question," Burrell said. "Jean-Baptiste Vorbe, the manager of the Smart Buy in LeAnn Grimes's neighborhood, called the station house this morning. He wants to file a complaint, and indicated it had something to do with the

Grimes investigation. Is this something *you* did?"

I thought back to my visit to the Smart Buy. I'd gone behind the store, and chased away the Asian tourists who'd wanted to have their pictures taken by the Dumpsters. I hadn't seen anyone watching, although you never knew.

"I don't think so," I said. "I didn't go into the store, and I didn't talk to anyone except some tourists who were hanging around outside."

"Exactly what did you say to them?"

"I chased them away."

"Why the hell did you do that?"

"They were ghouls."

Teeth clenched, Burrell looked at her watch.

"We'll continue this conversation later," she said.

"Yes, ma'am."

I got out of her car and watched Burrell pull away. I knew what was bothering her. Because I'd agreed to work with the police, she'd wrongly assumed that I'd play by their rules. But I played by my own rules these days. Sometimes it got me in hot water, but I slept better at night. It was a trade-off I could live with.

I entered Louie's thinking about the

manager at the Smart Buy. There was a chance he knew something, only Burrell hadn't sent anyone to speak to him, wanting to first find out if I'd harassed the guy. It was typical of how the police thought, and it gave me an idea.

I went to my office, and threw on the change of clothes I kept there for emergencies. Then I walked down the hall and knocked on Kumar's door. He told me to come in, and I found him sitting at his desk, working on the books.

"Jack, Jack, how are you? I hope things are going well," Kumar said.

"I had a little problem this morning," I replied.

Kumar raised his eyebrows in concern. "A problem?"

"A guy smashed up my car. It looks like I'm going to be without wheels for a couple of days."

"Would you like to borrow the company pickup truck?"

Everyone in the world needed a guardian angel. Mine was Kumar. He pulled a key ring from the center drawer in his desk and tossed it to me.

"Keep the truck for as long as you want," he said.

CHAPTER
TWENTY-FIVE

The cashiers inside the Smart Buy were looking at baby pictures when I walked in. The store was quiet, and I went to the help desk, and asked the young woman on duty for the manager. She made a call, then cupped her hand over the phone's mouthpiece. "He's kinda busy. Who are you again?"

"My name's Jack Carpenter," I said. "I'm working with the police. I'm responding to the manager's complaint."

The young woman relayed the message, then pointed to the rear of the store. "Mr. Vorbe's office is back there. Go to the meat section, and he'll come out and get you. By the way, no dogs are allowed in the store."

"He's K-9," I said.

I walked down an empty aisle to the meat section. The store's interior was another step back in time: narrow aisles, a limited selection, and tinny Muzak playing over the sound system. I was no financial genius, but I couldn't see the place making money.

Vorbe appeared through a swinging door. He was from one of the Caribbean islands, medium height and stocky, with a mouth filled with glittering gold teeth. He carried a scuffed metal cane and walked with a limp. He led me to his office.

Jean-Baptiste Vorbe's office was adjacent to the meat locker, and brutally cold. I saw Vorbe grimace as he dropped into his chair. I made Buster lie down and leaned against the wall.

"You must work undercover," Vorbe said in a beautiful lilting voice. "Your dog is a wonderful touch."

"Thanks," I said. "Did you hurt yourself?"

"Twenty years ago, I fled the revolution in my native Haiti in a boat made of bamboo and rubber tires. My limp is a souvenir from that trip."

Haiti had been the most beautiful island in the Caribbean until a group of brutal politicians had ruined the country. In south Florida there were thousands of refugees like Vorbe who'd risked their lives in order to escape.

"How long have you worked here?" I asked.

"Almost fifteen years," Vorbe said. "I got

my citizenship, then took a job here. I was the night manager back in ninety-six when the young woman's body was discovered in our Dumpster. I'm sure you heard of the situation."

I did a double take. "Are you the same store manager who saw Abb Grimes on the surveillance tape and called the police?"

"Yes. I guess you could say I set the wheels in motion," Vorbe said.

The store hadn't changed, and neither had its manager. I rarely found myself at a loss for words, but this was one of those times. I took out my trusty pack of gum and offered Vorbe a stick. We chewed in silence.

"It is said in my country that silence speaks volumes," Vorbe said. "Did what I just said bother you, Mr. Carpenter?"

Vorbe had a natural twinkle in his eye that I would have liked to have bottled and sold. I put my gum in its paper and tossed it into the trash. "I'm surprised you're still here. Most people would have moved on."

"I did move on. The store was shut down in ninety-seven, and the employees who wished to remain with the company were relocated. I went and managed another Smart Buy in Pensacola for five years, then came back."

"But you said this store was shut down."

"That is correct. The parent company attempted to sell the location to one of those big box stores, only the property was not large enough. Then they attempted to sell to a builder of strip centers, with the same results. The location remained vacant for five years. Then the parent company decided to open it back up."

"Why?"

Vorbe's eyes flashed and he smiled. "What other reason does a large company open a store? Profits!"

"Does this store make money? It seems rather small."

"Its size is deceiving. The neighborhood has many shut-ins and elderly people. We home-deliver to two hundred and fifty customers each week."

The phone on his desk lit up, and Vorbe took the call. It occurred to me that a real policeman might be calling soon, and that I needed to move things along. Vorbe hung up, and I said, "I was following up on the call you made to the police. What seems to be the problem?"

Vorbe steepled his hands in front of his face. "I have a rather delicate situation. Are you aware that LeAnn Grimes still lives in the neighborhood?"

I nodded.

"LeAnn is one of our delivery customers. I have known her a long time. I sometimes deliver her groceries and check up on her. She is a good woman."

Vorbe was beating around the bush. I pushed myself away from the wall. Buster lifted his head off the floor.

"Are you having a problem with her?" I asked.

"No, with her son, Jed."

"What happened?"

"Jed is a troubled young man. For several years he's been coming here on a regular basis, and hanging around the Dumpsters. None of the employees wanted to confront him. Finally, I could not tolerate it anymore, and I asked him to stay away."

"Did he?"

"For a while. Then this morning, an employee saw someone who looked like Jed sitting by the Dumpsters in a black sports car. I went outside to speak with him, but he sped away before I had the chance."

"Did you actually see him?"

"Just the back of his head."

"Was it him or not?"

Vorbe hesitated. "I *thought* it was him."

"What time was this?" I asked.

"Nine-fifteen, thereabouts."

"Was there someone in the car with him?"

219

"No, he was alone. I have known Jed since he was a little boy, and I don't want to cause problems. But he must stop coming here. He's scaring my employees. That is why I called the police station."

I saw something that I hadn't seen before, which was that Vorbe was scared. He knew something was wrong, even if he didn't know what it was. I probably should have called the police at that point, but I didn't. I wanted to first see for myself.

I clicked my fingers and Buster rose from the floor.

"Show me where Jed was," I said.

Vorbe escorted me through the back of the grocery. We stopped at a large sliding metal door, and he pressed a red button on the wall. The door automatically lifted, and blinding sunlight flooded over us. I followed him onto a loading dock. The Dumpsters were directly across from us. They were big and smelly and surrounded by buzzing flies.

We took a flight of stairs to ground level, and Buster immediately began to circle the Dumpsters. He'd locked onto a scent, and I saw him paw at a pancake-sized stain on the ground. Kneeling, I touched the stain with the tip of my finger. It was sticky and red. When blood is exposed to air it takes on the consistency of the gook on my finger. Vorbe stood behind me, breathing heavily.

"I need something to stand on," I said.

Vorbe got a milk crate from the side of the loading dock, and brought it to me. I stood on it, and used both hands to raise the Dumpster's lid. The smell that greeted me was a toxic blend of rotten fish and produce. Taking a deep breath, I looked inside. The interior was filled with black garbage bags. By law, garbage had to be put in plastic bags in order to be collected. I sifted through the bags while breathing through my mouth.

A bag in front caught my eye. It was covered with dirt, and made me think that it had been laid on the ground. I grabbed the corners, and pulled it out. My eyes fell on the bag directly beneath it. Something sharp was sticking through the plastic. I gingerly touched it. It was a woman's nose, small and perfectly shaped.

Shit.

I smoothed the plastic with both hands and gently pushed down. A woman's face appeared, her mouth frozen in a silent, never-ending scream. I stared at the face for what felt like an eternity, then tore the plastic away with my fingers.

Piper Stone stared up at me, her lifeless

eyes wide open. Her skin was cold to the touch, and she wore a necklace of ugly purple bruises. Her killer had broken her neck, then folded her up like a bundle of sticks, and tossed her away. Tears burned my eyes. I had only met Stone for an hour, but she had impressed me as one of the good guys. It made her death that much more painful, and I hopped off the milk crate.

"What did you find?" Vorbe asked.

"A body," I said.

Vorbe grabbed the milk crate I'd been standing on, and turned it into a seat. Falling onto it, he emitted an unearthly moan.

"I cannot believe this is happening again!" he declared.

CHAPTER
TWENTY-SIX

I stepped into the building's shade and called the mayor's office on my cell phone. A secretary answered in a hushed voice. In the background, I could hear the mayor yelling at the top of his lungs.

"I need to speak with Detective Burrell," I said.

"Detective Burrell is in a meeting with the mayor and cannot be disturbed," the secretary said.

"Tell her it's Jack Carpenter, and it's urgent. I'll hold."

Vorbe came out of the building with a white towel draped over his arm. I watched him climb onto the milk crate and cover Stone's face with the towel. The secretary came back on the line. "Detective Burrell says she'll call you back."

"I must speak with her," I said.

"She's with the mayor," the secretary whispered.

Back when I'd run Missing Persons, I'd come up with code words and expressions that had allowed the detectives in my unit to communicate with each other without anyone else being the wiser. I said, "I need for you to give Detective Burrell another message."

"Sir, I can't."

"Write this down. Elvis has left the building. She'll know what it means."

"But —"

"Just do it."

The secretary put me on hold. Thirty seconds later, Burrell came on the line. "Jack, I don't know what's gotten into you, but you're going to get me fired."

"Are you still with the mayor?" I asked.

"He's taking a leak. What do you want?"

"I just found Abb Grimes's defense attorney in the Dumpster where Abb put his victims. Her neck's broken."

I heard a sharp intake of breath.

"Does anyone else know about this?" Burrell asked.

"You're the first person I called."

"Give me directions to the grocery."

I had smoked on and off when I was a cop. It was the only thing that I'd found that calmed me down after finding a corpse. I was puffing on my second cigarette when

Burrell's Mustang pulled up behind the grocery with a bubble flashing on its dashboard.

Burrell jumped out. I introduced her to Vorbe and escorted her to the Dumpster where I'd made the grisly discovery. Without a word, Burrell climbed onto the milk crate and looked inside.

"What's her name?" Burrell asked.

"Piper Stone," I said. "She's an attorney at Crippen and Howe and was representing Abb Grimes. She told her boss this morning that she'd found information in the transcript of Abb's trial that indicated evidence had been destroyed. She went to Memorial Hospital and spoke with Ron Cheeks, then drove to LeAnn Grimes's place, and met with Jed Grimes. Not long after that, someone who looked like Jed was spotted by the Dumpsters by a store employee, and the manager called the police."

"Are you sure that's the right chronology?"

"Yes. It's all been confirmed."

Burrell climbed off the milk crate and dusted off her palms. "And then you met with Jed Grimes, and he ran away."

"That's right," I said.

"So, do you still feel Jed is innocent?"

I heard the accusation in her voice. Burrell thought I'd screwed up, and had let a killer get away. Still, my gut was telling me that someone else had done this. And until I had cold hard proof that showed me otherwise, I was sticking with my gut.

"Yes," I said. "I still think Jed's innocent."

Burrell called for backup on her cell. In what seemed like a few minutes but was probably longer, the grounds were swarming with dozens of uniformed cops and EMS. Burrell had the uniforms go to the front of the store, and seal off the property. It was a smart move, for it kept the media at bay, and let the police do their job without interference.

I stood next to the loading dock with my dog. A pair of medics lifted the garbage bag containing Stone out of the Dumpster and laid it on the ground. They cut the bag away, and lifted Stone's body onto a gurney, and wheeled her into the back of an ambulance. Stone was not wearing any clothes, and it occurred to me that she'd died almost identically to how Abb Grimes's victims had died. Twelve years had passed, yet it was like nothing had changed.

I felt a tap on my shoulder and turned around. A homicide detective named Chuck Cobb stood behind me. A lot of people used to think Cobb and I were brothers. Cobb was tall and had a dark complexion, swam competitively in his youth, and had a smart mouth. Personally, I didn't see the resemblance.

"Ready to get grilled?" Cobb asked.

"Sure," I said.

Cobb led me inside the supermarket to a windowless room half-filled with boxes. I sat in a chair with Buster at my feet, while Cobb leaned against a wall and faced me. Flipping open his notebook, Cobb had me recount the events that led to my finding Stone's body while carefully writing down my answers. It took a half hour.

Cobb then put away his notebook and turned on a camcorder. He repeated his questions, but this time taped my answers. Later, this tape would be compared to my written answers, in an effort to see if I was lying, or had unknowingly changed any facts about the case. This process took another half hour, and was draining.

Cobb shut off the camera. "All done. Anything else you can think of?"

"I think that's about it," I said.

"Next!" Cobb called out.

Vorbe came into the room, and took my chair. The morning's events had done a number on him, and he was visibly upset. If

I'd learned anything as a cop, it was that murder left a stain that never went away.

"I'm sorry you had to go through this," I told him.

"Thank you," Vorbe replied.

I went outside and stood on the loading dock. The area around the Dumpsters was a mob scene, with a small army of crime scene investigators scouring the grounds for evidence, which included removing every garbage bag from the Dumpster in which Stone had been found, and spreading its contents on the ground. I saw Burrell talking to an investigator, and tried to get her attention. To my surprise, she turned her back on me.

"Excuse me, are you Jack Carpenter?" I heard a voice ask.

I turned to see a man climbing up the loading dock stairs. He was about six feet and well built, with silver hair offset by piercing blue eyes. Despite the heat, he wore a black leather jacket zipped to his neck, and his clothes were wrinkle-free.

"Am I that easy to spot?" I replied.

"You're the only one here with a dog," he said.

"Who said this was my dog?"

"And a sense of humor. Is he friendly?"

I shook my head.

"How about his owner?"

"Sometimes," I said.

The man had reached the top of the stairs, and paused to dust away some dirt on his pants. Then he said, "I'm Special Agent Roger Whitley, FBI."

I'd heard of Whitley. He ran the FBI's Behavioral Sciences Unit in Quantico, and specialized in catching serial killers. One of his cases had been the basis for a really bad Hollywood movie, and had turned him into a household name.

"What can I do for you?" I asked.

"I need to speak with you about Jed Grimes," Whitley said.

CHAPTER
TWENTY-SEVEN

Hollywood had a way of distorting the truth that most cops didn't like. The movie based on Whitley's exploits was a good example of that.

Whitley regularly visited federal prisons around the country and interviewed serial killers who were willing to talk about their lives. These interviews were tape-recorded, and had allowed Whitley to build profiles that helped him catch serial killers still at large.

One day Whitley had paid a visit to the Attica Correctional Facility in upstate New York to interview a serial killer named "Nasty" Nate Savage. Savage had brutally killed eight people in the Buffalo area, several of whom he'd decapitated. When he'd been caught, Savage had been carrying a head in a bowling bag.

Savage was literally a giant, and stood an inch under seven feet and weighed over three hundred pounds. Because of the threat he posed to other inmates, he was kept in solitary confinement, where he spent his days reading comic books and playing solitaire.

Whitley's interview of Savage had lasted several hours, with Savage talking freely about his killing spree. Then, in a sudden shift, Savage had begun to act out his attacks, and had demonstrated to Whitley how he'd ripped the heads off his victims' bodies. Sensing that his life might be in danger, Whitley had pressed the call button for the guards.

"They're changing shifts," Savage had explained when the guards had failed to appear. "Might be a while before they come and get you. It's just you and me, pal."

Whitley had tried to shift the conversation to Savage's childhood, but the serial killer was having none of it.

"You know, I could go batshit in here, and you'd be in trouble," Savage had said. "I could screw your head clean off your body, and put it on the table to greet the guards. Wouldn't that be fun?"

Whitley had reacted with surprising calm. He'd warned Savage that he'd be in serious trouble if he murdered a federal official. Already serving ten consecutive life sentences, Savage had burst into laughter.

"What are they gonna do, take away my cigarettes?" he'd asked.

What had followed was a contest of wills. For each of Savage's vicious taunts, Whitley had thrown up a roadblock, and used his extraordinary behavioral insight to keep the killer at bay. At one point Savage had jumped out of his chair, to which Whitley had said, "You don't think I'd meet you without some way to defend myself, do you?"

"What you got?" Savage shot back. "A nail clipper?"

"Something a little more powerful than that," Whitley had said.

Whitley had feigned reaching for a side-arm, and Savage had retreated. Moments later, two guards entered the cell and took Savage away.

That was the story Hollywood had bought. But it wasn't what had ended up on the silver screen. In the movie, Savage had been a sympathetic character filled with justifiable rage. Taking Whitley hostage, he'd escaped from Attica, and gone home and killed everyone who'd ever wronged him, including his sadistic stepfather and a local bully. For the finale, he'd jumped into Niagara Falls as the police were closing in.

I had seen the movie, and left the theater wanting my money back. The cops had been the bad guys, while Savage was the hero. Whitley's name had been in the credits as technical adviser. It had made me think the guy had sold out.

Whitley suggested getting something to eat. We went to a nearby fast-food restaurant in his rental, and ate fried chicken sandwiches in the parking lot. I bought french fries for Buster, which I fed him through the seats.

"Detective Burrell contacted me yesterday after you discovered the dead guy in the orange grove," Whitley said. "Based upon the information she shared with me, I knew I'd better come down here. Unfortunately, I wasn't in time to save Piper Stone."

I'd never heard a cop say what Whitley had just said. I put my sandwich down on the wrapper lying in my lap. "Do you think you could have saved her?"

"Yes, I do," Whitley said.

"Would you mind telling me how?"

"By having Jed Grimes arrested. Jed killed the homeless guy in the grove, and he was going to kill someone again — all the signs were there. Stone happened to be the unlucky one."

"What signs?"

"Serial killers aren't born, they're made. If you accept that theory, then you can see the signs that tell you that someone is becoming one. Jed Grimes is an evolving serial killer. A tortured childhood, a string of arrests, likes to set fires, hates his father, and has a grudge against the law. It's textbook."

I wrapped up the rest of my sandwich, and tossed it into the bag on the floor. Whitley had told me he wanted to talk about Jed Grimes, but that wasn't true. He wanted to lecture me about Jed, and tell me where I'd gone wrong. I didn't like it, and I said, "Abb Grimes received a ransom note in prison. The note told Abb to stop talking to the FBI or his grandson would die. Are you telling me Jed sent that note?"

"Yes," Whitley said.

"What the hell for?"

"Part of Jed's evolution into a killer involves stepping free of his father's shadow. That can only happen when Abb Grimes is dead. My guess is that when Jed found out his father was trying to stall his own execution, he decided to kidnap his son."

Stall his execution. The words hit me hard.

"Was that Abb's motivation for talking to the FBI?" I asked.

234

"Yes. Death row inmates do it all the time."

"So you think Abb doesn't care about his grandson's safety?"

"I doubt he does," Whitley said.

"And that he's just a monster."

"That's right."

I stared through the sun-soaked windshield while thinking about my meeting with Abb. I'd come away believing that he cared about his grandson's welfare. So far, nothing that Whitley had said had convinced me otherwise.

"You think I got played for a fool, don't you?" I asked.

"I'm afraid so," Whitley said.

"Is that what you wanted to tell me?"

Whitley turned in his seat. We were close enough for me to see the road map of lines in his face. His brown eyes were hard and unyielding. "As of this afternoon, I'm officially handling the homicide portion of this investigation, while Detective Burrell is handling the search for the missing little boy. I know you've gotten yourself wrapped up in this, but I need you off the case."

I felt like I'd been kicked in the teeth, and spent a moment composing myself.

"You don't want to hear what I have to say, or the conclusions I've come to?"

Whitley picked up a paper napkin and wiped the corners of his mouth. He was looking at me the way an adult looks at a child.

"You still believe Jed is innocent, don't you?" he asked.

"That's right."

"Then no, I don't want to hear what you have to say."

If Whitley hadn't been with the FBI, I would have knocked the smug look off his face. Instead, I thanked him for lunch, got out of the car with Buster, and walked back to the Smart Buy to get my borrowed pickup truck.

CHAPTER TWENTY-EIGHT

The sunlight was beginning to fade as I pulled into the Sunset's parking lot, and I knew I didn't have much time left. Walking down to the shoreline, I pulled off my clothes, and dove headfirst into a wave.

The water was tepid, and tiny schools of minnows tickled my legs as I headed out to my regular spot. I'd gone swimming here the day my marriage had fallen apart, and it had given me the strength to get on with my life. The backstroke was my specialty, and I flopped onto my back, and began doing laps.

I searched for a cloud in the sky but couldn't find one. My body was tired and I could not find the rhythm to my stroke. I'd been looking for missing kids nearly all my adult life, and I'd never been forced to leave a case before it was finished. It made me angry enough to scream, so I did.

Soon it was dark, and I decided to head

in. Reaching the shore, I found a cold sixteen-ounce Budweiser half-buried in the sand next to my dog. I popped the top and let the beer pour down my throat. Then I threw my clothes back on, and went inside the Sunset. The bar was quiet, and I found Sonny watching the evening news.

"Where are the Dwarfs?" I asked.

"Over at the jai alai fronton, losing their money," Sonny replied.

I took a stool, and watched the TV. The news was showing the manhunt taking place in LeAnn Grimes's neighborhood, the police using bloodhounds and policemen on horseback to scour the alleyways and backyards in search of Jed Grimes. Toward the end of the segment, an aerial shot taken from a helicopter appeared, and showed bags of garbage lying on the ground next to the Dumpsters behind the Smart Buy.

The shot made me think back to my discovery of Piper Stone's body. Before her killer had tossed Stone into the Dumpster, he'd removed a bag of garbage, and put it on the ground. Then he'd tossed Stone in, and covered her with the first bag. It hadn't seemed significant to me at the time, but now it did.

The segment ended, and I slapped my hand on the bar. Sonny thought I wanted another beer, and placed a fresh can in front of me.

"Son-of-a-bitch," I swore.

"What'd I do?" Sonny asked.

I pointed at the TV. "I meant the killer."

"Oh. What about him?"

"I was there at the grocery, and I missed something. The killer had the presence of mind to cover his tracks. That's not normal."

"It's not?"

The beer had rushed to my head, and I took a deep breath and spoke slowly. "Not with a murder like this. The guy just strangled a woman. His heart is racing a hundred miles an hour. What is his mind telling him to do?"

Sonny scratched his chin and gave it some thought. "Run?"

"That's right, run. Only he had the presence of mind *not to.* Instead he took the time to remove a bag of garbage from the Dumpster, put it on the ground, then put his victim in, and cover her up. What does that tell you?"

Sonny wasn't too quick on the draw, and he gave it some more thought.

"That he's a master criminal?"

"He's more than that," I said. "Even master criminals lose their cool when they're committing a crime, especially a cold-blooded murder. This guy didn't lose his cool."

"You make him sound like a genius," Sonny said.

I looked down at the water-stained bar while playing back everything I knew. Whoever was responsible for these crimes had outsmarted the police every step of the way. He planned his crimes meticulously, and he didn't leave clues.

"He *is* a genius," I said quietly. "Only the police haven't figured that out yet."

"What a surprise," Sonny said. "Drink your beer."

The second beer went down way too easily, as did the third. Soon the Dwarfs appeared, and the place got noisy. I went upstairs and stretched out on my bed with Buster curled up beside me. Shutting my eyes, I was soon floating in that hazy area between sleep and reality.

"Jack."

The voice came out of nowhere. I opened my eyes, and found myself standing behind the Smart Buy next to the Dumpsters. Unearthly shadows danced across the property beneath a full moon.

"Jack."

I spun around, trying to determine where

the voice had come from.

"Jack."

I looked at the Dumpsters. The milk crate I'd used that morning was still there. I stepped onto it, and flipped open the closest Dumpster's lid. The interior was filled with black garbage bags that shimmered eerily beneath the moonlight.

"Jack."

A bag in the back caught my eye. A woman's face was pushing through the plastic. I pulled the bag toward me and tore it open.

"Hold on," I said.

As the plastic came away, Piper Stone's face materialized. Her mouth was still frozen, her neck ringed by her killer's hands. Her eyes snapped open.

"Jack!" she said.

I tried to reply, but the words were frozen in my mouth. Stone sat upright, and put her hands around my forearms. I tried to pull back, but her grip was like iron.

"Help me," she said.

Her eyes were hollow and black. Suddenly the other bags in the Dumpster came to life, the plastic shredding to reveal more dead women lying inside. They sat up, and stared at me with their lifeless eyes.

"Jack!" they all said.

241

I looked into their faces. The other dead women were young, and their necks had been ravaged by a killer's hands. The women started to cry, the tears rolling silently down their cheeks. I could not help myself, and began to cry as well.

A pounding on my door snapped me awake. The moon was peeking through my window, and Buster was up on my bed, licking my face.

"It's open," I said hoarsely.

Sonny stuck his head in. "You okay?"

I took several deep breaths. "Never better."

"I heard you yelling, and thought maybe something was wrong."

"Was I really yelling?"

"Only like someone was sticking a knife in you. Come downstairs and I'll buy you a beer. I was just cleaning up."

"What time is it?"

"About three-thirty."

"Was I really loud?"

"Shit, yeah. I almost called the cops."

My room had grown chilly, and I draped the bedspread over my shoulders, and followed Sonny downstairs. I took a stool at the bar, and tried to pull myself together. Stone's haunting voice still rang in my ears.

I could feel her hands, and the hands of the other dead women, clutching me like they were never going to let go.

Sonny served me a beer. "This will make you feel better."

"You think so?" I asked.

"It's always worked for me."

I took a swallow. The beer was cold and good, but it didn't make me feel any better. I pushed it away.

"What was I yelling?" I asked.

"I don't know. Something about being sorry."

"Being sorry about what?"

Sonny began to wipe down the bar. "It was weird. You were yelling 'I'm sorry! I'm sorry!' and your voice kept getting louder. Finally I ran upstairs and woke you up."

I thought back to the dead women. Each one had seemed real, and not just a figment of my imagination. So real that I'd felt compelled to tell them that I was sorry.

Then I understood what my nightmare had meant, and jumped off my stool.

CHAPTER
TWENTY-NINE

I sucked down coffee while driving through downtown Dania. The town's main traffic light was blinking red, and in the shadows dark figures lurked, some with sleeping bags thrown over their shoulders, others pushing shopping carts filled with junk, the homeless on parade.

Pulling out my cell phone, I retrieved Burrell's cell number, and hit Send. I knew Burrell wasn't happy with me, but I wasn't going to let that affect how I handled this. She needed to know what I knew.

Burrell's voice mail picked up. I ended the call, and hit redial. I kept doing that until I was heading north on the Florida Turnpike. When I was a few miles from the Pompano Beach exit, Burrell answered the call, her voice thick with sleep.

"Hello . . . ?"

"It's Jack Carpenter," I said.

"For the love of Christ, what time is it?"

"Four in the morning."

"What do you want?"

"I need to talk to you about the case."

Burrell snapped awake. "Listen to me, and listen good. You're off the case, and there's nothing I can do about it. Please don't argue with me. It wasn't my call."

"Whose call was it?"

"The mayor's. He decided you were a liability."

"Am I?"

"Please don't make me have this conversation," Burrell said.

"Did you stand up for me?"

"Of course I stood up for you. I did everything I could. I just couldn't tell you to your face. So I let Special Agent Whitley give you the bad news."

"How do you know Whitley?"

"I worked with him a few months ago."

"I still want to talk to you about the Grimes case."

Burrell let out a noise that was half-shout, half-scream. "You're not listening to me!"

"Whitley is wrong about Jed Grimes," I said. "Jed didn't commit these crimes. Someone else did, and they've killed before. We're dealing with another serial killer."

"Really? Where's your proof?"

"The victims are my proof."

"I'm not buying it."

A giant flock of seagulls loomed over the turnpike. There were several hundred of them, maybe more. It looked like a scene straight out of *The Birds,* their incessant cawing loud enough to awaken my dog.

"What's that noise?" Burrell asked.

"Birds," I said.

"Where are you? The beach?"

"I'm driving north on the turnpike."

"And I'm going back to sleep," Burrell said "Now stay off the case."

Burrell hung up on me before I could reply. I weighed calling her back, but decided there was no point. Her mind was made up. The Pompano Beach exit was in my headlights, and I dug the change for the toll out of my pocket.

The Pompano Beach landfill was the largest in south Florida, and was where garbage from Broward and Palm Beach Counties was brought to be buried. It was one of the few areas of the county not at sea level, and the man-made hills of garbage towered over many office buildings in town, and were covered in grass that was country-club green. During the day, thousands of birds feasted on the garbage, then flew back to their nests when the sun went down.

I drove down a gravel road and parked in front of the gate. I had been to the landfill many times as a cop. It was the last stop when I was looking for a missing person who might be dead. I was hoping an employee would remember me, and I wouldn't have to lie through my teeth to get in.

The guardhouse door opened, and a white-haired guard emerged. Although he was older, the starched white shirt and necktie told me he took his job seriously.

The guard came over to my window, and shone a flashlight into my face. "What can I do for you?"

"I'm Jack Carpenter," I said. "I don't know if you remember me. I used to run the Broward County Sheriff's Department's Missing Persons unit."

"Didn't your daughter play basketball?" the guard asked.

"You've got a good memory. She's now at Florida State on a full scholarship."

"Jessica Carpenter."

I smiled and nodded.

"You must be very proud of her," the guard said. "What can I do for you?"

"I'm working with the Broward police on a missing kid's case," I said. "I was wondering if I could come inside, and have a look around."

"There's a lot of garbage back there. What are you looking for?"

"Commercial garbage from Davie. It's from a supermarket."

"That would be section P. If you'd like, I can draw you a map."

"That would be great."

The guard drew me a map on a sheet of paper. The landfill was divided into sections that were identified by letters of the alphabet. Going into the guardhouse, he hit a switch, and the gate slid back. I waved to him and drove inside.

Following the guard's map, I drove down a bumpy dirt road that cut between the hills. It was pitch dark, and my car lurched uncertainly every few feet. There were no other people back here, and I found myself petting Buster as I drove.

Soon I came to a wood sign that read "Section P." The area was in the process of being filled, and several unfinished mountains of garbage stood in front of me. I grabbed my flashlight from the glove compartment, and got out with my dog.

Landfill excavation was a vital part of homicide investigations, and excavation teams used metal detectors, ground-penetrating radar, and Forward-Looking

Infrared (FLIR) technology to look for clues. When it came to looking for bodies, they also used dogs.

I led Buster to the freshest hill, and let him loose. He spent a minute peeing on everything in sight, then scurried up the side of the hill. I followed cautiously, my feet slipping on the mushy ground.

Reaching the top, my dog began to run in circles, having a field day with all the strange and wonderful smells. Then, he disappeared, and for a scary moment I thought he'd fallen down a hole.

Hearing his panting, I followed him down the other side of the hill. He was running fast, and I struggled to catch up. He ran straight to an older hill covered in grass, and went halfway up the side. Then he began digging with his front paws.

"What you got, boy?"

His digging turned frantic. Buster was the kind of dog that would do something until you stopped him, or it killed him. I ran back to my car and popped the trunk. I needed something to help him dig. All I found was a tire iron.

I drove back to the front gate, and found the guard sitting inside the guardhouse, reading a novel. He took off his glasses, and came outside.

"I need to borrow a shovel," I said.

"You want some help?" he asked.

I should have said yes — another pair of hands would have made my task a lot easier — but I was afraid of getting anyone else involved. I wasn't supposed to be here, and the fewer people who knew what I was doing, the better.

"No, but thanks anyway," I said.

I drove back to section P. Buster was still at it, and I plunged my borrowed shovel into the hill, and began to help.

There is no more difficult labor than digging a hole. Soon, sweat was pouring down my face, and I could barely see. I stopped to wipe the sweat away, and looked to the east. The sky was lightening, and I could feel the air beginning to warm up.

I went back to work, and pulled out the plastic bags buried in the earth, and sliced them open with the blade of my shovel. The smell they emitted was disgusting. Each time I inhaled, it felt as if a hole was being eaten into my brain. But I didn't stop.

Nor did my dog. Buster had locked onto a scent, and each time a bag came out of the hill, he stopped what he was doing to sniff the contents. It was hard to say who was more driven, him or me.

I was still digging when the sun came up. My shoulders were aching, my breathing labored. There was garbage strewn all around me, and the gulls had swooped down from the sky, and were picking at it.

I was beginning to think I'd made a mistake. I had pulled a huge portion of the hill apart, and there were no other bodies hidden in the garbage. Then I heard a car backfire, and saw a pickup truck pull up to the hill.

Four Mexicans jumped out, shovels in hand. They wore bandannas on their heads, and had smiles on their faces. I spoke to them in Spanish, and learned that the guard had sent them. I told them what I was looking for, and their smiles disappeared.

Together, we dug for another hour and a half, and took the hill apart. By now my muscles were screaming, and my mind was telling me to quit. I went and leaned against the pickup truck, and one of the Mexicans came over to see what was wrong.

"This is no good," I said.

My shovel was lying on the ground. He picked it up, and tried to give it to me. I didn't understand the gesture, and he pointed at the sky.

"Look," he said.

I shielded my eyes with my hand, and

stared upward. Hundreds of gulls were circling overhead, forming a cyclone of white.

"So what?" I asked him.

The Mexican pointed directly overhead. I had to squint, but finally saw it. A large black bird among the gulls, looking down at us.

"What is that?" I asked.

"Vulture," the Mexican said.

I took the shovel from his hands, and went back to work. Forty-five minutes later, we discovered the first body.

■ ■ ■ ■

PART THREE:
DON'T BE CRUEL

■ ■ ■ ■

Chapter Thirty

The body was of a woman who appeared to be about five-four, with wispy black hair and a silver cross hanging around her neck. Her eyes and skin were gone, and her mouth was twisted in a horrible smile. I was no expert on pathology, but I saw no signs of bullets or knives or blunt instruments having been used, and I guessed that she'd been killed the same way Piper Stone had died.

The vulture that had been circling overhead had landed on a garbage hill no more than thirty feet away. The Mexicans had taken turns throwing bottles at it, but the bird would not leave. I turned my back on it as I called Burrell.

"You need to get up to the Pompano Beach landfill," I said when she answered. "Tell the guard at the front gate you know me, and ask for Section P."

There was silence on the line, and for a

moment I thought we'd been disconnected.

"What did you find?" Burrell asked.

"Another victim," I said.

I heard a sharp intake of breath.

"For the love of Christ," she said.

I ended the call, then spent a minute petting Buster. My dog had bloodied his paws ripping through the earth, and now lay at my feet, exhausted.

Burrell arrived a half hour later. With her was Special Agent Whitley. They got out, and Burrell handed me a cup of coffee. I thanked her with a nod.

I led Burrell and Whitley to the body. I had covered it with a blanket that I'd found in the trash. I shooed the gulls away, and pulled the blanket back. Whitley took a tube of Vick's from his pocket, and dabbed some beneath his nostrils. Burrell did the same, and offered me the tube. I shook my head.

"How can you stand the smell?" she asked.

"You get used to it," I said.

Whitley knelt down to study the corpse. He wore a navy windbreaker with FBI printed in blazing white letters across the back. I wondered if he'd put the windbreaker on to remind me that he was still in charge of the investigation. He pointed at a number of items lying on the ground beside the body.

"Did you put these here?" he asked.

"Yes," I said.

"Did they belong to the victim?"

The garbage bag in which I'd found the corpse had contained several personal items. These included a lipstick, some coins, and two pieces of inexpensive jewelry.

"I think so," I said.

"How can you tell they were hers?" he asked.

"The lipstick is good, and the jewelry is wearable," I said.

"So they're not garbage."

"That's right."

Whitley picked through the items. "Anything else you want to share?"

"She's either a runaway or a homeless person," I said.

"Did you ID her?"

"I didn't have to ID her."

"Then how do you know that for certain?"

I pointed at the victim's feet. "She's wearing a pair of cheap Keds. That isn't a fashion statement. She was dirt poor."

Whitley examined the victim's sneakers. One of the sneakers had a slight bulge in it. Taking rubber gloves from his pocket, he snapped them on, and tugged the sneaker off the victim's foot. Then he held the sneaker up, and gave it a shake. Out dropped a Florida driver's license and several folded bills. He picked both up from the ground. The victim's name was Mary McClary, and she hailed from West Palm Beach. I'd dealt with hundreds of missing persons cases as a cop, and names that rhymed had always stood out.

"I remember her," I said. "She left home at age sixteen. Her father ran a moving and storage business. He called me every day for a few months."

"So she was a runaway," Whitley said.

"That's right," I said.

"Was she seen around Fort Lauderdale?" Whitley asked.

"Yes," I said. "That was why I was looking for her."

Whitley looked at Burrell, and I saw a knowing look pass between them.

"Like father, like son," Whitley said.

"Do you think Jed Grimes did this?" Burrell asked.

"Yes, I do," Whitley said. "He's taking over his father's legacy. I've seen a couple of cases like it in my career. It's called savage spawn."

I couldn't believe what I was hearing. Whitley had decided that Jed Grimes had killed this woman, even though there was no evidence linking him to the crime. Worse,

Burrell had fallen under his spell, and was going along with it. I exploded.

"Savage spawn," I said. "That sounds like the name of a movie. Do you think you can get us all parts?"

Whitley placed the driver's license into an evidence bag, then removed his gloves and tossed them on the ground. His eyes were on fire.

"You're not funny," he said.

"And you're a jackass," I replied.

We rushed each other at the same time. I got my hands on his windbreaker, and spun him around. Whitley's legs got tangled up, and he fell onto a pile of garbage, ripping his pants and messing up his haircut. He cursed me.

Burrell grabbed my arm and pulled me over to her car. She wagged a finger in my face. "Stop this or I'll cuff you, Jack."

"Whatever you say," I said.

Five minutes later an unmarked white van came rumbling into Section P, and disgorged a sheriff's department excavation team consisting of six men. Each man wore rubber gloves and a surgical mask, and carried a black duffel bag filled with equipment.

A flatbed truck carrying a pair of bobcats

came in behind the van. The bobcats were unloaded, and Burrell directed their drivers to start tearing apart the hill where I'd discovered the body. I stood off to the side with Buster and watched. My clothes stank of rotting garbage and sweat and death, and I guessed I'd have to throw them away.

Over the next hour, the bodies of five more women were discovered in the hills in Section P. The bodies were lined up next to Mary McClary's body, and covered with blankets. The scene was starting to resemble a disaster area.

I heard a loud noise and looked to the sky. A helicopter circled overhead, the markings on its underbelly belonging to a local TV news station. Burrell had her hands full, and I didn't want to be filmed or give her any more grief.

I hustled Buster into my car, and got behind the wheel. As I started to pull away, Burrell ran over to me.

"Jack!" she called out.

I hit the brakes, and made Buster climb into the back. Burrell opened the door, and slid onto the passenger seat.

"I want you back on the case," she said.

"You do?" I said.

"Yes. I'm sorry about what I said earlier."

"What about the mayor?"

"Fuck the mayor," Burrell said.

I looked through my windshield at Whitley, who was helping the evacuation team examine the bodies. During our scuffle, a piece of rotten fruit had gotten stuck in his hair, and ruined the image that he seemed so bent on cultivating.

"What about Mr. Hollywood?" I asked.

"Believe it or not, Whitley wants you back on the case, too."

"He does?"

"Yes. He thinks you have amazing instincts."

"Even if I think Jed Grimes is innocent?"

"Yes. The fact that we disagree doesn't mean we can't work together. I need you, Jack. Please say yes."

It had been a long time since anyone had told me that. I looked across the seat at Burrell, and saw that she meant every word of it.

"Okay," I said.

CHAPTER
THIRTY-ONE

There is always a glimmer of light when I
search for a missing person. That light is
sparked by the hope that the person is still
alive, and that I'm going to find them safe
and unharmed, and reunite them with their
loved ones.

There is no light when I'm dealing with
the dead. The color is always black, and
sometimes it's so deep and penetrating that
it swallows up everything around it.

I felt swallowed up in black as I drove
away from the landfill. It was a feeling that I
had to shake, and I drove due east until I
reached the ocean. The beach was filled
with people, and I stripped off my shirt,
and jumped into the water. I splashed
around until I got my sanity back, then lay
on the beach for a few minutes and let my
pants dry. Then I put my shirt back on, and
went looking for something to eat.

I found a McDonald's and bought breakfast. As I was sitting in my car unwrapping an egg biscuit, my cell phone rang. Caller ID said it was Sally Haskell, my former colleague who now ran security for the Walt Disney World Corporation in Orlando. I tossed Buster my food.

"Hey Sally," I answered.

"Hey, Jack. How's it going?" Sally replied.

"I'm working a case, and need your help."

"I know. I got an e-mail from Candy Burrell. I've been trying to reach her with no luck, so I figured I'd give you a try. What's up?"

"I'm looking for a little boy named Sampson Grimes. He's being held by a couple of drug enforcers in Fort Lauderdale. I got my hands on a photo of the kid taken inside a hotel room. One of your employees once helped me identify a hotel room from a photo, and I was hoping to use him again."

"That was Tim Small, our resident interior designer," Sally said.

"Is he available?"

"I'd like to help you, Jack, but Tim is dying of pancreatic cancer. He's in home hospice."

I leaned back in my seat. Ever since I'd started searching for Sampson, I'd been surrounded by the dead and dying. "How bad is he?" I asked.

"I spoke to his nurse a few days ago. He's got a week at best."

"Will you call him, anyway?"

Sally let out a gasp. "Jack, the man's at death's door. I'm not going to intrude on him at a time like this."

"Please."

"Jack! For God's sake, what's come over you?"

Buster was eyeing the hash browns sitting in my lap. I wasn't hungry anymore, and gave them to him. "The little boy I'm searching for is in mortal danger. If I don't find this kid soon, I'm afraid I never will."

"I'm sorry, Jack, but I can't make the call. Tim's in horrible shape. I can't put this kind of strain on him."

I took a deep breath. "Can I ask you a question?"

"Go ahead."

"If you knew you were about to die, and someone came to you, and begged you to help save a little kid's life before you checked out, would you do it?"

"Jack, don't do this . . ."

"Would you?"

"Jack!"

"I sure as hell would. Instead of making the decision for Tim Small, why don't you let him make the decision himself?"

Sally went silent. We'd butted heads many times when we'd worked together, and it had been like fighting with my sister, with lots of verbal pushing and shoving, and one of us usually getting our feelings bruised. But in the end we'd remained friends, and Sally knew that I wouldn't push her unless there was good reason.

"All right, Jack, I'll call him, but I can't make any promises," Sally said.

"Thanks, Sally," I said.

I drove up and down A1A smelling the salty ocean breezes while playing with the radio. I ended up listening to a talk show whose sponsor was a local moving company. It made me think of Mary McClary's father, whom I'd spoken to so many times. He'd been a decent man and a loving father, and I wondered if the Broward cops had contacted him with the tragic news about his daughter. Or would he hear about it the way so many families of the missing did, from the TV?

I decided to call him myself, and spare him any unnecessary grief. Pulling off A1A, I got the number for McClary Moving & Storage in West Palm Beach from information, and dialed it. A receptionist answered, and patched me through to the boss's office. McClary picked up on the first ring.

"This is Frank McClary," he said.

"Hello, Mr. McClary," I said. "This is Jack Carpenter."

Light jazz was playing in the background. Frank McClary killed the music, then in a tentative voice said, "You're calling with news about Mary, aren't you?"

"Yes, and I'm afraid it's not good," I said. "A woman's body was discovered this morning in the Pompano Beach landfill that was carrying your daughter's driver's license. The police will have to make a positive identification, but I wanted you to know."

McClary put down the phone and started to weep. The sound tore at my heart. After a few moments, he came back on the line.

"My daughter is with the Lord," he said.

"I'm very sorry for your loss," I said.

"May I ask you a question?"

"Of course."

"Do the police have any idea who did this?"

I hesitated. The police did have a suspect, only I knew it wasn't the right one. I didn't want to give Frank McClary any conflicting information, so I said, "The case is wide open, Mr. McClary. That's all I can tell you right now."

"Is there anything I can do?"

"Pray that they catch him," I said.

McClary fell silent, and I heard him blow his nose. Then he said, "I got a call from one of Mary's friends about a year ago. Mary had contacted her, and said that she was trying to get off the streets and find work. I took that as a positive sign, and told myself that one day Mary would call, and that she'd tell me she'd gotten her life straightened out."

Mary McClary had been looking for a job. It made me wonder if that was how she'd met her killer. "Did your daughter's friend say what kind of work?" I asked.

"Not that I remember."

"Did your daughter have any training?"

"No, she dropped out of high school."

"Did she work during the summer or on weekends?"

"She did some babysitting in the neighborhood, but that was about it. No, wait. Mary worked as a waitress and part-time cashier one summer at a hotel on the beach. She made a lot in tips, so I guess she was good at it."

McClary's voice cracked, and he again started to weep. I didn't like putting him through this, but I'd learned something important. His daughter might have tried to get a job at a restaurant before she died. I again told him I was sorry, and got off the line.

I left the McDonald's and drove back to the beach. I sat with my car facing the ocean and my windows down. I did not know what was worse, finding Mary McClary's body, or telling her father. They both ripped at my soul.

My wife believed that for every good deed there is a reward. Mine came a few minutes later when Sally Haskell called me back.

"Tim Small said he'll help you," she said.

CHAPTER
THIRTY-TWO

Tim Small lived outside of Melbourne, a seaside town an hour east of Orlando and two and a half hours north of Fort Lauderdale. Driving north on the Florida Turnpike, I pulled off at the first town I came to, went into an outlet store, and purchased a pair of khaki cargo pants and a lime-green Tommy Bahama shirt that was on sale for half-price. My old clothes smelled like death, and I did not regret parting with them.

Small lived on a street lined with ranch homes painted in vibrant Sun Belt hues. As I pulled down the driveway, I saw Sally Haskell leaning against her car. Sally was a honey-blond, blue-eyed Florida native who spent her free time running marathons. She was dressed in chinos and a pale blue sports shirt with the Disney logo embroidered on the pocket. We hugged as I got out of my car.

"You look like hell," she said.

"It's nice to see you, too," I said.

She gently pushed me back and put on her serious face. "I want you to know something before we go inside. Tim Small is a very dear person to me. I'm very protective of him."

"I'll be on my best behavior," I said.

"I know you will," she said. "But you're also going to push him. It's your nature. And if you push too hard, I'm going to put my foot down. Understand?"

"Yes, ma'am," I said. "Do you think he'd mind if I let Buster run in his backyard? He's been cooped up in the car for a few hours."

"I don't see why not. Tim adores animals."

I got a plastic dog bowl out of the trunk and filled it with water, then put Buster and the water in the backyard. My dog seemed happy with the situation, and began chasing a squirrel in a tree. I found Sally standing by the front door.

"You still haven't gotten back together with your wife, have you?" she asked.

"Whatever gave you that idea?"

"That dog acts like he owns you."

Sally rang the bell. The door opened, and a male nurse wearing a white uniform ushered us inside. He introduced himself as Danny, and we followed him into a spacious room off the foyer that was decorated like an old-time soda fountain.

"I'll go get Tim. Please make yourself comfortable," Danny said.

Danny disappeared into another area of the house. Sally took a stool at the shining Formica-topped counter, which contained several penny licks, a Hamilton Beach malt maker, and an old-fashioned root beer dispenser. Hanging on the wall were colorful signs for different ice creams and sodas, plus a photograph of a smiling man sitting atop a Good Humor delivery tricycle.

A minute later, Danny pushed the man in the photograph into the room in a wheelchair. Despite the mildness of the afternoon, the man was swathed in blankets and wore a knit hat.

"I'm Tim," the man said hoarsely.

Sally hopped off her stool, and kissed Small on the cheek. I smiled into the dying man's face. To my surprise, he smiled broadly back.

"I'm Jack Carpenter," I said.

"Nice to meet you, Jack," Small said. "Sally tells me you're looking for an abducted little boy, and that you're hoping I can help. I'll be happy to try, but I must warn you, my eyesight and memory are not what they used to be."

"I understand, Mr. Small," I said.

"Please call me Tim," he said. "Now, let's see the photograph."

I froze. I had forgotten to bring the photograph of Sampson Grimes. Sally came to my rescue, and fetched her laptop computer from her car. She retrieved the photo from her e-mail, and Small spent a long moment studying it.

Small shook his head, and I felt my spirits crash.

"The resolution is too weak for my eyes," he explained. "Perhaps you could send the photo to the computer in my bedroom. I just purchased the screen, and the resolution is much sharper."

"What's your e-mail address?" Sally asked.

"Goodhumorman@timsmall.com."

Sally typed in the e-mail address, and sent the photo to Small's computer. At Small's request, Danny left to check and see if the e-mail had arrived.

"Not yet," Danny called from the other side of the house.

"It should be here soon. I have high-speed Internet access." Small rested his hands in his lap and looked at me. "I saw you admiring my collection of ice cream memorabilia. Did you see anything that struck your fancy?"

My face reddened. Had Small sized me up as a petty thief and thought I was going to steal something from the room? I started to reply, only he spoke first.

"My question is a sincere one," Small said. "I have no family to bequeath my things to. I've donated the soda fountain to the Smithsonian, and Sally's agreed to take an ice cream maker, but there are many pieces that have no place to go. I want them to have good homes, where they'll be used and appreciated. Please tell me you'd like something."

"I live in a small apartment," I said. "I wouldn't have anywhere to put something."

Small twisted his head and spoke to Sally. "It looks like I've offended your friend."

"He's got a tough skin. He'll get over it," Sally said.

"I'd like to show you something," Small said to me. "Would you mind pushing my chair to the other side of the room?"

"Not at all," I said.

I wheeled Small across the room. He pointed at a door marked "Employees Only," and I opened the door and pushed him into an air-conditioned garage that housed more of his collection, including an old telephone booth, a row of antique gumball machines, and practically every Wurlitzer jukebox ever made.

"Those are my babies in there," Small said. "When I die, they'll either be auctioned on eBay, sold at a yard sale, or thrown away. Do you know how sad that makes me feel?"

"It must be hard," I said.

"I'd like you to have something. Please."

The final wish of a dying man was hard to ignore. Out of respect I took my time looking around, and I found myself drawn to a wall-mounted jukebox. It was filled with 45 records by Jerry Lee Lewis, Little Richard, and dozens of other old-time rock and rollers. I punched in a selection, and we listened to Roy Orbison singing to the lonely.

"This is a nice piece," I said.

"Would you like it?" Small asked expectantly.

"I live above a bar. The place could use some music."

"Take it," Small said.

"You're sure you want to part with it?"

"Nothing would make me happier."

A toolbox sat on the floor. I found a screwdriver and unscrewed the jukebox from the wall. There were tears in Small's eyes as I carried the jukebox out the door.

Sally was waiting when I came back inside. She led me to a bedroom in the rear of the house, which had been set up with a hospital bed. My host was facing his computer, and I came around his wheelchair to see the photo of Sampson sitting in a dog crate on the screen, the resolution much sharper than Sally's laptop.

"Recognize anything?" I asked.

Small nodded while staring at the screen. "The carpet and wall coverings are from a defunct hotel chain called Armwood Guest Suite Hotels. Most of their properties were located in the southern United States. Armwood tried to capitalize on the corporate business traveler and fell victim to the last recession. If I'm not mistaken, the entire company was sold off."

"Did they have many hotels in Fort Lauderdale?" I asked.

"Yes. They were quite big in Broward County."

Small's voice had grown weak, and he paused to gather his strength. "Now, there are some little things that this photograph is telling me. I don't know if they're significant, but I'm happy to share them."

"Please," I said.

"The carpet is frayed, and appears to be quite old. I'm guessing it's original, and was never replaced. That's unusual, even more so if the property is in south Florida, where you have to replace the carpets every few years because of mold and mildew. The wall coverings are probably original as well."

"Excuse my ignorance, but what does that mean?" I asked.

"More than likely, whoever bought the hotel in this photograph is not presently using it as a hotel. It's too downtrodden."

"What would it be used for?"

"It could be used for a variety of things. Perhaps to house welfare recipients, or maybe a religious organization bought it to lodge their members. It might also be empty, and your kidnapper is using a room without the owner's knowledge."

"Anything else jump out at you?" I asked.

"There was one other thing," Small said. "Behind the boy there is a night table, which is next to a wall. I believe that was where the telephone in all Armwood rooms was placed. In this photograph, there is no phone."

I looked at the screen and saw the empty night table. "Are you sure there was a phone there?" I asked.

"I believe there was. However, there's one way to know for certain."

"How?" I asked.

"Print the photograph, and we'll see if there is a phone jack on the floor."

With Small's help, I printed the photo off his computer onto a laser copier, and we both scrutinized the spot on the floor beneath the night table. There was *something* there, but neither of us could be certain what it was.

"Danny, please get my magnifying glass," Small said.

The nurse went into another room and returned with a magnifying glass. Small held the magnifying glass up to the photo with a trembling hand.

"I was right," Small said. "Have a look."

I took the magnifying glass and looked for myself. It was small, but I could see a phone jack screwed into the baseboard on the floor.

"Someone removed the phone," I said.

"It certainly looks that way," Small said.

His voice had dropped to a whisper. Sally shot me a look, and I realized it was time for us to leave. I folded the photo into a square, and put it in my pocket.

The nurse pushed Small into the foyer. Sally kissed him good-bye, and I thanked him for his help. Small looked like a mummy in his sheets and his sickly state, but when he gazed up at me, the expression on his face told me he was still very much alive.

"Good luck finding the boy," he said.

CHAPTER
THIRTY-THREE

I followed Sally to a Cracker Barrel near the turnpike, and we got a booth. After our waitress delivered our coffee, Sally spoke up.

"I never ate at a Cracker Barrel until you told me about the waitress who helped you find that missing little girl. Then I started eating at them, and decided I like the food."

There were fifty-four Cracker Barrel restaurants in Florida, and all of them were located near major highways. Whenever a child had gone missing in Broward and a vehicle had been involved, I'd sent a Be on the Lookout e-mail to every Cracker Barrel. The BOLO had included the child's photo and physical description, plus a description of the abductor if one was available. The waiters and waitresses had spotted so many missing kids in their restaurants that it had become standard procedure.

"Are you still seeing Ralph?" I asked.

Sally rolled her eyes. "What day is it? Friday? Yes, I'm still seeing Ralph. Ask me tomorrow, and you'll probably get a different answer."

"The last time we talked, it sounded like you guys were getting serious."

"That's an understatement. Ralph asked me to marry him."

When Sally had lived in Fort Lauderdale, she'd dated an assortment of guys, with each one being a bigger loser than the last. I'd been hearing about Ralph the subcontractor for a while, and had been rooting for it to work out.

"So what are you going to do?" I asked.

"I told him I wasn't ready for marriage."

"How did he take it?"

"About as well as you are. Stop looking at me like that."

"How am I looking at you?"

"Like I'm the Wicked Witch of the West. His proposal took me by surprise. I told him I wanted to think about it. We didn't have a fight."

I blew on my coffee. "Did he give you a ring?"

"I don't want to talk about this anymore, okay?"

"Did he?"

Sally balled up her napkin and threw it at

my head. "Damn it, Jack, you're like a flipping dog with a bone. Let it go. Okay?"

It was well known that men didn't understand women. What wasn't as well known was that women didn't understand men. I leaned across the table and lowered my voice. "The hardest thing I ever did was ask Rose to marry me. It took me an entire week to gather up the nerve. When I gave her the ring, she started crying. I thought she was upset with me, and I nearly threw up. Thank God she said yes."

Sally drew back in her seat. "What are you telling me? That I wounded Ralph, and destroyed our relationship?"

"I'm just telling you how he feels. How you deal with it is up to you."

We finished our drinks and settled the check. I followed Sally to the parking lot and watched her smoke a cigarette.

"So what should I do?" she asked. "Cook him a fabulous dinner and sleep with him?"

I put my hand over my mouth to stop the laughter. Sally punched me in the shoulder so hard I nearly hit the pavement.

"It's not funny, Jack. What should I do?"

"Go home, go to bed, turn off the lights, stare into the darkness, and listen to your heart," I said.

"Where did *that* come from?"

"My grandmother told me that. It was her solution to all of life's great problems."

"Does it work?"

"It works better than anything else I've tried."

Sally ground her cigarette into the pavement. I wasn't ready for the long embrace, or the smooch that came with it.

"Sometimes the strangest things come out of your mouth," she said.

I drove south on the turnpike while punching Burrell's number into my cell phone. Burrell hadn't had much to cheer about lately, and I wanted to share the lead I'd gotten from Tim Small.

"Hello, Jack." Her voice was flat and dead.

"What's wrong?" I asked.

"I'm having the day from hell," Burrell said. "A sick newborn was abducted from Broward General Medical Center this morning. Chip Wells with Action Eleven News found out, and got on the air and called Fort Lauderdale the missing kids capital of the United States. The chief has made me drop everything to find this baby. Every detective in Missing Persons is looking for him."

"Who's handling the excavation at the landfill?" I asked.

"Whitley has taken over."

"Who's looking for Sampson Grimes?"

Burrell paused. "No one right now. I'm sorry, Jack, but you know how things work."

I punched the dashboard in anger. Chip Wells was one of the reasons I was no longer on the force. He'd written untrue things about me that had helped destroy my career while advancing his own, and I could see him doing the same thing to Burrell.

"I can find your sick baby," I said.

"You can?"

"Yes. I handled three sick baby abductions when I ran Missing Persons. The abductors were identical. I'm willing to bet yours is as well."

"You think so? Describe the abductor."

"Your abductor is female, between the ages of twenty and forty-five, overweight, and was posing in the maternity ward as a nurse."

Burrell gasped. "Jesus Christ. You just described our prime suspect."

"Thank you very much."

"Stop being a jerk. Is she violent?"

"No, but she is delusional. This is not your normal child abduction."

"How do you know that, Jack? How can you be so certain?"

"Because the baby was sick," I said.

"Is that the clincher?"

"Yes. It tells you everything you need to know. I'll help you find the baby, but I want something in return."

"Name it."

"Sally Haskell's guy pulled through. The drug enforcers who are holding Sampson Grimes are keeping him in an Armwood Guest Suite Hotel in Fort Lauderdale. The hotel is old and run-down, and probably isn't being used as a hotel anymore. If you'll assign the detectives from Missing Persons to track down all the Armwood hotels, I'll find this kid."

I heard Burrell breathing heavily into the phone.

"Why do I feel like I'm being black-mailed?" she asked.

"Because you are," I said.

CHAPTER
THIRTY-FOUR

I knew the Broward General Medical Center like the back of my hand. Jessie had been born there, and I'd spent an unplanned vacation in its IC unit after being stabbed in the leg by a suspect. Because of its proximity to busy downtown Fort Lauderdale, its maternity ward was a target for people looking to steal babies, and I'd spent many hours training the nursing staff and doctors on how to thwart abductions.

Like so many hospitals in south Florida, the parking lot was half the size it needed to be. I trolled the aisles until I spied someone leaving, then fought another car for the spot. My snarling dog convinced the competing driver to retreat, and I parked.

I leashed Buster and we headed across the baking macadam. Standing beneath a green canopy by the back entrance I spotted Burrell, talking on her cell. The expression on her face was best described as frozen dread.

She folded the phone as I got close.

"Getting browbeaten by the mayor?" I asked.

"How did you guess?"

"You look ready to throw up."

We went inside to the admissions area. The atmosphere was zoo-like, with a mob of ailing people besieging a pair of frantic receptionists. I didn't see any reporters, and guessed that Burrell had decided to freeze out the media for the time being.

Burrell showed her badge, and we were allowed to pass. Our footsteps followed us down a long corridor to Obstetrics.

"Have you been able to maintain the crime scene?" I asked.

"Barely," Burrell said.

Crimes in hospitals always posed problems for the police. If the crimes took place inside high-traffic areas like emergency rooms or maternity wards, it was impossible to keep staff and patients from trespassing on the crime scene.

"How about witnesses?" I asked.

"We've got a candy striper who thinks she saw the abductor, and the mother, who handed her child off to a woman posing as a nurse early this morning. The mother's name is Lonna Wakefield. Her son's named Martin."

"What's wrong with the boy?"

"He was born three weeks premature, and was put in the neonatal intensive care unit. This morning he was cleared to leave NICU, and brought to see his mother."

"His mother's still a patient in the hospital?"

"Yes. She had complications giving birth."

"How's the mother taking it?"

"Not well. She started screaming when she heard the news. The father was in the room, and he started punching the walls. We almost had to arrest him."

"Have you ruled the parents out as suspects?"

We had reached the maternity ward, and I put my face inches from the thick glass and stared at the newborns lying in bassinets. Burrell slapped her hand on my shoulder, and I turned and looked into her tired face.

"How long did I work for you, Jack?" she asked sternly.

"Six years," I replied.

"Did I learn anything in all that time?"

"You learned plenty."

"Glad to hear it. Yes, I've ruled the parents out as suspects. They didn't sell their baby or decide to get rid of him. They're innocent young kids. Now, let's get this show on the road."

Burrell started walking toward a room down from the ward. I gave the newborns a final glance, and saw a tiny guy in the front raise his clenched hand like he was saluting me. I couldn't help myself, and waved back.

Lonna Wakefield and her husband were having a good cry when we entered the room. Lonna was sitting up in bed, a petite, fair-skinned young woman with wide, childlike eyes, while hubby sat beside her, a husky, corn-fed guy with a face as round as a barn owl. The wall beside the bed looked bruised.

Burrell introduced me to the couple. They both looked at me suspiciously, then did the same to my dog. Burrell picked up on their apprehension.

"Jack is an expert at finding abducted children," she explained. "He's offered to help us find your son."

The husband frowned. "No offense, Detective, but we don't have money to pay for this guy."

"Jack won't charge you," Burrell said.

The couple's faces lit up. I made Buster lie down, then crouched beside the bed so I was looking into Lonna's face. Burrell was an excellent judge of character, but I still had to be sure that the Wakefields weren't trying to pull the wool over our eyes. More than one sobbing couple had been responsible for selling their kid to pay off a debt, and I had to be certain these two were being honest.

"I'd like to ask you some questions about the woman who took your son," I said. "Take your time with your answers. The more you can remember, the easier it will be for me to find your baby."

Lonna rested her hand on her husband's wrist. "I'll do whatever you want, mister."

"Let's start from the beginning. How many days have you been here?"

"Three," Lonna said. "I started having my contractions early, and Jimmie rushed me to the hospital on Tuesday night."

"Detective Burrell told me that a woman came into your room this morning, and you gave her your son," I said. "Why did you do that?"

Lonna winced, and I thought her husband was going to come out of his chair.

"She didn't do it on purpose," Jimmie Wakefield said angrily.

I ignored him, and continued staring into his wife's eyes.

"I thought she was a nurse," Lonna replied softly.

"Was she wearing a nurse's uniform?" I asked.

Lonna's eyes flickered as she brought up the memory. "Yeah, but she wasn't wearing a nurse's badge around her neck. I should have noticed that."

"You had other things on your mind. Had you seen this woman before?"

"I saw her hanging around the maternity ward. I really didn't notice her, not right away. There are so many people, between the doctors and nurses and volunteers and visitors. There was even a newborn class one day. She sort of blended in."

"Had she visited your room before?"

"Yes. She popped in after Martin was born to see how I was doing."

"Can you describe her?"

Lonna closed her eyes. "She was about thirty-five, Italian, maybe five-six or five-seven, kinda plump, wore her hair tied back in a bun, pleasant face."

"Was she nice to you?"

She opened her eyes. They had welled up with tears, and Jimmie grabbed a tissue and handed it to her. "She was sweet," Lonna said. "She reminded me of my mom."

"Which was why you felt comfortable handing her your son."

"Yeah, but I didn't want to at first."

"Then why did you?"

"My baby was coughing, and needed to

get his medicine. She offered to take him. I thought I was doing the right thing."

Lonna had just described the classic abductor of newborns: a pleasant woman impersonating a hospital employee who ingratiates herself with a mother in order to get her hands on the mother's newborn child. I decided that the Wakefields hadn't done anything wrong, and rose from my crouching position. Both parents relaxed.

"Is there anything else you remember about this woman?" I asked.

"She called herself Tessa," Lonna said. "She really fussed over Martin."

I found myself nodding, and went to the door. Then I had a thought, and turned back to face the couple. "Did Tessa know the name of the medications Martin was being given?"

"Yes," Lonna said. "She asked me what they were called, and wrote it down. She said she wanted to be sure the doctor was giving Martin the right drugs."

"What were their names?"

"Albuterol and theophylline."

I borrowed a pen and slip of paper from Burrell, made Lonna spell the drugs for me, and wrote them down.

"Is that important?" Lonna asked.

I didn't like to tell grieving parents any

more than I had to during an investigation, only Lonna and Jimmie Wakefield were sick with worry, and deserved to hear even the tiniest bit of good news. I said, "This is going to sound strange, but that's the best thing you could have told me. Tessa loves your baby. That's why she stole him, and that's why I should have no trouble tracking her down."

CHAPTER THIRTY-FIVE

I walked outside Lonna Wakefield's room and let my eyes scan the hallway. The floor had been recently mopped, and it reflected my shadow, as well as that of my dog's and Burrell's, both of whom stood behind me. My eyes locked on an emergency exit at the hallway's end. Without conscious thought my feet took me to it, and my hand grabbed the door handle that would lead me outside. Burrell called out in alarm.

"Jack, you're going to set off the sirens," she said.

"This is the exit that Tessa took when she escaped with the baby," I said.

"We don't know that for certain. There are other exits in the building."

I shook my head, still grasping the door handle. I heard Burrell's shoes clop on the floor as she caught up to me. "Tessa took the path of least resistance, which happens to be this door," I said. "My guess is, she dismantled the siren earlier, and parked her car outside. She was gone before anyone knew the baby was missing."

"You're sure about this," Burrell said.

"Bet you a buck."

"You're on."

I've been hunting down kids long enough to know when I'm right. I pushed open the emergency exit and waited. No siren went off. Burrell let out an exasperated breath.

"It must be hell being right all the time," she said.

I entered a dimly lit stairwell and had a quick look around. On the opposite side was another door that led outside. I went to it, and grabbed the handle.

"Want to bet another buck?"

"Not with you."

I opened the door and sunlight flooded the stairwell along with the clamorous noise of traffic on nearby Andrews Avenue. Buster scurried out between my legs and made a beeline for a line of garbage cans hugging the side of the building. I began pulling off the lids and quickly found a drab gray nurse's uniform stuffed into one. The tag inside the collar said X Large. Burrell took the uniform and held it up to the light.

"You never cease to amaze me," she said.

"Check the pockets," I said. "She was in a

hurry, and probably didn't bother to clean them out."

Burrell emptied the pockets while I tried to determine where Tessa had parked her car. We were on the eastern side of the hospital, and parking was limited to cars reserved for doctors and high-ranking hospital employees. A small strip of grass separated the parking area from the street, and I found tire imprints in the grass.

"Tessa parked her car here," I called to Burrell. "Judging from the space between the tires, she's driving something pretty small."

"She parked in the grass? Isn't that a little risky?"

"Desperate people do desperate things," I said. "Find anything?"

"A receipt from Publix. She purchased eighty-six dollars' worth of groceries two days ago, paid cash. Judging from the items she bought, she definitely is married."

"Lots of beer and frozen pizza?"

"Yes. They like to eat."

Burrell stuffed the uniform beneath her arm. "We still don't know her name, or where she lives, or anything else. I don't mean to sound pessimistic, but how do we track her down? Have your trusty dog run down the highway, and pick up her scent?"

Buster had found something smelly in the grass and was rolling in it. I clicked my fingers to no avail, then answered her. "You need to contact all the local pharmacies and hospitals, and ask them to be on the lookout for any woman who's registered a home birth. They also need to be looking for any prescriptions for albuterol and theophylline. Tessa may have stolen a doctor's script, and written out a prescription for Martin's medicine."

"You think she's going to claim Martin as her own?"

"Yes. Tessa is starting a family."

"This woman isn't your normal criminal, is she?"

"She's probably never broken a law in her life. But apprehending her is still going to be tricky."

"Is she dangerous?"

"Yes."

Burrell's cell phone was ringing. She yanked it out, and made a face. I didn't have to ask her who it was. She said, "Save that thought. There's a Village Inn up the road. I'll meet you there when I'm done with this call, and you can explain this to me."

"Tell the mayor I said hello," I said.

"I'll do that."

I pulled Buster out of the grass. He'd

rolled in something dead, and I dragged him to my car.

I got a towel out of the trunk and cleaned Buster's fur. Dogs rolled in bad smells to cover their own scent and keep their enemies guessing. Right now, I was guessing that Buster needed a bath.

As I put Buster into the car, I saw Jimmie Wakefield coming across the parking lot. He was a huge guy, and his puffed-up chest and face made him look even bigger. He halted a few feet from where I stood, and pointed a finger in my face.

"Why did you say that to Lonna?" he demanded.

"I don't know what you're talking about," I said.

"You said you'd have no trouble finding our son. That's bullshit. You don't know who this nurse was, or what she's going to do with him. You filled my wife with false hope, you crummy son-of-a-bitch."

It was common for parents of abducted children to fly into rages, and siphon their anger against the very people who were trying to help them. It was part of coping, and something I'd experienced many times.

"You need to calm down," I said.

Jimmie cocked his fist. "What I need to

do is punch your lights out."

He looked strong enough to kill me. I didn't want to pull my gun and risk shooting him. He was a victim, and needed to be treated that way. I stepped toward him with my arms still at my sides. "What I told you and your wife was true. I *will* find your baby."

"How can you know that?" he bellowed. "That nurse might have driven Martin down to the Miami airport, and sold him to some couple that's already halfway around the world. I've seen those shows on TV — people steal kids and sell them all the time. It's a big business. How can you stand there and tell me that didn't happen to my son?"

Tears were streaming down his cheeks and his whole body was shaking. I decided to tell him the truth. It was going to hurt, but I had to tell him anyway.

"People don't buy sick babies," I said.

Jimmie blinked, then blinked again. He lowered his fist.

"They don't?" he replied.

"There's no market for them."

"There isn't?"

"None whatsoever. People who traffic in children look for strong, healthy babies to steal. That's their main criterion. Your son is sick and needs attention and medicine for

297

his lungs. That rules him out."

"If people don't steal sick babies, then why did the nurse steal Martin?"

"We won't know for certain until we track her down. But I can give you my best guess. The woman who stole your son wants a baby of her own, but is incapable of having one. That was her motivation. She bought a nurse's uniform, and started visiting maternity wards at different hospitals to become familiar with the procedures. She's been planning this for a long time."

"But Martin's *sick*."

"That's right. And because he's sick, he had to be moved around the floor to get his medicine. That meant different nurses got to put their hands on him. That let this woman step in, and grab him."

Jimmie stared at me. The rage had left his body, leaving a scared and bewildered young man. I stepped toward him, and placed a consoling hand on his shoulder.

"Now I get it," he said.

CHAPTER
THIRTY-SIX

A toasted bagel was waiting for me when I slipped into the booth at Village Inn. Burrell had also ordered a pot of coffee, and was pouring herself a fresh mug.

"You remembered," I said.

"Jack's rules," she said. "First one orders."

I bit into my bagel. Back when I was a cop, I'd established a number of different rules for the detectives in my unit, one of which was that the first person to a restaurant was required to order for everyone else. It was a great time saver and also forced each detective to be familiar with the others' preferences.

"I would have ordered for your dog, but I don't know what he likes," Burrell said.

"That's easy," I said. "He likes doggie bags."

She smiled at my joke. "I want to hear why the woman who apprehended the Wakefield baby is dangerous. You said she probably isn't a criminal. Arresting someone like that should be easy."

"Not necessarily," I said. "She's been living a lie for the past nine months. That makes her dangerous."

"What do you mean, living a lie?"

"She plans to keep Martin, and claim him as her own child. Babies don't fall out of the sky. Nine months ago, she told her husband and friends and her family that she was pregnant. She's been living that lie ever since."

"And by arresting her, we're going to shatter that lie."

"That's right. Based upon past experience, she'll probably lose it when we arrest her. We have to make sure she doesn't harm the child when that happens. We also have to make sure her husband or boyfriend doesn't go ballistic on us. She's sucked him into this lie, and he probably thinks that Martin is his son."

The sounds of crashing waves filled the air. It was the ring tone to Burrell's cell phone, and she answered it. Moments later she had a pen out, and was scribbling on a napkin. She said, "Got it," and ended the call.

"A woman named Teresa Rizzoli reported a home birth to her doctor this morning,"

Burrell said. "This same woman also filed a prescription for albuterol and theophylline at the pharmacy in her neighborhood. Now here's the clincher. The detective who called me ran a background check, and discovered this same woman got arrested for shoplifting last month. Guess what she got caught stealing?"

"Baby clothes," I said.

Burrell yelped so loudly it made the people in the next booth jump.

"Damn it, can't I get anything by you?" she asked.

Teresa Rizzoli lived in a development called Weston. We decided to take one car, and Burrell drove her Mustang across the clogged lanes of 595 and down the pitched exit ramp. Burrell had called for backup before leaving the restaurant, and I looked for a cruiser as we neared Rizzoli's apartment building.

In Fort Lauderdale, a good parking place had everything to do with shade. Burrell parked in a cool spot next to Rizzoli's building, and we both got out. The air was still, and we stood beneath the building's canopy. Burrell checked her watch.

"Where's a cop when you need one?" she asked half-jokingly.

"I'll be your backup," I said.

"Are you armed?"

"Yes."

Burrell considered it. "All right, but don't draw your weapon unless I do. While I'm arresting Rizzoli, I want you to find little Martin Wakefield and get him safely out of the apartment. I'll deal with the rest."

"You're the boss."

"And watch your dog. I don't want him biting anyone."

Buster was glued to my leg, and I looked down at him.

"Hear that, boy?" I said. "No biting."

"You're a funny guy, Jack."

Burrell clipped her badge to her purse, and I followed her down a breezeway filled with bikes and baby carriages. She stopped at apartment 78, and banged on the door with her fist. Next to the door was a window with curtains draped across it. The curtains stirred, and a woman's face appeared. I moved my body to block Burrell from her view.

"Teresa Rizzoli?" I asked.

The woman looked at me suspiciously. Italian with a pleasantly plain face, she fit the description Lonna Wakefield had given.

"Who are you?" she asked through the glass.

"Sunshine Florists. I've got a delivery of flowers for Teresa Rizzoli."

Her face melted into a dreamy smile. "Really?"

"Yes, ma'am. Two dozen red roses for Teresa Rizzoli. They're going to wilt if you don't get them into some cold water."

Rizzoli pulled away from the window, and we listened as the deadbolt on the front door was thrown, and several security chains pulled back.

"That was mean," Burrell whispered.

"Mean works," I replied.

Rizzoli opened the door expecting something wonderful. What she got instead was a detective's badge shoved in her face, and Burrell informing her that she was under arrest for the kidnapping of Martin Wakefield. Rizzoli backed up into the living room of her apartment. She wore a black shift that hung to her ankles, no makeup, and was barefoot. Her eyes shifted between Burrell and me.

"I don't know what you're talking about," she protested.

Burrell removed handcuffs from her purse. "Put your hands where I can see them."

"You're making a mistake," Rizzoli said.

A baby's cries came from the back of the apartment, and my dog took off. I started

303

to follow, and Rizzoli sprang toward me with her hands extended like claws. I ducked just in time to save my eyes from being gouged, and wrestled her to the couch. I got her arms behind her back, and Burrell cuffed her.

"Get the baby," Burrell said.

I followed the cries down a hallway to a bedroom and halted in the doorway. The bedroom's walls were painted sky blue, and contained dancing unicorns and fire-breathing dragons straight out of a fairy tale. The floor was a minefield of baby toys, and I hopped over them to reach the crib in the corner.

"Hey, kiddo," I said.

Martin Wakefield lay in the crib, punching the air with his tiny fists. He didn't weigh more than five pounds, and had expressive eyes and a head full of dark hair. As I lifted him into my arms, Buster sniffed his diaper and whined approvingly.

I held Martin against my chest and started down the hall. A door in front of me opened, and a shirtless guy with a beer belly came into the hall. He looked half-asleep, and his eyes went wide in disbelief.

"What are you doing with my son?" he asked.

"I can explain," I said.

"Like hell you can."

He ducked back into the room. Seconds later he reappeared holding a .38 Smith & Wesson, which he aimed at my head.

"Give me my son," he said.

Guns frighten me as much as anyone else. The trick was not to show it.

"Are you Teresa Rizzoli's husband?" I asked.

"What if I am?"

"I'm with the police," I said. "There's a detective in the living room with your wife. She'll explain everything to you."

"Give me my son or I'll shoot you."

"Please don't do that. You might hurt Martin."

"Who the hell is Martin?"

I looked down at the baby cradled in my arms. "His name is Martin Wakefield. He was born at Broward General Medical Center a few days ago. A woman matching Teresa Rizzoli's description stole him from his mother this morning."

His face twisted in confusion. *Like he'd known something wasn't right.* Without another word, he moved backward down the hall, then sideways into the living room.

"Police! Drop your gun!" a pair of voices rang out.

I ran down the hallway clutching Martin

to my chest, and halted at the entrance to the living room. Two of Broward County's finest stood by the front door, pointing their guns at Teresa Rizzoli's husband, who had not complied with their warning.

"No!" I yelled out.

Burrell had wrestled Teresa to the floor, and was sitting on her.

"Don't shoot him," Burrell said.

Rizzoli's husband stood in the center of the living room with a dazed expression on his face. I came into his line of sight, and held my hand out for his gun. I was taking a huge risk, but I didn't want to see him die because the woman he loved had lied to him.

"Give me your weapon," I said.

His face twisted in shock and his chin sagged.

"Did you steal this little baby, Teresa?" he asked his wife. "You gotta tell me the truth."

"Yes," Teresa said, still lying on the floor.

"He's not ours?"

"No."

"Oh, sweet Jesus," he said.

He dropped his gun into my hand. The uniforms rushed across the living room, and shoved him against the wall. I laid the gun on the couch, and took Martin into the breezeway. The baby had started to cry, and

I rocked him against my chest.

"Welcome to the world," I said.

CHAPTER
THIRTY-SEVEN

I remained in the breezeway with Martin while the police arrested Teresa Rizzoli and her husband, and read them their rights. As the police led the Rizzolis past me, Teresa stopped to look lovingly at the child she'd tried to make her own.

"I gave him his meds at noon," she said. "He's not due again until four. I used to be a physician's assistant. I know what I'm doing."

"How was his coughing?" I asked.

"It was okay. I was going to take him to a doctor this afternoon."

One of the cops pushed Teresa down the breezeway, and I went into the apartment. Burrell was talking to Martin's real mother on her cell phone. She placed the phone next to the baby, and I tickled Martin's belly and made him giggle. Through the phone I heard Lonna Wakefield laugh and cry at the same time. Burrell lifted the phone to her face.

"We're bringing your baby back to the hospital. See you soon."

"Thank you, thank you!" Lonna Wakefield shouted through the phone.

Burrell folded her phone. "Let's go."

"Not so fast. He's got a smelly diaper."

"We'll lower the windows."

"Great. I'll drive and you hold him."

"On second thought, let's change his diaper."

We went to the baby's bedroom, where I laid Martin on a changing table and began to undress him. When Jessie was born, I stayed home for two weeks and got to know my kid. I hadn't lost my touch at changing a diaper, and Martin was soon good to go. As I picked him up, Burrell's cell phone rang. She looked at the caller ID and groaned.

"The mayor?" I asked.

"Who else?" Burrell said.

"Don't talk to him."

"Why not? I've finally got some good news to share."

"He'll go to the hospital, and steal your thunder."

"You really think he'd do that?"

"Absolutely. You rescued this baby and

deserve the credit, not him."

"Let's be honest, here. *You* rescued him, Jack."

I handed Burrell the baby. "The official version of events is that you found him. I was along for the ride. Got it?"

Burrell shot me a funny look. She was honest to a fault, which could be a real character flaw when you were rising up the ranks of the police department.

"Whatever you say," she said.

I drove Burrell's Mustang to Broward General Medical Center with Burrell in the backseat cradling Martin. I normally paid scant attention to the insane traffic that defined Broward's highways, but today there was more at stake, and I put Burrell's flasher on the dash and turned it on. The spinning blue light had a magical effect, with cars slowing down to safe and normal speeds. A block from the hospital, I glanced at Burrell in the mirror.

"You ready?" I asked.

"For what?" she replied.

"My guess is, Jimmie and Lonna Wakefield have told everyone in the hospital the good news. It probably leaked out, which means the hospital is swarming with reporters. You're about to become everyone's

310

favorite cop."

"Is that a problem?"

"It all depends on how you handle it. Have you ever held a news conference before?"

Burrell shook her head.

"I'll give you some pointers. Make sure you have the parents with you, plus the hospital staff. You want smiling faces standing behind you. This is a joyous event. The baby's fine, the parents are happy, life is wonderful."

"Make it into a celebration," Burrell said.

"Exactly. Also make sure that you have the reporters' credentials checked before you start. There are a lot of nuts out there, and you don't want someone lobbing a crazy question at you, especially if there are cameras rolling."

"No nuts."

"That's right. Now, here's the tricky part. How do you talk about Teresa Rizzoli? The reporters will want to know how you plan to prosecute her."

"Why is that tricky? She stole a baby."

"You still don't want to demonize her. There are plenty of women who can't have children who can empathize with her situation."

"Don't speak about her like she's a criminal."

"Exactly. Tell them she's a confused woman, and that police psychologists will be dealing with her. I wouldn't mention the charges she's facing, or that she might do hard time."

"What about her husband pulling the gun on us?"

"I wouldn't mention that, either."

"Keep it upbeat, huh?"

"Happy time," I said.

I pulled into the hospital's emergency entrance in the back of the building, and threw the Mustang into park. Getting out, I walked around and opened Burrell's door. She smiled at me with her eyes as she climbed out with the baby.

"One more thing," I said.

"What's that?" she said.

Burrell's detective's badge was still clipped to her purse. I removed it, shined it on my sleeve, then pinned it on her chest so it was in plain sight.

"Just so everyone knows who's in charge," I said.

CHAPTER
THIRTY-EIGHT

I parked and went inside the hospital. There was a pharmacy on the first floor, and I strapped myself into the free blood pressure machine to check my blood pressure and pulse. I'd had guns pointed in my face before, and I knew how it affected me.

My blood pressure and pulse were both sky high. I went to my car, popped James Taylor's greatest hits into my tape deck, and started petting my dog. After a while, I started to feel better. Then my cell phone rang.

"I just wrapped up my news conference," Burrell said. "You should come inside. The Wakefields want to thank you."

"Tell them I'll take a rain check," I said.

"What's wrong?"

"There's another little boy who needs to be rescued."

"I'll be out in five minutes."

I drove Burrell to the Village Inn to

retrieve my car, and neither of us spoke a word. Then I followed her to police department headquarters on Andrews Avenue. Finding a parking space, I rolled down the windows for my dog.

"I've had every detective from Missing Persons tracking down the Armwood hotels in Fort Lauderdale," Burrell said as we crossed the lot. "I didn't forget our deal."

"I know you didn't," I said.

Burrell had me cleared at the reception desk, and we headed upstairs to the War Room on the top floor. The War Room was used as a communications center during emergencies like hurricanes and wildfires, and was outfitted with a bank of telephones and a wall of high-resolution TVs. It also had a panoramic view of the county. Although the building was smoke-free, people still occasionally smoked in the War Room, and a recent cigarette lingered in the air as we entered. Standing around an oval table were the six detectives from my old unit.

"Good afternoon," Burrell said.

They broke out of their huddle. A detective named Tom Manning was holding a remote. He pressed a button, and on every TV appeared a clip of Burrell from the news conference. The detectives broke into applause.

"Thank you very much," Burrell said. "Now, I'd like to hear what progress you've made tracking down Armwood hotels."

A sunburned detective named Bob Smith stepped forward. Smith was the first detective I'd ever hired, and he knew how to get things done. He pointed at the map of south Florida spread across the oval table. The map was covered in red thumbtacks, and there were a lot of them.

"We were in the process of identifying all the Armwood Guest Suite Hotels in south Florida when you walked in," he said.

"How many have you found?" I asked.

"Ninety," Smith replied.

The number gave me pause. Tim Small had indicated there were forty Armwood hotels in south Florida. Searching forty hotels for a kidnapped child was manageable; searching ninety wasn't.

"I was told there were less," I said.

"It's an inflated number," Smith said.

"What do you mean, inflated?" Burrell asked.

"At one time, Armwood owned forty hotels in south Florida," Smith explained. "Then their parent company bought another chain of hotels called Leisure Inns, which were quite big. When Armwood got sold, the Armwood properties and Leisure

Inns were listed on the bill of sale under the Armwood name. We're working off the bill of sale, because it's the only record we could find."

"So fifty of those thumbtacks are Leisure Inns, only you have no way of knowing which ones," I said.

"That's right," Smith said.

I turned to Burrell. "Can we search all of them?"

"We'll have to," she said.

"There's another problem," Smith said.

"What's that?" I asked.

"Many of these hotels are welfare houses and crack dens, and are dangerous places," Smith said. "We're going to need a small army to properly search them."

"Define small army," I said.

"If we're going to conduct the searches at the same time, which is the best way to go, we'll need a few hundred people at least," Smith replied.

"Do we have that kind of manpower available?" I asked Burrell.

"Let me find out," she said.

While Burrell made some calls, I talked with the detectives from my old unit. I'd had little contact with them since leaving the force. The case that had cost me my job had cast a dark cloud over Missing Persons, and I hadn't wanted to hurt their careers by staying in touch. But I still cared about them, and always would.

Burrell hung up the phone and came over to where we stood.

"No go," she said. "Every available cop is searching for Jed Grimes."

"What about FBI or FDLE agents?" I asked.

"They're looking for Jed, too," she said.

It was rare for three different law enforcement agencies to search for a single suspect, and I suspected that Special Agent Whitley had convinced them that Jed was responsible for the bodies in the landfill. Cops worked on priorities, and right now, finding Sampson wasn't as urgent as finding his father.

Except to me.

I studied the map. The two men who were holding Sampson hostage were known drug enforcers. That made it likely that they would use a crack den as their hideout.

"Which of these hotels are crack dens?" I asked.

Smith pointed out the known crack dens. Lonnie Lowman had said that Sampson was being kept in Fort Lauderdale, so I removed all the thumbtacks on the map except for the known crack dens in Broward. There were seven.

"Sampson is being held in one of these locations," I said.

"Are you sure?" Burrell asked.

"Positive. The eight of us should be able to find him."

Burrell looked at the map, then shook her head. "We need to know which hotel Sampson is in. If we raid one, and he's not there, the drug dealers will get on their cell phones, and alert their friends. We could end up getting ambushed if we're not careful."

"What are you suggesting?" I asked.

"We wait until we have more people, then raid them all at once," Burrell said.

"How long will that be?"

"I wish I could tell you, Jack."

I tried to imagine Sampson Grimes living in a crack den. The kid was a survivor, but I didn't see him lasting forever in an environment like that. No one could.

I kicked a trash can across the War Room on my way out the door.

CHAPTER
THIRTY-NINE

Back when I was a cop, I'd often go home after a bad day, and lie on the couch in the living room with my head resting in my wife's lap. Sometimes I'd listen to music on the stereo, but more often than not, I'd let the silence of my house calm me, while Rose gently ran her fingers through my hair.

These days, I didn't have a house to escape to, and Rose was living three hundred miles away, so I settled for sitting at the Sunset's bar with the Seven Dwarfs. My mind had latched onto the image of Sampson Grimes being held in a crack den, and wouldn't let it go. I crushed my empty beer can against the bar.

"You doing okay?" Sonny asked.

"I've had better days," I admitted.

"Can I do anything?"

"Tell me some good news."

"A new guy came in last night and started buying drinks, and became everyone's new best friend. I think he's going to become a regular."

The Sunset operated on a shoestring budget, which was largely paid for by the drinking habits of the Seven Dwarfs. A new regular was a cause for celebration.

"Is he suitable for Dwarfdom?" I asked.

"I think so. Check him out. He's over there on the last stool."

I followed Sonny's eyes down the bar. Sitting on the last stool was an old, unshaven man with watery eyes and a drinker's nose, what locals call a salty dog. He wore a long-sleeved denim shirt with the right sleeve tucked into his pants pocket.

"No right arm?" I asked.

"Says he lost it in a car accident," Sonny said. "His name is Mitch, but he goes by Lefty. He's a good guy, until he starts singing. Then he gets pretty unbearable."

I ordered dinner. Sonny served me a bowl of the house chili, and I took a table overlooking the ocean, and ate while watching waves slap the pilings that held up the bar. In their pale reflection I could see the daylight slowly fading, and the blackness of night meet the blackness that lay below. Looking into the water's depths, I felt a twisting in my gut. For every hour that passed, the chances of Sampson being rescued grew slimmer. I couldn't just sit here and wait for the police to act. I had to do something.

I removed the photo that I'd printed off Tim Small's computer, and laid it on the table. In the photo, Sampson was sitting in a dog crate. It occurred to me that of all the child abduction cases I'd worked, I couldn't remember anyone putting a kid in a dog crate. I wondered what Sampson had done to make the men holding him do this.

An ugly sound broke my concentration. Turning around in my chair, I saw Lefty standing in the middle of the room, belting out a drunken ballad. He sounded like a cat being strangled.

"Hey," I called out.

Lefty stopped singing. "What's your problem, mate?"

"I think it's your voice," I said.

"Don't you like music?"

"That's not music."

The Dwarfs hooted and hollered. Lefty glared at me.

"Can you do better?" Lefty asked.

I couldn't sing worth a damn. But if I didn't respond, Lefty was going to think he'd won, and go back to torturing me. Then I remembered the jukebox sitting in the trunk of my car.

"Give me a minute, and I'll let you hear what real music sounds like," I said.

"Sure you will," Lefty said.

With Sonny's help, I mounted the jukebox onto a wall in the bar, and plugged it in. As colored neon flowed magically through the glass tubes, the Dwarfs crowded around me, oohing and awwing like a bunch of dumbstruck kids.

"Play something," one of them said.

The playlist contained dozens of classic rock 'n' roll songs. I dropped a dime into the machine, and Elvis Presley's "Don't Be Cruel" filled the bar. The Dwarfs danced in place and clapped their hands. I returned to my chair, and Sonny served me a cold beer.

"You made Lefty's day," Sonny said.

I glanced across the bar. Lefty was dancing by his stool, and having more fun than anyone in the room. His voice didn't sound nearly as bad singing backup, and he winked at me as he belted out the lyrics.

An alarm went off inside my head. I lowered my drink to the table, and picked up the photograph of Sampson. For a long moment, I simply stared at it.

Sampson was being held in a hotel room with a telephone jack, but no telephone. He was also being kept in a dog crate. The two things hadn't seemed connected, but now I realized that they were. Sampson had used the phone in the hotel room to call 911, only the drug enforcers had caught him. Fearful that he'd try again, they'd taken the phone out of the room, and stuck him in a dog crate. The kid had nearly rescued himself.

The song ended, and Lefty came over to where I sat.

"Still don't like my singing?" he asked.

I stood up and hugged the old drunk.

"It's beautiful," I said.

Standing in the parking lot beside the bar, I called Burrell on my cell. My heart was beating so fast I could hear a bass line in my ears. With a little help from Burrell, I was going to find Sampson. Her voice mail picked up. I left a message saying it was urgent, and asked her to call me back.

I waited a few minutes, and called again. Still no answer. I scrolled through the address book of my cell, and discovered I didn't have her home number.

The stairs groaned as I ran upstairs to my rented room. From my closet I removed the cardboard box containing the crap from my police department days, and dumped it on the bed, praying my address book hadn't

323

gotten lost. My address book contained the phone numbers of every cop I'd ever worked with. Work numbers, cell numbers, and home numbers. The home phone numbers were all unlisted. Finding Burrell's, I punched it into my cell, and heard the call go through.

"Pick up the phone," I said.

She didn't answer. Her home address was also in my book. Burrell lived on Sheridan Street in Hollywood, just a few miles away.

I ran down the stairs, Buster on my heels.

CHAPTER FORTY

I arrived at Burrell's apartment building a few minutes later. The architecture of south Florida was of two distinct schools: before the great land grab of the eighties, and after. The stuff built before was low-key and charming, the stuff after towering and harsh. Burrell's building was six stories of concrete and glass, and I waved to the dozing guard inside the booth and drove in.

I found Burrell's Mustang and parked beside it. She was home, and I wondered why she hadn't picked up her phone. It gave me a bad feeling, and I grabbed Buster and went inside the building.

Burrell lived on the first floor, and I walked down a hallway filled with dinner smells while trying to remember the last home-cooked meal I'd eaten. Reaching her door, I stopped and banged a greeting. When she didn't answer, my nervousness grew.

I went to her neighbor's door and knocked. The door opened, and a young woman holding a kid appeared.

"Who are you?" she asked suspiciously.

"I'm a friend of Candy's," I said. "Have you seen her around?"

"Boyfriend?"

"No, just a friend. We used to work together."

"You a cop?"

"Ex-cop. I'm worried about her."

I've been told that I wear my emotions on my sleeve. The woman decided I was telling the truth and went into her living room, leaving the door open. With her palm she banged on the wall separating her apartment from Burrell's.

"Hey, Candy, some guy's here checking up on you!"

I thanked the woman and went to Burrell's door. It opened, and Burrell greeted me wearing a fluffy white bathrobe and slippers. Her hair was pinned up, the expression on her face a cross between disgust and pure anger.

"Jesus Christ, Jack, what is it now?" she asked.

"I guess I caught you at a bad time."

"Whatever gave you that idea?"

My ability to state the obvious was a sore

point with every woman I'd ever known. Burrell crossed her arms and glared at me. I was hoping she'd ask me inside, and when she didn't, I looked up and down the hallway to make sure it was empty.

"I know how to find the hotel where Sampson Grimes is being kept," I said.

"You do? How?"

From my pocket I removed the photograph printed off Tim Small's computer, and gave it to her. "Sally Haskell's guy figured out that there's a phone jack in Sampson's room, but no phone. I think Sampson tried to call 911, and the drug enforcers caught him. I need you to check all interrupted 911 calls that occurred after Sampson's abduction, and backtrack them to their place of origin. If any match the address of an Armwood hotel that's now a crack den, we'll know where Sampson is being held."

While Burrell studied the photo, I glanced into her apartment. A candle was burning on the dining room table next to a bottle of wine. Then I looked at her. Her hair was doing the tango, and her skin emitted the heady aroma of sex. She'd been dating another detective in Missing Persons for a while, and I guessed he was visiting.

"It's worth a shot," she said. "We need to

go to headquarters, and put a trace on those calls."

"I'm ready when you are," I replied.

An awkward silence followed. I realized Burrell wasn't going to invite me inside, but didn't know how to say it without offending me. I decided to save her.

"I'll go walk my dog, and meet you in the parking lot," I said.

She smiled thinly and shut the door.

I followed her Mustang to headquarters, and we went upstairs to the War Room. A skeleton staff worked the night shift, and Burrell got on the phone and put them to work. A short while later, a deputy came into the War Room, and handed Burrell a printout of all interrupted 911 calls on the days since Sampson's disappearance.

"How many calls are there?" I asked.

Burrell ran her finger down the page. "About a hundred each day. I'll start with the first day, and read them aloud while you look for a match."

The sales transcript for Armwood hotels lay on the oval table in the room's center. As Burrell read off the address of each interrupted 911 call, I looked through the transcript for a match. Several times Burrell stumbled, and had to repeat herself.

"Still not wearing glasses, huh?" I said.

"My vision is fine," she said testily. "This print is faint."

"Wal-Mart has a special going on, three pairs of reading glasses for ten bucks. They have an eye chart right there in the store."

"Shut up, Jack."

At midnight, we had reached the third day of interrupted 911 calls and still hadn't gotten a hit. Burrell's eyes betrayed her weariness.

"I don't know about this," she said.

"I'll bet you it's the last call on the page you're looking at."

"You think so?"

"Yes. It's how the gods punish us."

Burrell read the last address. It was on Broward Boulevard, and I pored through the transcript and found an Armwood hotel at the same address.

"It's a match," I said.

We consulted the map of south Florida spread across the table. The seven thumbtacks showing known crack dens in Broward were still stuck in the map. I pointed at the thumbtack on Broward Boulevard.

"The call came from here," I said.

"I know that address," Burrell said. "It's in one of the worst sections of town."

My wife believed that everything happened for a reason. There was a reason that I'd found Sampson's whereabouts when I had, and I knew that I needed to rescue him right away. I started across the room.

"Where are you going?" Burrell said.

"Where do you think I'm going?" I replied.

"Cool your jets. I'm calling for backup."

Burrell got on the phone and ordered reinforcements. The War Room had a panoramic view of the county, and my eyes scanned the sea of shimmering lights until I'd found Broward Boulevard, and the block where Sampson was being held. He was right around the corner, and I was going to bring him home.

Burrell appeared by my side. "Everyone's in bed, and can't get over here for an hour or more. I know you're not a fan, but what would you think if I called Whitley?"

I clenched my teeth. Whitley had done nothing to help the investigation. But if he was the only person available, I wasn't going to say no.

"Go ahead," I said.

CHAPTER
FORTY-ONE

We went downstairs to the parking lot and waited for Whitley. I had worked with the FBI on busts before, and it was always the same. They talked, and you listened.

Whitley pulled into the lot driving a black SUV with tinted windows. He got out of his vehicle, said hello to Burrell, and nodded to me. His leather jacket was unzipped, and I spied a big sidearm strapped to his waist. He looked ready for bear.

"Let's go," he said.

I pointed at my car on the other side of the empty lot.

"Let's take my vehicle," I said. "It's in the worst shape."

"Does that make a difference?" Whitley asked.

"Some crack dens have lookouts on the roofs," I explained. "My car won't arouse suspicion if someone sees us coming."

"Whatever you say," he said.

I drove north on Andrews to Broward Boulevard, then hung a left and headed due east. On every corner I passed drug pushers, and hookers basked beneath the streetlights. South Florida was known for fun and sun, but at night, a much different creature emerged.

I found the Armwood hotel on Broward Boulevard, and slowed down as we drove past. It was a two-story building painted in tropical pink with a flashing Vacancy sign. Whitley was riding shotgun, and he counted the people lurking by the entrance.

"Three," he said. "Two looked like women, but you can never tell these days."

"Let me handle them," I said.

"How do you plan to do that?" he asked.

"I'll use my dog."

Whitley glanced into the backseat at Buster, who sat at stiff attention beside Burrell.

"Okay," he said.

I parked on the next block, and headed down the sidewalk with Buster on a leash. As I neared the hotel, I let Buster sniff the bushes. A pair of black hookers stepped out to greet me. They were tall and ravishingly beautiful, and swung their hips seductively.

"Looking for a good time?" one hooker asked.

"Who isn't?" I replied.

"You came to the right place, sugar. What kind of doggie is that?"

"A mean doggie."

"Does he bite?" she asked.

"Only people he doesn't like."

The hookers eyed me warily. Sensing trouble, their pimp emerged from the shadows. He was a bruiser, and sported a shiny gold ring on each finger. Buster began to bark ferociously, and the pimp raised his arms.

"Beat it, and take the glitter twins with you," I told him.

The pimp looked me over, and decided he didn't like what he saw. He put his hands on his girls' shoulders. "Come on, ladies. Time to hit the road."

I watched them disappear into the night. Moments later, Burrell and Whitley joined me on the sidewalk.

We entered the hotel. A zoned-out man lay sleeping on the floor of the foyer. Stepping around him, we entered the registration area. A large Hispanic male was at the front desk, eating chicken and yellow rice from a Styrofoam container. A sign on the desk identified him as the hotel manager.

"Get that fucking dog out of here," the manager said.

Burrell flashed her badge while Whitley came around the counter with his weapon drawn. The manager lifted his arms and Whitley frisked him.

"I want to ask you some questions," Whitley said.

"I don't know nothing," the manager said.

"I think you do," Whitley said.

The manager laughed in Whitley's face. His eyes were glassy and he acted high. He wasn't going to tell us anything unless we did something drastic.

I came around the counter with Buster, who was straining at his leash. The manager started backing up, and didn't stop until he was pinned in the corner. I guess he didn't like dogs.

"There's a little boy being kept prisoner in this hotel," I said. "Help us find him, and nothing will happen to you. Don't, and I'll let my puppy loose."

The manager was breathing hard, and sweat dotted his brow.

"I think he's upstairs," the manager said.

"Why do you think that?" I asked.

"A couple of guys keep a dog crate up there, only they don't own no dog. I asked one of them what the crate was for, and he told me to shut my fucking mouth."

"Describe these two guys," I said.

"They're from South America. One's really skinny, the other's sort of fat."

It sounded like Pepe and Oscar, the drug enforcers I'd chased on I-95. But before we went upstairs and broke down their door, I decided to run a quick check.

"Which room are they in?" I asked.

"Number forty. It's at the end of the hall."

I walked over to the manager's desk, which was covered in papers and shoved in the corner. An old-fashioned switchboard sat on it.

"Come here," I said to the manager.

The manager crossed the room with Whitley holding a gun on him. Buster was snarling, and the manager looked petrified. I made him sit at the switchboard.

"I want you to call number forty," I said. "If someone answers, hang up. Got it?"

"Whatever you say," the manager said.

"Jack, what are you doing?" Burrell asked.

"Sampson's room doesn't have a telephone," I said. "If room forty is where he's being held, we shouldn't get an answer."

I crouched beside the manager as he made the call. He let the phone ring a dozen times, and no one picked up.

335

"No answer in forty," the manager said.

I stood up and faced Whitley. "We need to lock this guy up before we go upstairs."

"Why, don't you trust him?" Whitley asked.

I saw Whitley grin, and realized this was his idea of a joke. Whitley pushed the manager into a coat closet, and handcuffed him to a water pipe. He was still grinning when he came out of the closet.

The stairwell was next to the reception area. The three of us stood at the bottom, and listened to the crackheads getting high on the second floor. Cops called situations like this a hornet's nest. It was hard to step into it without getting stung.

I drew my Colt. "I'll go first."

"It's all yours," Whitley said.

CHAPTER
FORTY-TWO

The stairwell was poorly lit. With each step, I heard the sickening sound of glass crack pipes crunching beneath my shoes. Reaching the landing, I peered down a hallway strewn with empty pizza boxes.

"What a hellhole," Burrell whispered.

Buster was the brave one, and led us to the hallway's end. I stuck my ear to the door of number forty, and heard a TV playing Telemundo inside. Grabbing a pizza box off the floor, I held it against my chest so my Colt was hidden. With my shoe, I knocked.

"Pizza for number forty," I announced.

Burrell and Whitley pressed their bodies against the wall. The door opened, and a skinny Hispanic missing his two front teeth stuck his head out. He was about thirty, and wore striped boxer shorts and nothing else. It was Pepe.

"What you want?" he asked, smothering a yawn.

"You order a pizza?" I asked.

"Nope."

"Damn. It's going cold. You want it? I'll sell it to you for five bucks. It's got extra cheese."

"I'll give you four."

"You've got a deal."

Pepe pulled out a roll of bills, and peeled off four dollars. He took the box out of my hands, and I showed him my Colt.

"Shit," he said.

Whitley swept into the room, throwing Pepe against the wall. I followed and did a visual sweep. The room had a single bed with a night table, and a closed door leading to a bathroom. Lying on the bed were boxes of children's cereal and candy.

"Where's the kid?" I asked.

"In the closet," Pepe replied.

My heart was pounding as I opened the closet door. Filling the space was a dog crate holding a terrified African-American girl with cornrows in her hair and wearing a yellow dress. She looked about five, and held up her hands to block the light.

Buster pressed his nose against the bars, his tail wagging furiously. She lowered her hands, and touched my dog through the bars. I knelt down.

"What's your name?" I asked.

"Tyra," she said fearfully.

"Do you know a little boy named Sampson?"

"Yeah."

"Where is he?"

"Oscar took him away."

Something hard dropped in the pit of my stomach. I untied the piece of twine on the crate door while looking over my shoulder at Pepe standing with his hands pressed against the wall. "Why is she here?" I asked.

"Collateral for a drug deal," Pepe said.

"Why did your partner take Sampson away?"

"Kid kept trying to escape. We couldn't handle him."

"Who hired you?"

"Dunno."

"What's that supposed to mean?"

"Oscar dealt with the guy."

Before I could ask him where Oscar was, a toilet flushed, and Oscar emerged from the bathroom. Also shirtless, his most distinguishing feature was the automatic pistol tucked down the front of his pants. Seeing us, he drew his weapon.

Whitley was in Oscar's line of fire. Without hesitation, the FBI agent pumped three bullets into Oscar's chest. The bullets went clean through Oscar's body, killing him instantly, while also penetrating the plaster wall behind him. In the room next door, someone let out a blood-curdling scream.

"Get on the floor!" Whitley shouted.

I continued to untie the crate door.

"Do it!" Whitley said.

A bullet came through the wall and whistled past my head. It was quickly followed by another. Then I understood. Next door was shooting back.

I hit the floor while Whitley returned the fire. Tyra was huddled in the corner of the crate, crying her eyes out. I hugged the bars, and prayed that no bullets hit her.

Gunfire does something to your nervous system that's hard to explain. I saw my life flash by several times, and found myself regretting all the things I'd yet to do.

The shooting stopped, and the room fell deathly still.

The fog of gunpowder made it difficult to breathe. Whitley put a fresh clip into his gun, and hurried into the hallway. Pepe had taken a slug in the chest, and was sitting with his back to the wall, his eyes blinking rapidly. Burrell checked his pulse, then shook her head.

"We need to get Tyra out of here." I opened the crate door, and held my arms out. "Come on, honey."

The little girl rose to her feet. Her eyes were wide with fear, and she bolted out of the crate, and ran right past me to the room's single bed, and scurried beneath it.

"For the love of Christ," Burrell said.

Going to the bed, I knelt down, and stared at Tyra huddled in the darkness.

"Go away!" the little girl screamed.

I said her name, and told her I was going to take her home.

"Leave me alone!"

I knew what was happening. Tyra no longer trusted strangers, and was going to stay hidden until she encountered someone she knew. From out in the hallway came another round of gunshots. Whitley ran into the room.

"Every person in this hotel has a weapon," Whitley said. "We need to move."

"The kid's hiding under the bed," Burrell told him.

"So move the bed," Whitley said.

Whitley ran back into the hall. Burrell and I tried to move the bed away from the wall, and found that it was bolted in place.

"What are we going to do?" Burrell asked.

"Call her parents," I said.

"Are you serious?"

"They're the only ones she'll listen to."

341

Burrell knelt down next to Pepe. "Tell me who the little girl's parents are."

Pepe's eyes darted to the TV. Burrell picked up a notepad lying on the set, and read from it. "Her name is Tyra Lawson, and she lives on Magnolia Lane."

"Let's hope the number's listed," I said.

Burrell called information, and got the Lawsons' phone number. She dialed the number, and handed me her cell phone.

"Hello?" a woman answered.

"Is this the mother of Tyra Lawson?" I asked.

The woman made a fearful sound. "Yes."

"My name is Jack Carpenter, and I'm with the police. Your daughter is hiding under a bed in a crack house. I'm going to slide the phone to her. I want you to tell her to come with me. Do you understand?"

"Is my baby all right?" the woman asked.

"So far. Ready?"

"Yes — yes!"

I stuck my head beneath the bed. "Tyra. Your mother wants to talk to you. I'm going to slide you a phone. Okay?"

Tyra didn't answer me. I slid the phone beneath the bed, and heard the little girl pick it up.

"Mommy?"

I heard her mother's anguished answer.

"Tyra? Oh darling, I miss you!"

"Mommy, I'm scared!"

"You listen, and you listen good. I want you to crawl out from underneath that bed, and do whatever this man tells you to do. Do you understand?"

"But people are shooting at me!"

The mother's voice started to crack. "That man is going to save you. I want you to go to him. Please, honey."

"But they're scaring me!"

"Go with him. Please, Tyra, darling. For me."

There was a short silence. On the other side of the room, Pepe let out a dying gasp, and slumped over. Tyra crawled out from beneath the bed, and climbed into my arms. I kissed the top of her dirty little head while running out the door.

CHAPTER
FORTY-THREE

In the hall, I found a black man swimming in a pool of blood with a machine pistol clutched in his hand. He had been shot in the chest, and appeared to be dead. I made Tyra shut her eyes, and hopscotched around him.

Hurrying down the hallway with Buster, I glanced into several open doorways. Each had bloodied bodies lying inside, their hands clutched around high-powered, automatic weapons. Burrell was behind me, and I heard her gasp.

Whitley met us in the landing. He had secured the floor, and was waiting to escort us down. By my count, he'd killed six people, and hadn't broken a sweat. I wondered if he had ice cubes in his veins.

"Let's go," Whitley said.

I followed him downstairs and out of the hotel. Broward Boulevard was quiet, and I crossed the street and walked into an open

7-11. Tyra would be taken to a hospital, and given all sorts of physical and psychological examinations, but right now she was going to get a treat. Treats were good when rescuing kids. It was an easy way to tell them that things were returning to normal.

"Hey, Tyra. Your mother made me promise to buy you ice cream," I said, searching through a refrigerated bin. "What flavor do you like?"

Tyra pulled her head off my shoulder. "Vanilla."

"That's my favorite flavor, too. Do you like Dove bars?"

"Yeah."

"Want something to drink?"

"Coke."

I bought four vanilla Dove bars and a Coke, and went outside. Burrell and Whitley stood in the parking lot, facing the hotel. A cigarette passed between them.

"Ice cream," I called out.

They came over and joined us. I gave them Dove bars, and we ate our ice cream and let Buster lick the sticks. It was starting to feel like a backyard barbecue when an unmarked black van screeched to a stop in front of the hotel entrance. A Broward County Sheriff's Department SWAT team jumped out, and swarmed inside.

Tyra had seen enough, and I carried her down the sidewalk to my car. I unlocked the car, and climbed into the backseat with her clinging to me like my own child.

Minutes later, Burrell tapped on the glass. I rolled down my window.

"Everything under control?" I asked.

"Whitley's got it covered. I'll drive you to the hospital."

Burrell got behind the wheel, and I passed her the keys. As she started to pull away, Tyra lifted her head.

"Where are we going?" the little girl asked.

"To the hospital," I said. "We want the doctors to examine you."

"Will my mommy be there?"

Burrell pulled out her cell phone. "I'm calling her right now."

"Will my daddy be there?" Tyra asked. "I don't want to see Daddy."

She was looking at me now, her eyes wide and fearful.

"Why don't you want to see your daddy?" I asked.

"Daddy was mean to me. He gave me to those men as part of a deal. My daddy said he'd come back to get me, but he never did. He's mean."

I saw Burrell's eyes in the mirror. She had lowered her cell phone, and was hanging on

Tyra's every word.

"Tell me something, Tyra," I said. "What happened to Sampson?"

"Oscar took him away," the little girl said. "Sampson tried to escape from the room a bunch of times. One time, he even called someone on the phone. Sampson said if he got free, he'd come back and rescue me. I liked Sampson."

There was a spot of ice cream on her chin, and I licked the tip of my finger and wiped it away. "Did Sampson tell you who brought him there?" I asked.

"Yeah," Tyra said.

"What did he say?"

"Sampson said he had a secret friend," Tyra said. "His secret friend came to his bedroom, and took Sampson away. He gave Sampson to the men at the hotel, and they put him in the cage with me."

"Was Sampson mad at his secret friend?" I asked.

"Yeah."

"Did Sampson say who his secret friend was?"

"He called him Big Daddy."

We had reached the Broward General Medical Center. Burrell drove around to the rear of the building, and pulled up to the emergency entrance. I opened my door and started to get out. Tyra squeezed her arms tightly around my chest.

"Are you going to find Sampson?" she asked.

"Yes. I'm going to find him."

She burrowed her head into my chest. "Good."

Hospital emergency rooms were hell on kids. People who've been shot, stabbed, and beaten up filled them late at night, along with drunks and druggies. If kids weren't traumatized going into one, they usually were when they left.

I carried Tyra into the emergency room and found a quiet seat in the corner. The place was filled with hard-luck cases, many of whom were bleeding and battered. I made eye contact with every one, and watched them drift to other parts of the room.

Burrell brought a female doctor to where we were sitting. The doctor checked Tyra's pulse, listened to her heartbeat, and looked into her ears without the little girl letting go of my chest. Burrell took the chair next to mine.

"I contacted HHR," she said quietly. "They're sending someone over."

"Has Tyra been reported missing?" I asked.

Burrell shook her head no. By not reporting her daughter missing, Tyra's mother had made herself an accessory in her daughter's kidnapping and would be arrested, while Tyra would be turned over to an agent with Health and Human Resources.

"Where's my mommy?" Tyra asked.

"She's on her way," Burrell said reassuringly.

"You said that before," the little girl said.

"I'm sorry, honey," Burrell said.

Tyra started to cry. Burrell went outside to see if the mother had arrived. She returned with a black woman dressed in shorts and flip-flops and wearing the vacant expression of someone strung out on drugs. I rose from my chair holding the child.

"Hey, Tyra, look who's here," I said.

The little girl turned her head. *Mommy!*

I passed Tyra into her mother's arms. The woman let out a sob, and crushed her daughter's head into her bosom. A uniformed cop was stationed at the door. Burrell told the cop to watch Tyra's mother, and make sure she didn't leave with the child.

"Yes, ma'am," the cop said.

Burrell motioned to me. "Let's go outside.

We need to talk."

Burrell walked out of the emergency room. I started to follow, and glanced back at Tyra, who was still in her mother's arms. I hoped that her future didn't include any more crack dens, or living in dog crates, or parents who used her in drug deals. I wanted her to have a normal life, with school buses and days at the beach and report cards and all the stuff a child growing up was supposed to have. She deserved a better life, and in my prayers I'd ask God to give her one. It seemed the least I could do.

CHAPTER FORTY-FOUR

I stood with Burrell beneath a green canopy by the emergency entrance. A punishing rain had started to fall, and thunder rolled ominously in the distance.

"I want to ask you a question, and I want an honest answer," Burrell said.

The tone of her voice told me I was in trouble again. I thrust my hands into the pockets of my cargo pants, and waited.

"Based upon what Tyra told us in the car, do you think Jed Grimes is responsible for these crimes?" Burrell asked.

"No," I said.

"So Jed isn't Big Daddy."

I shook my head.

"But he's the child's father. Wouldn't it make sense for him to call himself that?"

"It could be a family friend or someone who works in the neighborhood."

"If I told you that we'd interviewed every single person who was around that child, including LeAnn Grimes's neighbors, and Jed's neighbors, and employees of every store, and they were clean, would you change your mind?"

"No," I said.

"But *everyone* was clean."

"You missed someone."

Her frown grew. "No, we didn't. We looked at everyone, and they all checked out. The only person who didn't check out was Jed. That makes him our primary suspect."

"So you're buying Whitley's savage spawn theory?"

"It's the only one that works."

Lightning crackled and flashed above our heads. Dozens of people died during thunderstorms in Florida every year, yet neither of us moved from our spots. Burrell had made up her mind, and she wasn't backing down. I didn't want to lose her as a friend, but I wasn't going to retreat, either.

"Let me see if I've got this figured out," I said. "You and Whitley are going to combine your investigations, since you're convinced you're looking for the same person. You were hoping that I would help you, and now you're pissed."

"I'm pissed because you're going down one road, while everyone else is going down another," Burrell said.

"Do you want me off the investigation?"

Burrell crossed her arms and stared at the ground.

"Is that a yes, or a no?" I asked.

I heard the unmistakable sound of a transformer being hit by a bolt of lightning. The lights in the parking lot flickered, then went off.

"I want you to reconsider," she said quietly.

"There's nothing to reconsider," I said.

"Please, Jack."

"You missed someone. Go back and interview everyone again."

"I'm not going to do that."

I couldn't help myself, and held her shoulders, looking deep in her eyes.

"You're making a *terrible* mistake."

Burrell shoved me away. She started to say something, then bit her tongue. The door slid shut as she went inside.

I had stepped over the line. I should have felt bad, but instead I told myself she'd get over it. The rain was starting to ease up, and I ran to my car, having no idea how prophetic my words to her would become, or the nightmare I was about to enter.

■ ■ ■ ■

PART FOUR:
THE NIGHT
STALKER

■ ■ ■ ■

CHAPTER
FORTY-FIVE

The storm followed me home.

I entered the Sunset to find the jukebox playing the Isley Brothers' "Twist and Shout." The Dwarfs sat at the bar clapping their hands and swaying their bodies in unison. They were not feeling any pain, and I wondered if they'd even noticed that I'd been gone.

I took a stool at the end of the bar, and Buster curled up at my feet. Sonny pulled a cold Budweiser out of the cooler, and I drank it and listened to the rain. It was loud enough to compete with the music, and made the bar feel smaller than it was.

It had been a brutal day. I'd had a gun pointed inches from my face, and a couple of bullets fly right past my head. I was going to wake up the next few nights in a cold sweat, thinking about my own mortality. I always did when I nearly got killed.

A clap of thunder shook the building, and

made me shudder. I didn't want to wake up alone, thinking about death. I wanted someone beside me who I could draw close to, and hold in my arms.

The jukebox went silent. I crossed the room, and flipped through the playlist. The Doors' "Love Her Madly" jumped out at me, and I dropped a dime and hit the play button. Moments later, Jim Morrison's whiskey-pure voice came belting out of the speakers, and several Dwarfs shouted their approval.

I returned to my stool and listened to the song. All it did was make me think of Rose and how much I missed her. Grabbing my dog, I headed upstairs.

Sitting on my bed, I dialed Rose's number. It was an ungodly hour to be calling some-one, but I couldn't help myself. I wanted to hear my wife's voice, and I felt my heartbeat quicken when she picked up.

"Hey, honey," I said.

"Oh, Jack, I'm so glad it's you," Rose replied.

"Is something wrong?"

"Yes. Where are you? It's so noisy."

The music was trailing up from down-stairs. I hopped off the bed, and shut the door with my foot. "I'm at my place. What's going on?"

"I just got off the phone with our daughter," Rose said. "Jessie has been talking to Heather Rinker. She wanted to see how Heather was doing. Heather said the police are following her wherever she goes. Heather also thinks her cell phone is being tapped. She told Jessie that she saw a policeman with a rifle on the roof across the street from her mother-in-law's house. Heather thinks the police are using her as bait to draw out Jed."

"Heather saw a sharpshooter?" I asked.

"That's what Jessie said."

It had been a long, shitty day, and what my wife was saying made it that much worse. The Broward cops never used sharpshooters. This was the FBI's doing. Whitley had decided to lay a trap for Jed.

"I'm calling Jessie right now," I said.

"Please let me know what happens."

"I will. There was another reason I called."

"What's that?"

"I miss you."

"I miss you, too," Rose said.

I called my daughter and got voice mail. I left a message for her to call me back. Then I went to my window, and watched the storm churn up the ocean. Sharpshooters on the roof meant that the FBI was planning to take out Jed once they laid eyes on him. They didn't want to hear his side of things, or give him due process. Maybe they thought he was too dangerous. Or maybe Whitley was looking for another scalp to add to his collection.

My phone rang. Caller ID said JESSIE.

"Hey, honey," I answered. "I just got off the phone with your mom. She told me what was going on."

"Can you do something?" my daughter asked.

"I'm going to try," I said. "I want to ask you something. Do you think Heather has been talking to Jed? If so, the FBI is probably listening to their conversations. It would explain why the FBI is using her as bait."

"Heather made me swear not to tell, but yes, she is."

"Okay, then here's what I want you to do. Call Heather, and tell her that I think Jed is innocent, and that I'm willing to take him to the police, and guarantee his safety."

"You'll do that?"

"Yes. Jed will be much safer in police custody than he is in hiding. If one of those FBI sharpshooters spots him, it's all over."

"Should I tell Heather that?"

"Do whatever you have to do," I said.

I stood by my window and listened to the rain pound the roof. It sounded like a thousand tiny hammers on my skull, and I felt the anger and frustration inside of me rising to the surface.

Jed Grimes had been set up. I didn't know who was responsible, or what their motivation was. What I did know was that he'd done a masterful job of convincing the police and the FBI. If I didn't get to Jed first, he was history.

My phone rang, and I pulled it from my pocket. Caller ID said UNKNOWN.

"Carpenter here," I answered.

A car horn blared in the background, along with other street noises. Then a young woman said, "Mr. Carpenter, this is Heather Rinker. I'm standing at a pay phone next to a convenience store two blocks from my mother-in-law's house. I wanted to call you without the FBI listening in."

"I guess you spoke to Jessie," I said.

"Yeah. She explained your offer to help Jed. I thought it was a good idea, so I came over here and called him. Jed wants to do it."

I breathed a sigh of relief. "Good."

"Come to the store, and I'll take you to where Jed's hiding out."

"That sounds like a plan, Heather. I'm

361

leaving right now."

"No. Wait until it gets light."

"Why?"

"There are too many FBI agents hiding in the neighborhood. They've got rifles. Jed's scared of getting shot, and so am I."

The fear in her voice was almost palpable.

"All right," I said.

"I'm going to give you my cell number. Call it when you leave. I'll slip out of my mother-in-law's house, and meet you at the convenience store. Then we'll go see Jed."

I grabbed a pen and piece of paper off my night table. "Go ahead."

She gave me her cell phone number. Her voice was strained, and I sensed that she was holding something back. "Is there something you want to tell me, Heather?"

"I'm just afraid," she said.

"Nothing is going to happen to Jed. You have to believe that."

"I do. It's just . . ."

"Just what?"

She started to reply, then hung up.

CHAPTER
FORTY-SIX

I lay on my bed and did ceiling patrol for a few hours, thinking about Jed. His father was about to be executed, his little boy had been kidnapped, and he was being hunted by the FBI. I needed to get him out of harm's way, and figure out who was behind these crimes. And I needed to do it fast.

At six a.m. I dragged myself out of bed, and took a long, hot shower. It woke me up, and I threw my clothes on while listening to the rain.

I drove over the short steel drawbridge to the mainland with a cup of coffee in my hand and Jimmy Buffett's *Songs You Know by Heart* album playing on the pickup's tape deck. The roads were treacherous, and I crawled through town and headed north to the interstate.

As I drove, I visualized the convenience store in LeAnn Grimes's neighborhood. It sat on the corner of a busy intersection and had two gas pumps. I didn't like meeting people in places that weren't out in the open, not even people that I knew. Call it my survival instinct. I decided that the store was a good meeting place.

As I exited the interstate, I called Heather.

"It's Jack Carpenter," I said. "I'm five minutes away."

"Let me call you back," she said.

"Is something wrong?"

The line went dead. It was the second time she'd hung up on me. It gave me a bad feeling, and I glanced at Buster, who sat at stiff attention in the passenger seat.

I navigated my way down the flooded streets to the convenience store. When I was a block away, I pulled off, and put my blinkers on. Then Heather called me back.

"We're on," she said.

"Good," I said.

"I'm going to need about ten minutes."

"I'll be there."

Ten minutes later I arrived at the store. The parking lot was a lake, and contained no cars. Parking so I faced the front door, I grabbed the Marlins' baseball cap off the backseat and stuck it on my head. I hadn't followed the Marlins until they'd won the

World Series. Now they were my favorite team.

Out of habit I touched the Colt resting in my pants pocket. It gave me a sense of security that only a gun can. Then I glanced at Buster. His ears were pinned straight back.

"I'll be right back, partner."

I dodged raindrops going inside. The store was empty, save for the Cuban manager eating breakfast behind the counter. I coughed and he looked up.

"I'm looking for a girl," I said. "She's supposed to be meeting me here."

He nodded toward the bathroom. "She's in there. You want something?"

"No, thanks."

He pointed at the sign on the counter. It said "No Loitering." I pretended to fill out a Lotto ticket while waiting for Heather to emerge. The bathroom door opened, and a barefoot woman who looked like a street person sauntered out.

"Hey, big boy," the woman said.

"Sorry, I thought you were someone else," I said.

"Sure you did."

She cackled like a witch and left the store. I went to the front window, and pressed my face to the glass. I didn't see Heather.

"You want something?" the manager asked.

"Give me a cup of coffee," I said.

"Cuban coffee?"

"Why not?"

The coffee was strong enough to wake the dead. Sipping it, I went to the door. Two black SUVs had pulled into the lot, and I watched eight shotgun-wielding FBI agents climb out. I knew they were FBI because it was printed in bold letters across their baseball caps. Nothing like free advertising, I thought. They surrounded the pickup and aimed their weapons at Buster, who was sitting behind the wheel. At the same time, a black helicopter swooped out of the sky, and I saw a door open, and a man clutching a high-powered rifle aim at the roof of the pickup.

I burst out of the store. "Don't shoot!"

It was the wrong move. Two of the agents spun around, and aimed their weapons at my chest. I froze, and they threw me to the ground. I dropped my coffee and banged my head. A shotgun found my rib cage.

"Don't move," one of them said.

"Wouldn't dream of it," I said.

The other agent knelt down, and ripped off my Marlins' cap. "It's Carpenter."

"Jesus Christ," the first agent said.

I got to my feet. My clothes were covered in dirt and spilled coffee, and I was seeing double. I waited for my vision to return, and stared into their faces. It was Burrell and Whitley. Burrell wore a baseball cap that said Broward Police, and looked ready to kill me.

"What are *you* doing here?" she demanded.

"Getting breakfast," I said.

"Don't push me, Jack."

"You should try their coffee. It's really good."

"Is Jed here? Or Heather?"

"They never showed."

"Get in your car and follow us," she said.

Whitley shouted a command, and the agents lowered their weapons, and got back into the SUVs, while the chopper lifted into the clouds. I got into the pickup and hugged Buster. I didn't know who I was angrier at: Heather for setting me up, or myself for letting it happen. I turned the key in the ignition so hard it made the engine scream.

One of the SUVs got in front of me, the other behind, and we drove to LeAnn Grimes's neighborhood. At the entrance to RichJo Lane, we came to a roadblock manned by six heavily armed FBI agents, and were waved through.

We drove to a house directly across the street from LeAnn's. The grass was knee-high, and partially obscured the "For Sale" sign on the lawn. I followed Burrell inside.

The house was old and musty, and had creaky hardwood floors. There was no furniture except for the sophisticated monitoring equipment the FBI had installed in the living room. Two FBI techs were staring at a bank of flickering video monitors showing LeAnn's house as we came inside.

Burrell led me to a back bedroom, and shut the door with her foot. Yanking off her cap, she shook out her hair. She was still livid with me.

"You two make a nice couple," I said.

"I should arrest you," she said.

"On what charge?"

"I'll think of something."

"Do you want me to tell you what happened back there?" I asked.

"Be my guest."

"Heather gave you the slip. Check your surveillance tapes if you don't believe me."

"Stay here."

Burrell hurried to the front of the house. She came back to the bedroom with an angry look on her face.

"How did you know Heather ran out on

us?" she demanded.

"Can I see the tape?" I asked.

"Explain yourself first."

"I offered to bring Jed in, and turn him over to the police. Heather agreed, and told me to meet her at the convenience store, where she'd take me to see Jed. Then she conned the FBI into believing Jed was coming to the store. The FBI took the bait, and Heather used the opportunity to run."

"Why did she do that?"

"I guess because she loves him. Now can I see the video?"

Burrell led me to the living room. Whitley had come inside and was staring at the monitors with an unlit cigarette dangling from his lips. A surveillance tape was playing showing a person wearing a faded jean jacket and workman's cap walking down a dirt path behind LeAnn's house. The person turned, and one of the techs froze the image. It was Heather, dressed in her husband's work clothes.

"Do we know where she went?" Whitley asked the tech.

The tech unfroze the image, and we watched Heather disappear from the screen.

"No," the tech said.

"Shit," Whitley cursed.

"I know where Heather is," I said.

Everyone in the living room stared at me.

"She went to be with Jed," I said. "And I know who can tell us where Jed is."

"Who?" Whitley asked.

I went to the window and cranked it open. Through the glass shutters I stared at LeAnn Grimes's house with its "No Trespassing" signs scattered across the lawn. LeAnn and Jed had impressed me as having a special bond born out of years of shared adversity. If anyone knew where Jed was hiding, it was her.

"If you think LeAnn Grimes is going to help us, forget it," Whitley said. "I tried to speak with her, and she slammed the door in my face."

"That's because you're a cop," I said. "She'll talk with me."

"How can you be so sure?"

"She trusts me."

An uneasy silence filled the room. I glanced over my shoulder, and saw Burrell and Whitley exchange looks. They were going to have to work on their signals, because I knew what Burrell was going to say before the words came out of her mouth.

"Please, Jack," she said.

CHAPTER
FORTY-SEVEN

As I came outside, Buster exploded out of the bushes and followed me across the street to LeAnn's house. I made him lie on the grass, then knocked on the door.

"It's Jack Carpenter," I said.

I heard a deadbolt being drawn back, and LeAnn filled the doorway. She wore a shapeless black housedress, and her eyes were filled with dread.

"I need to talk to you about Heather," I said.

"Heather's in trouble," she whispered.

LeAnn fell heavily against the door. She was in shock, and I escorted her to the living room and made her sit on the couch. From the kitchen I got a glass of cold water, and placed it beneath her lips. She drank the entire glass.

"Tell me what happened," I said.

She pointed at the cell phone lying on the coffee table. It was right in front of her, only she didn't want to touch it. I picked it up.

"Is there something you want me to hear?" I asked.

"Heather left me a voice message," she whispered.

I sat beside her on the couch, and made her show me how to access her messaging service. Dialing in, I entered her password, then listened hard. At first, I heard nothing. Then Heather's voice ripped through the phone.

"Help me! Please, somebody help me!"

Her attacker was beating her, and I could hear the blows. Heather's screams grew louder, then suddenly stopped altogether. I strained to pick up any background noises, and heard another voice. It was small and strong.

"Leave my mommy alone! Leave her alone!"

It was Sampson, and he was fighting back. I listened as the killer dragged him across the room, and heard a door slam. Then the call ended.

An icy finger ran down my spine. The message was similar to Piper Stone's last call. The killer had sent that message, along with this one. He was taunting us.

"Sweet Lord, have mercy on their souls," LeAnn whispered.

"Where did Heather go?" I asked.

"To buy some things for Jed."

"What things?"

"I don't know. They talk on walkie-talkies, and sometimes it's hard to make out what they're saying."

"Was she stopping someplace in the neighborhood?"

"I think so."

"But you don't know where."

LeAnn shook her head.

"I need to talk to Jed."

"I don't know where my son is," she whispered.

"I think you do," I said.

Tears ran down LeAnn's cheeks, and she balled her hands into fists and bounced them on her lap. I touched her sleeve, but she refused to look at me.

"Your son has a hiding place in the neighborhood, someplace where he goes when he wants to escape from the world," I said. "He's been going there for a long time, and you've always known about it, even if you haven't talked about it. Am I right?"

She nodded stiffly.

"This secret place bothered you, so you watched him, and tried to figure out where he went. You wanted to know, and probably came up with some ideas, didn't you?"

"Yes," she said softly.

"Tell me your ideas," I said.

She took a deep breath. "It was nearby. I knew because he never took his bike or the car. For a while I thought he was going to a mall where his friends hung out. Then I realized that wasn't so."

"How did you know that?"

"His clothes. Whenever he went to his secret place, he wore the worst clothes. He didn't do that when he went to the mall."

"Did he invite his friends there?"

"Yes, all the time. I used to hear him on the phone."

"So other kids knew about it."

"Yes, they knew."

"Do you remember anything else?"

"Jed always took a shower after he came home. One day I confronted him in the hall. That's when the smell hit me."

"The smell?"

"It was rancid. He smelled like he'd been rolling around in something dead."

"Do you think he's hiding in a barn?"

"He didn't smell like horses."

"Then where?"

She fell silent and stared at the framed photo of Jed on the coffee table. "I just figured he'd dug a big hole in the ground somewhere. Where else could he be going?"

■ ■ ■ ■

I went outside and called Jessie on my cell phone. A veil of storm clouds had descended over the neighborhood, and a harsh rain was falling.

"Hi, Daddy," my daughter answered. "How did it go with Heather?"

"Not good," I said. "Heather's in trouble. I need to find Jed."

"What can I do?"

"You grew up with Heather, and shared a lot of friends. I want you to call them, and ask them if they remember a secret hiding place that Jed had. Maybe there's an old bomb shelter buried in someone's backyard, or an abandoned garage. Jed's got a hideout, and he's had it for a while. Hopefully, one of Heather's friends will know where it is."

"I'll call them right now," my daughter said.

I folded my phone. Across the street, a small army of FBI agents wearing bulletproof vests and carrying rifles had gathered on the sidewalk. Whitley was with them, barking out orders, and I watched the agents break into groups, and begin a house-to-house search of the neighborhood. Seeing me, Whitley crossed the street.

375

"We just picked up a message on LeAnn Grimes's voice mail," the FBI agent said. "You can hear Jed beating up his wife. We're going to find him before he kills her."

I started to protest, then clamped my mouth shut. Whitley had made up his mind that Jed was guilty, and nothing I could say was going to change that belief. I watched him hurry away. Then Jessie called me back.

"I just got off the phone with Cinda Bowe, one of Jed's old girlfriends," my daughter said. "Cinda said that Jed's neighborhood used to be on private well and septic, but got switched over to city water and sewer. Most of the houses kept their septic tanks, and Jed spent a summer cleaning several out, and connecting them with underground tunnels. Cinda said Jed even ran electricity down there."

"Did Jed ever take Cinda there?" I asked.

"Cinda went there once and smoked pot with Jed. She said it stank like a sewer, so she never went back."

"Did she remember where it was?"

"Cinda said it happened when she was a kid. She forgot the exact location, but said it was a couple of blocks away from Jed's mom's house."

Cinda Bowe wasn't old enough to be forgetting things like that. My daughter's

376

friend wasn't telling the whole truth, probably because she didn't want her name coming up. We were running out of time, and I decided to press her.

"Give me Cinda's number," I said.

"But, Daddy —"

"Give it to me."

"She'll freak out if you call her."

"Good. I always enjoy a freakout."

"Let me call her. Please. I can make Cinda talk."

I hesitated. I needed to get to Jed first. It was my only guarantee that he wouldn't get shot.

"All right, but you can't let Cinda off the hook," I said.

"I won't let you down," my daughter promised.

CHAPTER
FORTY-EIGHT

A minute later, Jessie called me back with exact directions.

The property where Jed had his hideout was owned by an elderly couple named Dodd. The Dodds were snowbirds, and spent six months of the year living in south Florida, the other six in their native Montreal. Jessie said they were hard of hearing, and that Jed had come and gone for years without them knowing it.

I thanked my daughter and ended the call. The rain was coming down sideways, and I crossed the street to the house being occupied by the FBI. Before I could knock, Burrell came onto the porch.

"Come with me," I said.

"I can't. I'm helping the techs watch the monitors," Burrell said.

"I know where Jed is hiding."

"You do? Did you tell Whitley?"

I shook my head. "We're going to do this

378

my way."

"You can't act outside the law, Jack."

"I'm not," I said. "You're going to help me."

"I am?"

"Yes. Now get your gear."

Burrell started to protest. I stepped off the porch and began walking down the sidewalk with my head bowed and my dog by my side.

Burrell caught up to me moments later. She had thrown on a bulletproof vest that was a size too big for her, and was cradling a shotgun between her arms.

"Slow down," she said.

I slowed my pace. "You need to lose the shotgun."

"Why should I do that?"

"Because we're going into a hole in the ground. You can't turn around in a confined space with a shotgun. Sidearms only."

Burrell's jaw clenched, and I saw her blink.

"Anything else you'd like to share with me?" she asked.

"Yes," I said. "LeAnn told me when Heather left the house, she went to get something for Jed. I'm guessing it was food."

"So?"

"Yesterday I spoke with the father of Mary McClary, one of the victims at the landfill.

He told me his daughter was looking for work, and had worked as a waitress."

"I'm still not reading you."

We came to the corner and both stopped. I was going to make Burrell understand if it was the last thing I did, and I turned so I was facing her.

"Our killer works in a restaurant," I said.

The Dodds lived in a tiny bungalow made of cinder blocks. The front yard was a jungle, the grass knee-high. I banged on the front door, and, when no one came out, checked the mailbox. It was filled with promotional flyers.

"Looks like they're away," I said.

I led Burrell to the back of the property. The lot was long and narrow, and had several ripening citrus trees. I picked up a stick and began poking at the soggy ground.

"What are we looking for?" Burrell asked.

"A septic tank," I replied.

We searched the property. Several times, I saw Burrell drop to her knees and dig in the earth, only to turn up a water sprinkler, or something hidden in the dirt. Soon we were done.

"Are you sure this is the place?" Burrell asked.

"Yes," I said. "Keep looking."

There was an art to finding a concealed space, and even the best searchers missed things. I retraced my steps while tuning out the storm. Buster was lying beneath a lemon tree, and raised his head each time I passed him.

"Some help you are," I said.

My dog let out a whine, and began to dig with his front paws. Etched in the dirt beneath the tree was the faint outline of a small door. I'd passed the spot several times, yet somehow missed it. Kneeling, I dug my fingers into the dirt, and the door came free.

"Over here," I said.

Burrell came over, and stared into the hole with her flashlight. She pulled out her cell phone.

"I'm calling Whitley," she announced.

"Why?" I asked.

"Because he's in charge."

"Are you afraid of bringing Jed in yourself?"

"Of course not."

"Then call Whitley when you're done," I said.

Burrell acted like I'd slapped her across the face.

"You're out of line, Jack," she said.

She started to make the call. I picked

Buster up in my arms, and held him over the opening. The drop looked about five feet. I lowered him as far as I could without falling in, then released him. He landed on all fours, and took off running.

"What are you doing?" she asked.

I followed my dog down the hole. I was inside an empty septic tank. The air was toxic, and I tried not to puke.

"Wait!" she said.

Burrell jumped down the hole so she was standing beside me.

"Don't do that again," she said.

I pointed at the passageway on the other side of the tank.

"That way," I said.

"Jack, I'm warning you. Don't do that again," she said.

"Yes, ma'am."

We went down the passageway. The ceiling was low, and we both walked like crabs. It led to another septic tank with bleached walls and breathable air. A Coleman lantern hung from the wall; beneath it several pieces of mismatched furniture were arranged like a living room. Hanging from the walls were posters of James Dean and Kurt Cobain, and I spied an old bong on the coffee table with cobwebs on it.

Burrell pointed at a black door on the

other end of the tank. It had a half moon painted on it, and appeared to be a bathroom. She drew her weapon, and aimed at the door.

"Don't shoot him," I whispered.

"Don't tell me what to do," she whispered back.

"Does this look like a killer's lair?" I asked.

Burrell glanced around the tank. "No."

"Let me open the door."

"Go ahead."

I went to the door and jerked it open. The bathroom was empty.

"Where the hell is he?" Burrell asked.

I looked around the tank. There had to be another way out, only I wasn't seeing it. Then I realized that I didn't know where Buster was.

"Where's my dog?" I asked.

"He was ahead of me, then disappeared," Burrell said.

I let out a shrill whistle. Through the walls I heard a sound that was half whine, half dying breath. I tore through the living room, and did not stop until I found a secret door hidden behind a piece of cloth painted to resemble the wall. Tearing the cloth back, I stared down another passageway, and made out two forms at the other end: Jed Grimes, dressed in a pair of blue jeans and nothing else, and Buster. Jed had gotten a chain around my dog's neck, and was strangling him. Buster's tongue was sticking out of his mouth, his body hanging limply by Jed's side. My head scraped the ceiling as I ran toward them. "Let him go!" I shouted.

Jed released my dog, and scurried up a ladder against the wall. Reaching him, I grabbed his bare foot, which was dangling above me.

"He's here!" I yelled.

Jed kicked me in the face. I heard my nose break and saw pools of black before my eyes. I fell onto my dog, and tried to regain my senses. Buster lay beneath me, his body limp. I found his face in the dark, and ran my hand across it.

He was dead.

Burrell's voice brought me back to reality.

"He's getting away!"

I forced myself to stand. My head felt like a balloon, and I was having a hard time seeing clearly. Burrell stood in the passageway with her weapon drawn. There was not enough room for her to pass, and she grabbed my shoulder and shook me.

"Wake up, Jack!" she said.

I filled my lungs with air. A ladder was attached to the wall, and I grabbed a rung and started climbing until I was standing in an unfamiliar backyard. The rain was coming down in sheets, and I spotted Jed scaling a picket fence. I took off after him.

"Jed! Stop!" I shouted.

He looked over his shoulder at me, then disappeared. I hurled my body over the fence, and landed in a flower bed. Jed was twenty feet ahead of me, and running for a gate that led to the front of the property. I yelled for him to stop, and he ignored me.

I came through the gate running as fast as my legs would go, and found Jed standing on the front lawn of the house, surrounded by five FBI agents. The agents were pointing their weapons at him, which consisted of three rifles, one shotgun, and one pistol. Jed was dancing around like a boxer, trying to find an opening to escape through.

"No!" I screamed.

One of the agents' heads snapped in my direction. It was Whitley. He was holding the automatic pistol, and had his free hand stuck in the air. When he dropped his hand, the agents were going to fire. His eyes met mine, and I saw him squint.

Whitley's arm came down as I jumped. I tackled Jed directly above the knees, and brought him down hard. Jed grunted, and I felt his body go still. I hugged the ground as bullets flew around me.

"Get up," Whitley shouted.

My ears were ringing as I rose to my feet. Whitley pulled me to the side while two of his men frisked and handcuffed Jed, who remained facedown on the ground. The air was thick with gunpowder, and I was having difficulty breathing.

"You're a stupid son-of-a-bitch," Whitley said.

I tasted blood, and brought my hand up to my face. It was trickling out of my left nostril. I'd gotten my nose busted a few times as a kid, and it hadn't killed me.

"Do you have anything to say for yourself?" Whitley asked.

I shook my head. The agents pulled Jed to his feet, and walked him to the curb.

A black SUV pulled up, and Jed was hustled into the backseat. As the door was closed, his eyes met mine. He looked terrified. I hadn't wanted Jed to get shot, and although the price had been more than I'd bargained for, I'd succeeded.

"Did you find his wife or son?" Whitley asked.

I shook my head. Whitley climbed into the passenger seat of the SUV. Its tires squealed as it pulled away from the curb.

I found Burrell in the backyard next door. She was sitting on the ground and had something furry clutched in her arms that looked like a giant teddy bear.

"The FBI has Jed," I told her.

"Is he alive?" she asked.

"Yes."

"Good. Now help me."

I got up next to her, and saw that she was holding my dog.

"He's still got a pulse," she explained.

CHAPTER
FORTY-NINE

I gathered up Buster in my arms, and carried him down the street. He was out cold, his breathing faint. Burrell made a call on her cell, and a police cruiser appeared. I loaded Buster into the backseat.

"Where do you want me to take him?" the driver asked.

As a cop, I'd taken injured animals to different clinics around the county, and one clinic had stood out above the others for the care it had shown.

"Hollywood Animal Clinic on Hollywood Boulevard," I said.

"Will do," the driver said.

I watched the cruiser drive away. I'd always ridiculed people who were overly attached to their pets, but now that I was close to losing mine, I wanted to crawl into a hole and die. Burrell edged up beside me.

"I won't be offended if you leave," she said.

I loved Buster, but I also had a job to do, and it wasn't finished.

"I'm not going anywhere," I said.

Bowing my head to the rain, I followed Burrell back to Jed's hideout.

We took our time, and searched the hideout thoroughly. Every piece of furniture and accessory felt like something a nineteen-year-old boy would own. Nothing we found indicated that Heather or Sampson had recently been there. Nor was there any evidence of Jed having killed anyone. Serial killers were notorious for keeping trophies of their victims, and we didn't find a single item that looked suspicious.

"Jack, look at this," Burrell said.

I stopped what I was doing. Burrell sat on the couch with an old book in her lap.

"What is it?" I asked.

"Take a look."

She handed me the book. It was falling apart, and I carefully opened it. It was a Bible, and on the first page I saw the names of every member of the Grimes family who had owned it over the past hundred years. At the bottom of the page was Jed's name.

"Not the kind of thing you expect to find in a serial killer's hideout, is it?" I said.

"No, it isn't," Burrell said.

I noticed something stuck in the Bible's pages, and pulled it out. It was a photograph of Jed standing next to a priest with a turned collar. The priest was bowed over from age, with wisps of silver hair that danced on his head. The priest had his hand on Jed's shoulder, and they were both smiling.

I flipped the photo over. There was a date written on the back. It had been taken a year ago. I showed it to Burrell.

"Jed's priest," I said.

Burrell studied the photograph, and shook her head. "Have you ever heard of a serial killer having a priest?"

"No," I said.

"Whitley needs to see this, and the Bible."

"Yes, he does."

Burrell's cell phone rang. She answered it, then looked at me.

"Buster's going to live," she said.

I pulled out my keys. My job was done here.

"Let me know how it goes," I said.

I drove to the Hollywood Animal Clinic in the pouring rain. A receptionist with silver thunderbolts painted on her fingernails greeted me from behind a Plexiglas panel.

"Can I help you?" the receptionist asked.

"I own a dog that was brought in earlier," I said.

"The Australian Shepherd that was involved in the manhunt?"

"That's right."

She led me to an examination room, and told me the vet would be in shortly. While I waited, I looked at the horse photographs hanging on the walls. They showed a pretty woman with short spiked hair sitting on a chestnut stallion with ribbons hanging around its neck. The horse's name was Charley Horse, which brought a smile to my face.

The vet came in wearing a white lab coat. It was the same woman from the photos. Her name tag said Dr. Chris Owens.

"The police tell me your dog's a hero," Dr. Owens said.

No one had ever called Buster that before, much less anything nice.

"How's he doing?" I asked.

"He regained consciousness a short while ago, but is still groggy," Dr. Owens said. "He seems to be all right, but I'm concerned about his skull. I don't think it's cracked, but I won't know for certain until I run a series of X-rays."

I'd been to enough emergency clinics to know how they operated.

"How much are we talking about?" I asked.

Dr. Owens worked up the cost on a pocket calculator, and showed me the figure. Three hundred and twenty bucks for a lousy pound mutt.

"Run the X-rays," I said.

"I'll need you to sign a form agreeing to the procedure," Dr. Owens said.

I removed the money from my wallet, and stuffed it into her hand.

"Right now," I said.

"He's a special dog, isn't he?" she asked.

No one had ever called Buster that before, either.

Dr. Owens returned to the examination room holding a handful of X-rays, which she held up to the overhead light for me to see. "Your dog has suffered a mild concussion. It could have been worse, but he's got a thick skull."

"Can I take him home?" I asked.

"I don't see why not."

I followed her down the hall to the X-ray room, where Buster lay on a table. His eyes were at half-mast, and I saw his tiny tail wag.

"You need to keep him quiet for a few days," Dr. Owens said. "I know that's hard with an Aussie, but you don't want him running around. I'm giving you some pain pills. Give him two every four hours until they run out."

I carried out Buster with his cold nose pressed against my neck. The waiting area was filled with people with ailing pets, and a woman stroking a Siamese cat spoke to me.

"Is it true what the receptionist said about your dog?" the woman asked.

"What's that?" I asked.

"That he helped the police catch that horrible serial killer Jed Grimes?"

I hadn't mentioned Jed's name to the receptionist, and I wondered how the woman had made the connection. Then I spied a TV in the corner of the room. Whitley was on, and was wearing fresh clothes, and had slicked back his hair. He was holding a press conference for the local media, and talking about Jed's apprehension. People accused of crimes were supposed to be innocent until proven guilty, only Whitley was calling Jed a killer, and giving himself and his agents the credit for apprehending him.

I walked out of the clinic without replying.

CHAPTER FIFTY

I found Burrell standing in the clinic parking lot. She asked after my heroic dog.

"He's going to be okay."

"I'm glad. We need to talk," she said.

Burrell offered to drive me home in my pickup, with a police cruiser following us. I agreed, and climbed into the passenger seat with Buster in my arms. He was coming around, and seemed to be enjoying all the attention I was giving him.

It was still raining like it was the end of the world. Burrell crawled through a tricky roundabout in the center of town, then turned her head to look at me. "You told me something the first day I came to work for you," she said. "You said, 'Listen to your brain, but follow your heart.' I've never forgotten that."

"Is your heart telling you something now?" I asked.

"Yes. I think we arrested the wrong person."

"Did you talk to Whitley?"

"I called him, and told him about finding the Bible and photo of the priest in Jed's hideout. Whitley said it was meaningless. He blew me off."

Burrell didn't try to hide the anger in her voice.

"What's the deal between you two?" I asked.

"I thought we were in love," she said.

"Thought?"

"Whitley and I have been seeing each other for about a year. He told me he was leaving his wife. The story changed a few hours ago."

"I'm sorry."

"Don't be."

We crossed the Hollywood Bridge, and took A1A north to the Sunset. The streets were deserted, the bars and restaurants empty. I had Burrell pull into the Sunset's parking lot, and park by the entrance. The cruiser did the same.

"Earlier you told me that you thought someone who worked in a restaurant was our killer," Burrell said. "Do you have a profile?"

Buster was whining to get out of the car.

Opening my door, I laid him onto the pavement, and watched him teeter down to the shoreline and relieve himself.

"Our killer works in a restaurant," I said, closing my door. "He might be the night manager, or maybe even the owner. He's a loner, and has lived in LeAnn's neighborhood for many years. He also has a connection to Abb Grimes, although I haven't figured out what it is. He's smart, but impulsive."

"A classic serial killer," Burrell said.

"That's right."

"If I run a background check on every restaurant employee in the area, would you take a look at them, and see if you could pick him out?"

I stared at the waves crashing on the beach. My nose was throbbing, and I was exhausted to the point that I could hardly keep my eyes open.

"Sure," I said.

Burrell leaned across the seat, and kissed me on the cheek. "Thanks, Jack."

Buster froze at the bottom of the stairwell leading to my room. I carried him upstairs, and laid him on the bed. Then I examined myself in the bathroom. My nose was turning purple, and had a nasty bump over the bridge. No more *GQ* covers for me.

I went downstairs to the bar. Two teenage girls were dancing in front of the jukebox while the Dwarfs ogled them from their bar stools. The girls were both slurping Diet Cokes, and I spoke to Sonny.

"They legal?" I asked.

"Naw. Tried to pass off some fake IDs, but I made them," Sonny said.

"Why didn't you throw them out?"

"Because I'm horny."

I went upstairs and found my detective's badge. The department had let me keep my badge after I'd quit. You could say it was one of the few decent things they'd done. I went downstairs and pulled the girls off the floor. Going outside, I made them stand in the pouring rain while I read them the riot act. By the time I was done, the makeup had washed off their faces, and they'd promised to stay out of bars until they were legal.

"Spoilsport," Sonny said when I returned.

"You have any pain pills?" I asked.

Sonny fed me some Advil. I drank coffee, and waited for them to kick in. It took awhile, but I finally started to feel normal.

The local news came on. The lead story was about Jed's capture, and showed him doing a perp walk outside the police station. The images faded into a blaring head-line.

WHAT WENT WRONG?

On the screen a familiar face appeared. It was Ron Cheeks, wearing his best suit and a smug look on his face. The pills churned in my stomach, and I grabbed the remote off the bar. Cheeks's voice came booming out of the TV.

"Jed Grimes was our number one suspect from the start," Cheeks said. "All the evidence pointed to him. He abducted his son, and we knew it."

"Why didn't the police arrest him before now?" a female reporter asked.

Cheeks did a slow burn. "I was going to. Unfortunately, a medical condition forced me off the case, and another detective took over."

"Who was that?"

"Detective Candice Burrell."

"Is she to blame?"

"Detective Burrell is a fine police officer, and in no way is responsible for what has happened with this investigation," Cheeks replied.

"Then who is?"

"A consultant the police hired to work the case."

"A consultant?" the reporter asked.

Cheeks raised his hands in mock surrender. "It wasn't my idea."

"Can you tell us who this consultant was?"

"It was a former detective named Jack Carpenter," Cheeks said. "Carpenter was hired by the family to find the boy, then hired by the police department as well."

"So there was a conflict of interest," the reporter said.

"I would say so," Cheeks said.

"Do you blame Jack Carpenter for what went wrong?"

"He let the case drag on, and now Sampson Grimes *and* his mother are missing. Yes, I blame him."

I looked for something to throw at the screen.

"Temper, temper," Sonny said.

The interview ended. Sonny took the remote out of my hand and killed the picture.

"How's your nose?" he asked.

"It's starting to hurt again," I said.

Sonny fed me two more pills. I swallowed them while looking into the future. Cheeks was campaigning to get his old job back. Considering how badly the case had gone, it just might happen. I could not imagine a more cruel injustice, and punched the bar.

I went outside and stood by the shoreline. The lightning made it dangerous, but I didn't care. My cell phone rang, and I answered it hoping it was Burrell.

"Carpenter here," I said.

"Mr. Carpenter, my name is Father Tom Kelly," the caller said. "I'm a priest at Starke prison."

The wind was blowing in my face, and I moved inside the bar's open doorway, and sat at the bottom of the stairwell.

"Let me explain why I'm calling," Father Kelly said. "I counsel death row inmates at the prison. One of those inmates is Abb Grimes. I was watching the news, and saw that Abb's son, Jed, had been arrested for murdering his father's lawyer, along with many other crimes. I called LeAnn Grimes, and she told me to call you."

"What can I do for you?" I said.

"I wanted to tell you that I think Jed is innocent."

"You do?"

"Yes. I was there when Jed was saved."

I thought back to the photograph of the elderly priest I'd seen in Jed's album, and realized this was the same man.

"Saved how?" I asked.

"Let me tell you what happened. A year ago, Abb told me that he wanted to see Jed before he died. I called Jed, and arranged a meeting. Jed came to the prison, and the warden let us meet in a cell, and eat a meal. Abb had asked me to wear my prayer shawl, which was given to me when I became a priest.

"When our meal was over, Abb held my prayer shawl, and told Jed he was ready to meet his maker. Abb asked Jed to hold the shawl, and forgive him for his sins. It was hard, but Jed did it. He forgave his father. Then we prayed.

"God was with us that day. Abb invited God into that cell by accepting his sins, and Jed accepted God by holding the shawl, and telling Abb he forgave him. God was there. I felt his presence.

"Jed changed after that. He started giving his wife money, and got shared custody of his son. The transformation was real. Jed's not a killer."

The rain blew through the open doorway onto my face, and a crash of lightning shook the building.

"I know, Father," I said.

"Then you must prove that Jed is innocent. Based upon what I saw on the news, the evidence against Jed is circumstantial. Yet, the police are making Jed out to be a criminal, and saying he was breaking laws before this happened. You need to set the record straight."

"How am I going to do that?"

"There is a detective named Ron Cheeks. Start with him. Cheeks destroyed a piece of evidence in Abb's case."

"You mean the missing slippers," I said.

"Yes, the slippers. Jed found out, and confronted Cheeks. Ever since, Cheeks has been on a mission to destroy Jed. He pulled Jed into the police station fifty times, and arrested him for crimes he never committed."

"You think Cheeks is trying to frame Jed?"

"Yes," the priest said.

I rose from the stairwell. Something had happened twelve years ago that had caused Cheeks to destroy evidence, and he'd been covering it up ever since. If I could find out why, perhaps it would lead me to the person behind these crimes.

"I'll see what I can do," I said.

CHAPTER
FIFTY-ONE

With a promise from Sonny to watch Buster, I drove to Tugboat Louie's. The pain in my nose had turned to a dull, aching throb, and I stopped by the kitchen to get an ice pack. One of the cooks made a joke about my battered state.

"You should see the other guy," I said.

I went upstairs to my office with the ice pack pressed to my face. Lying on the blotter was the transcript from Abb Grimes's trial, the word *slippers* highlighted in bright yellow in the evidence log. Piper Stone had also tried to discover the secret behind the slippers, and now she was dead. I needed to find out why.

I booted up my computer, and went online. Using Google, I typed in Abb Grimes's name, and hit Search. Within a matter of nanoseconds, the search engine had pulled up more than seventy-five thousand different websites where Abb's name was referenced.

I scrolled through the sites. I was looking for one that had the surveillance video of Abb carrying his bloodied victim in the Smart Buy parking lot. The video had become public domain, and was regularly shown on TV documentaries. I felt certain that one of the sites would have it.

I found a site called ragingmaniacs.com, and clicked on it. The homepage was done in bloodred, and was painful to the eye. The site was devoted to famous serial killers, and included a collection of videos taken at their trials.

I quickly found the video of Abb on the site. It was simply called "The Night Stalker." I clicked on it, and Windows Media Player filled the screen.

Like most videos shot through a surveillance camera, the quality was poor. The tape showed Abb walking around the parking lot of the Smart Buy with his female victim draped in his arms. His face was masked by shadows cast off by the building, and at times he appeared to be laughing, although it was hard to tell. He walked stiffly, his arms holding the dead girl like she'd fallen out of the sky.

I put my face next to the screen, and

studied Abb's footwear. As the clip ended, Abb's right shoe was briefly exposed. It was in the frame for a few seconds, then vanished. Just long enough for me to see *something.*

I walked down the hall to Kumar's office and knocked on the door. He'd recently bought a new computer, and the screen had a much better resolution than mine.

"It's open," he called out.

I poked my head in. Kumar sat at his desk, buried in spreadsheets.

"Jack, Jack! What happened to your nose?" he asked.

"I got kicked in the face," I explained.

"Does it hurt?"

"Only when I breathe. How would you like to play detective for a little while?"

Kumar swept the spreadsheets to the floor. "Yes!"

"First, I need you to help me burn a DVD."

"I can do that. My five-year-old daughter showed me how to burn DVDs the other night. What is it you wish to burn?"

"A tape from the Internet."

Kumar got on his computer, and I directed him to the raging maniacs website. Soon "The Night Stalker" video was playing on the screen.

"This is what I need burned," I said.

Kumar popped a fresh DVD into the computer, and typed in the instructions so the video was burned onto the DVD. I replayed the video, this time off the DVD.

"What are we watching? An old horror movie?" Kumar asked.

"It's a tape of a serial killer named Abb Grimes."

"How gruesome. What am I looking for?"

"I want to see what he was wearing on his feet."

We watched "The Night Stalker" video in silence. Toward the end, Abb's right foot appeared from beneath his pants, and Kumar froze the frame. The picture was much sharper on Kumar's screen, and I could see that Abb was indeed wearing a slipper. There was an image on the side of the slipper, and I strained my eyes to make it out.

"Any idea what that is?" I asked.

Kumar typed a command on his keyboard, and blew up the image. Then he fitted on his reading glasses and stared. "It looks like a cartoon."

"Are you sure?"

"Yes. Why are you so skeptical?"

"This guy was arrested for murdering eighteen women," I explained.

"So he must have been crazy," Kumar said.

"I need a copy of this," I said.

Kumar used the mouse to hit the print icon. Moments later, a four-color photo of Abb's right slipper spit out of the laser copier. I held the photograph beneath the light on the desk, and studied it. Kumar was right; the image on Abb's slipper resembled a cartoon.

"I need to blow this up," I said.

"Not a problem," Kumar said.

Kumar placed the photo into the copy machine behind his desk, then programmed the machine to blow up the image. The copy machine began to print, and I grabbed the sheet before it hit the tray.

Kumar came up behind me, and we both stared. The slipper now filled the page, and the cartoon was plainly visible. It was the smiling face of Fred Flintstone.

CHAPTER
FIFTY-TWO

I drove to LeAnn Grimes's neighborhood with my mind reeling. Abb Grimes had been wearing a pair of kid's cartoon slippers the night he'd murdered his last victim, which was a clear indicator that something was wrong with him. Yet no evidence about his mental state had ever been presented at trial. I had to find out why.

The storm had passed, and the sun was shining. I parked in front of LeAnn's house. Now that Jed had been captured, the FBI had pulled up stakes, and I spotted a lone police cruiser with two officers parked a few houses away. My windows were rolled down, and I could hear the officers discussing the police's ongoing search for Heather and Sampson. The tenor of their voices told me that they didn't expect to find either of them alive.

I knocked on the front door. It swung open, and I found myself standing face-to-face with LeAnn. She wore a somber black dress, and was dragging a suitcase.

"May I come in?" I asked.

LeAnn stepped onto the front stoop. Her eyes were ringed from lack of sleep, and her movements were slow and painful.

"Please get out of my way," she said.

"I need to speak with you. It will only take a minute."

"I have to go see Abb," she said.

Then I understood the suitcase. She was driving to Starke to see Abb get strapped on a gurney and have a needle filled with a powerful cocktail of narcotics and life-ending drugs pumped into his veins. She was going to say good-bye to her husband.

"I need to speak with you about the evidence that was destroyed in your husband's case," I said. "It will only take a few minutes."

A flicker of life came into her otherwise lifeless eyes. She dropped her suitcase in the doorway, then turned around and went into the house. I picked up the suitcase and put it in the foyer, then followed her inside.

She dropped onto the couch in the living room. The bun in her hair had come undone, and as her hair fell onto her shoulders, I glimpsed the woman she'd once been.

"What do you want to know?" she asked.

I pulled up a chair. In my pocket was the photo of Abb's slipper with the cartoon of Fred Flintstone I'd printed off Kumar's computer. It was folded into a square, and I smoothed out the creases before showing it to her.

"Your husband was wearing these slippers the night he was filmed in the grocery store parking lot," I said. "Do you recognize them?"

LeAnn's eyes briefly studied the page. Then they locked onto me.

"Let me tell you something about those slippers," she said. "They were a birthday present from Jed to his daddy. Abb adored them, and wore them whenever he was home. After my husband was arrested, those slippers were taken and destroyed by Detective Cheeks, the man who arrested my husband."

"Why would Cheeks do that?"

"Because he knew something was wrong with Abb. We all did."

"We?"

"Me, the neighbors, even Jed — and he was just a little boy back then."

"How old was Jed?"

"Seven."

"But he understood what was going on."

"Yes. You see, Abb suffered from insomnia.

410

It got so bad that I took him to a clinic, where the doctor prescribed a new experimental drug. The drug let Abb sleep, but bad things started to happen. I'd wake up at night, and hear Abb banging around the house. One night I went into the kitchen, and all the chairs were turned upside down. I tried to get him back to bed, and he nearly took my head off. The next morning, I talked to him about it over breakfast, and Abb acted like it hadn't happened."

"You said the neighbors knew something was wrong with Abb," I said. "How did they know?"

"Abb left the house at night and strolled around the neighborhood. One of my neighbors caught him peeking in their windows; another found him sitting in their car. He was scaring the daylights out of them."

Her voice had grown weak, the memories draining her. I didn't want to make her suffering any worse, but I had to get to the truth.

"What was the drug?" I asked.

"I don't remember."

"Did you contact Abb's doctor to find out?"

"The clinic went out of business. I tried to track the doctor down, but never found him. It was another dead end."

"Did you tell Abb's defense attorney this?"

"His attorney knew everything. He was appointed by the court because we didn't have any money to hire a lawyer. He seemed resigned to my husband losing in court."

I thought back to the evidence log from the trial. It had contained everything that the police had taken from the Grimes's house.

"Did the police take the drug as evidence?" I asked.

"Yes. It disappeared with the slippers."

"Do you think Detective Cheeks destroyed it?"

LeAnn laughed under her breath, giving me my answer.

"Did Jed know about the drug?" I asked.

"Oh, Jed knew. It was so painful for him. He used to walk up to police officers when he was a little boy and say, 'My daddy isn't a bad man! He isn't bad!' When he grew older, the reality of what Detective Cheeks had done hit him, and Jed tried to confront Detective Cheeks. That's when Detective Cheeks started to haul him in, and accuse him of crimes he hadn't committed."

I leaned back in my chair. Everything Father Kelly had told me was true. Jed had been painted as a monster by Cheeks, and

412

all because he knew the truth about his father.

"Now, if you'll excuse me, I must go," LeAnn said.

She went into the hallway to retrieve her suitcase. I tried to carry it outside for her, and she wrestled it from my grasp.

"No, thank you," she said.

I watched her throw the suitcase into an old Chevy parked in the driveway beside the house. It was an eight-hour drive to the prison, and I found myself wishing she didn't have to go it alone.

LeAnn backed down the driveway. The tailpipe was making horrible sounds that disrupted the quiet morning. She braked before reaching the street, and motioned to me. I hustled over to her open window.

"Would you like to know what *I* think?" she asked.

I said that I did.

"Detective Cheeks railroaded my husband, and now he's railroading my son," she said. "If you don't believe me, ask the manager of the Smart Buy."

"You mean Mr. Vorbe," I said.

"Yes. He told me so this morning while delivering my groceries. Detective Cheeks came to his store, and tried to coerce him into saying untrue things about Jed. Ask him if you don't believe me."

Her car rattled and clanked as she drove away. The noise it was making was loud, but not nearly as loud as the alarm going off inside my head. Cheeks had destroyed evidence in one murder investigation, and now he was coercing witnesses in another.

I ran to my car.

The Smart Buy was open for business, and I went inside to the help desk. The young lady manning the desk was the same one who'd assisted me the other day. I asked for Jean-Baptiste Vorbe, and she made a call to his office.

"I think Mr. Vorbe is outside with the police," she said.

I thanked her, and went outside the store. There weren't any cops in the front of the building, and I walked around to the back. A police cruiser was parked by the Dumpsters, and I saw two cops standing on ladders, poking through the garbage with long sticks. Several torn bags lay on the ground. I looked for Vorbe, but didn't see him.

"She isn't here, and neither's her kid," one of the uniforms said.

"Keep looking," the other said.

"We should have brought some fly spray."

"Tell me about it."

I climbed the stairs to the loading dock, and found Vorbe standing next to the building. He wore a white shirt and black tie, and was leaning on his cane. His brow glistened with sweat, and his graying hair looked electrified in the midday sun.

"Mr. Carpenter," Vorbe said.

"I need to speak with you," I said.

"Of course."

"I hear Detective Cheeks came to see you yesterday."

Vorbe looked at me in alarm. "Who told you this?"

"LeAnn Grimes. She said that Detective Cheeks tried to coerce you into saying untrue things about her son. Is that true?"

Vorbe glanced at the cops picking through the Dumpster, and lowered his voice. "Detective Cheeks was acting very ugly, very crude. He peppered me with questions about Jed Grimes — Did I remember how many times he'd visited my store? Had I ever seen him with a woman named Piper Stone? Did I know where he might have hidden his wife and son? — and then asked me if I'd testify against him at his trial. When I hesitated, Detective Cheeks yelled at me. I felt like . . ."

His voice trailed off and I pressed him. "Like what?"

"I do not feel comfortable saying this."

"Say it anyway."

"I felt he was trying to intimidate me."

Vorbe lowered his eyes. My gut told me that he wasn't telling me everything that had happened. I put my hand on his sleeve, and felt his body tense up.

"What else happened?" I asked.

"Else?" he said.

"The rest of it."

Vorbe hesitated, then the words poured out. "Detective Cheeks said that I should not talk to any other police officers about the case. He was emphatic about this. He said that if I did, I would pay. Then he told me he would be back."

"Was his tone threatening?"

"Very."

Down below, the cops had finished their search and had climbed off their ladders. They retied the torn bags of garbage lying on the ground and hoisted them back into the Dumpster. Then they came over to the loading dock, and thanked Vorbe for his help. Their cruiser kicked up loose gravel as it drove away.

I faced Vorbe. He was still sweating, and his eyes were glassy. Cheeks had done a real number on him. The police were supposed to protect the weak and the innocent, and

Cheeks was threatening them instead. I decided it was time to find out why.

"I'm sorry Cheeks put you through this," I said.

"I don't want any more trouble," Vorbe said. "Especially from Detective Cheeks."

"I'll take care of Cheeks," I said.

CHAPTER
FIFTY-THREE

Plantation was in the northwest section of the county, and was still green. Horses galloped behind three-board wood fences, and red-roofed barns towered behind elegant ranch houses. Someday it would be paved over like the rest of south Florida, but for now it was still country.

Finding Cheeks's place took awhile. I'd gone there once for a Super Bowl party, but I'd forgotten how similar the houses in his neighborhood looked. Luckily, his SUV was parked in his driveway, the same one we'd driven around in a few days ago.

I parked on the street and killed the engine. My daddy had been fond of saying that any argument between two men could end in death. I drew my Colt and checked the clip, then returned it to the holster in my pants pocket.

My heart was pounding as I walked up the front path. Putting my ear to the door, I heard loud music coming from the back of the house. I guessed Cheeks was on the lanai, recuperating from his fake heart attack. I decided to surprise him.

I walked around the side of the house to the backyard. The music was loud enough to cover my footsteps. Eric Clapton's Miami album, *418 Ocean Boulevard.* The cut was one of my favorites. "Motherless Children."

The lanai was attached to the back of the house, and contained an eating area, a barbecue, and a swimming pool. I pressed my face to the screen. Cheeks sat with his back to me on a reclining beach chair. On his lap was a blond woman wearing a teardrop bikini. She had fake stripper tits and platinum stripper hair and was coming on to him the way only a stripper can. Seeing me playing peek-a-boo, she let out a shriek, and hopped off Cheeks's lap.

"Ronnie, there's someone here!"

Cheeks tried to jump out of the chair, only his erection wouldn't let him. He was wearing a flimsy pair of shorts, and they were popping out in the wrong places. The stripper ran into the house, and slammed the slider behind her.

"Get out of here," Cheeks growled.

I found the screen door in the lanai and went inside. Cheeks came forward with his fists cocked. He was big and hairy and looked like something that had washed up on the beach. I wasn't going to beat him in a fight, only fighting wasn't what I had in mind.

"You heard me," Cheeks said. "Get off my property."

"First you're going to answer some questions."

Cheeks started to circle me, and I pointed an accusing finger at him.

"Why did you destroy evidence that proved Abb Grimes was insane?" I asked.

"I told you, those slippers were lost," Cheeks said.

"What about Abb's sleeping medication? Was that lost, too?"

Cheeks's eyes narrowed and his jaw clenched. It was the look of a trapped animal. I went in for the kill.

"Jed Grimes knew what you did to his father, and has been haunting you for twelve years, hasn't he?" I asked. "Jed knew you were a dirty cop, and kept telling everyone who would listen. It scared you, and you wanted to shut him up. Then his little boy got abducted, and you decided to frame him to get Jed off your back, once and for all."

"That's bullshit."

"That's why you kept ignoring evidence

in the case, and why you faked a heart attack when it became apparent that Jed wasn't the kidnapper. You had your doubts about Jed, but you refused to tell anyone else. You wanted the kid to go down."

"No!"

"I'm taking it all to the police. You've got a lot of explaining to do, Ron."

With a roar Cheeks charged across the lanai like a mad bull. I adroitly stepped to the side, stuck out my leg, and sent him headfirst into the pool. As he flew past, his arm shot out.

Before I knew it, I was underwater with him.

I landed upside down in the deep end of the pool, and stared into watery space. The water was overly chlorinated, and made my nose and eyes burn. Cheeks was beside me, standing upright on the pool floor.

I righted myself in the water. Through a torrent of air bubbles I saw Cheeks's face. His eyes were popping out of his head, and made him look rabid. He grabbed my throat, and began to strangle me.

I brought my arms up and broke his grip around my neck. Then I grabbed his forearms and held him. He outweighed me by at least fifty pounds, and was probably a lot stronger than I was. On land, he had the advantage, but underwater I was the better man. Through years of swimming, I could hold my breath for a minute at a time, something that I doubted he could do.

I waited him out.

Cheeks tried to wrestle with me, and we moved back and forth across the pool floor. I could feel his arms growing weak as the oxygen in his lungs burned up. Each time he tried to move toward the shallow end of the pool, I pushed him back into the deep end. Fear spread across his eyes as he realized what I was doing. The look turned to desperation, then one begging forgiveness.

I was having none of it.

His mouth opened, and he began to suck down water. A single word came out. It was loud enough for me to hear.

Help.

I did not let him go.

Before my eyes, he began to die, his gaze fixed on some faraway place that only the departed know. His body went slack, his arms fell away, and he turned as limp as a rag doll in my hands. He was a dirty cop, and I told myself that the world was a better place without him. I let him go, and watched him start to float.

A numbing sensation coursed through my

body. I'd never let anyone die before. The sensation was unlike any I'd ever felt. It was cold and utterly brutal. I was stepping over to the dark side, to a place that once I ventured, I knew I could never return from.

I was many things, but a cold-blooded killer was not one of them. Sticking my hands beneath his armpits, I pulled Cheeks to the surface.

I dragged him to the shallow end of the pool, threw his body against the stairs, and whacked him on the back. Moments later, he was retching up pool water.

Movement inside the house caught my eye. His stripper girlfriend was standing in the kitchen, yelling into a cordless phone. I didn't think she was ordering takeout, and I guessed the police would be arriving soon.

"I want you to answer my questions," I said.

Cheeks nodded violently.

"You destroyed Abb Grimes's slippers and his sleeping medication. Why?"

"Didn't want them coming up at trial," he gasped.

"Because they showed he was crazy?"

"Yeah. Didn't want him copping an insanity plea."

"Why did that matter?"

Cheeks rolled on his back, and stared at

the revolving ceiling fan above his head. "If a jury saw those slippers, and knew he was taking some crazy drug, they'd pity him. I wasn't going to let that happen."

"You wanted him to die."

"Damn straight. I saw what he did to those girls."

"What was the sleeping medication called?"

"I don't remember."

"Stop lying."

More water came up, and Cheeks puked it across the pool. The sliding door opened, and the stripper clopped out in her plastic high heels.

"You okay, sweetie?" she asked.

Cheeks fell back on the stairs. "Just having a chat with my friend."

The stripper looked at me, then back at him. "You know this guy?"

"We used to work together."

"I called the police," she said.

"Fuck," he said under his breath. Then in a normal voice, "Thanks, honey. Now go back inside so we can finish our talk."

The stripper clopped inside, and the slider closed behind her. I didn't have much time, and I grabbed his arm. "I want to know the name of that drug."

"I told you, I don't remember."

"Want to go for another swim?"

Cheeks stared at me, and saw I wasn't kidding. He gave it some thought.

"It was some experimental drug that was being used for people with insomnia," he said. "Some weird name beginning with a Z. I asked a doctor I knew about it. He said it produced a hypnotic effect in some patients, and gave them delusions."

"Piper Stone figured this out, didn't she?"

"Yeah. She confronted me when I was in the hospital. She was a smart kid."

"Last question. Why did you frame Jed with his son's abduction?"

"It didn't start out that way," Cheeks said. "When we got the call that Sampson was missing, everything pointed to Jed. So that was the direction I went."

"It was the wrong direction. Someone else snatched that kid."

"I know," he mumbled.

I pulled myself out of the pool. I was going to meet the cops outside, and let them hear my side of the story first. A guy I'd once busted had told me this was your best chance to get the cops to believe you. Cheeks looked at me as I started to walk away.

"We need to get our stories straight," he said.

"Our stories?" I said.

"Yeah. You know what I mean."

"You think I'm going to lie for you?"

"Why not? I'll tell them we were having a disagreement, and I don't want to press charges. In return, you don't mention what I did."

I considered dragging Cheeks back into the water, only I was too damn tired. Instead, I walked outside to the front yard, and waited for the police to come and arrest me.

CHAPTER
FIFTY-FOUR

The police sirens were faraway and sounded like a baby's cry. I took out my Colt, and laid it onto the roof of my car. I'd never gone swimming with my gun before, and had no idea how much damage the water had caused. Seeing that my gun was about to be taken away from me, I supposed it didn't really matter.

I got my cell phone from the car and punched in my wife's number at work. Even though Rose was in Tampa, she was still the most dependable person in my life, and I was relieved when I heard her pick up the phone.

"Rose Carpenter," she answered.

"Hey, honey," I said.

"I was just thinking about you."

"I'm in trouble and need your help."

"What's wrong?"

"The police are going to haul me in, and I

427

may need to post bail. I hate to ask you this
—"

"Of course I'll bail you out of jail. What happened?"

"I got into a brawl with a dirty cop."

"Are you all right?"

"Never felt better in my life."

"What will you be charged with?"

"Assaulting a police officer, possibly breaking and entering."

"Oh, Jack, this sounds serious."

The sirens were getting closer. I stepped away from my car, and stood in a neutral pose on Cheeks's front lawn. I needed to put away my cell phone so the cops didn't think I was brandishing a weapon. More than one suspect had gotten shot for clutching a cell phone the wrong way.

"I need to go now," I said. "What's the best number for me to reach you at?"

"Call my cell. I'll leave it on."

"Here they come. I'll call you later."

"I love you," my wife said.

"I love you, too."

A pair of cruisers turned down the street with their bubble lights flashing, and came hurtling toward me like a pair of rockets. My world was about to turn ugly, and I slipped my cell phone into my pocket, and stuck my arms into the air.

The cruisers braked on the street in a perfect V, and four uniformed cops jumped out. Two went inside to check on Cheeks, while the other two arrested me. I was frisked and cuffed and made to stand on the hot macadam while I was read my rights. As I gave my version of what had happened, the uniform who was taking my statement shut his notepad, and glared at me.

"Don't make allegations you can't prove," the uniform said.

"Ron Cheeks is dirty. Pass it on," I said.

I was driven to the station house and booked. My clothes and possessions were confiscated, and my body cavities were checked for hidden drugs and weapons. The booking procedure was designed to strip people of their dignity, and I dealt with the humiliation by cracking jokes that no one laughed at.

Next stop was the basement. Instead of being put in a holding pen with a bunch of lowlifes and psychopaths, I was shuttled to an interrogation room, and left by myself. The room had two plastic chairs that were hex-bolted to the floor, and a large mirror covering the wall. It smelled like someone had taken a piss in it.

I went to the mirror and stared at my reflection. My lower lip was bloody, my nose swollen and bruised, and my eyes had a trapped look that I didn't like. The mirror was two-way, and I wondered who was on the other side watching me. Probably the chief, trying to figure out what he was going to do with me.

"I know my rights. I want to make my phone call," I said.

I folded my arms and waited. Whoever was on the other side could hear me. There were hidden microphones in the ceiling that were sensitive enough to hear a person's stomach growl. When no one came into the room, I raised my voice.

"Come on. Let's get this show on the road."

I waited another couple of minutes. The cops were trying to intimidate me. It worked on most suspects they brought in, and knocked them down a few pegs. But it didn't work on me.

Peeling off my shirt, I threw it into the corner, then undid the drawstring in my prison jammies, and let them drop. Wearing nothing but my boxers, I got down on the floor, and started doing push-ups.

■ ■ ■ ■

Five minutes and a hundred push-ups later, I was sitting in the chief's office on the top floor, staring at the man himself behind his desk. The chief's navy suit looked like he'd slept in it, and clumps of gray whiskers were sprouting out of his face like weeds. Burrell flanked him, and made brief eye contact with me.

"Goddamn it, Carpenter," the chief swore. "The department has more problems than it can handle, and you're running around town beating up my men."

"Cheeks is dirty," I said. "You should have arrested him, not me."

The chief picked up a spiral notebook lying on his desk. It looked like the same notebook the uniform had used when interrogating me outside of Cheeks's house. He waved it in front of my face. "I read your allegations, and they're totally false. Cheeks didn't destroy evidence in the Abb Grimes case. It got lost. Cheeks didn't frame Jed Grimes for his son's abduction. Jed was the logical suspect, and still is our only suspect. And Cheeks didn't threaten the grocery store manager. He may have leaned on him a little bit, but he didn't threaten him."

431

"The manager told me he threatened him," I said.

"I don't care what the manager said," the chief snapped. "Cheeks knew we were shorthanded, and spoke to the manager as a favor to me. He's trying to help us find Heather Rinker and her son, which is more than I can say for you right now."

The chief was giving me the company line. He wasn't going to haul Cheeks in and question him, but he was willing to humiliate me. I folded my hands in my lap, and waited him out.

"Look, Jack, I need *help*," the chief said. "Heather Rinker and her son are gone, and I don't have a single clue as to where they might be. You're the expert at finding missing people. Help us find them, will you?"

"I can't," I heard myself say.

"Why not?"

"Because I'm under arrest."

"Cheeks has said he doesn't want to press charges. I'm willing to give you a pass. In return, you'll help us. Do we have a deal?"

I'd broken enough laws to have myself put away for a long time. The chief had to be pretty desperate to let me skate. I glanced at Burrell, then back at him.

"Deal."

"Good." The chief leaned forward in his

chair, and clasped his hands in front of his face. "Let's play pretend for a minute. If this was your investigation, what would you do?"

I stared down at my jailhouse flip-flops, and gave it some thought. Jed had spoken to Heather right before she had disappeared. According to LeAnn, her son had asked Heather to get something for him to eat, and probably knew where Heather had gone.

"I'd do everything possible to make Jed talk," I said.

"We tried that," the chief said. "Our best interrogators have worked him over, along with an interrogator from the FBI. Jed won't say a word."

"Jed hates cops. You need someone who isn't a cop," I said.

"Any suggestions?"

"How about his mother?"

"LeAnn Grimes left town, and her cell phone is turned off."

"Any other relatives?"

"They're all dead."

The room fell silent. Jed Grimes didn't have many fans, except for one. I pointed at the phone sitting on the chief's desk.

"Let me make a phone call," I said.

"To who?" the chief asked.

"His priest."

CHAPTER
FIFTY-FIVE

Dialing information, I obtained Father Kelly's phone number in Starke. I called the number, and a woman answered who identified herself as his wife. She was polite, and gave me the number of his parish office in town. I called it, and let the phone ring a dozen times. Father Kelly answered sounding out of breath.

"I was just leaving for the prison to be with Abb," Father Kelly said. "What can I do for you?"

It took me a moment to realize what Father Kelly meant. He was Abb Grimes's priest, and was going to be at Starke Prison when Abb was put to death.

"I'm calling about Jed," I said. "I think he might be able to lead the police to his missing wife and son, but he's refusing to talk to anyone."

"Do you want me to talk with him?"

"Yes."

"Consider it done."

I asked Kelly to stay by his phone at the parish, and told him someone would call back soon. Kelly promised to be there and hung up. I handed the chief the phone.

"Put Jed into a room with a telephone, and leave the rest to me," I said.

I went downstairs to the booking area and retrieved my clothes and personal items. A long line of perps was waiting to be processed. Looking in their faces, I saw the same desperate look I'd seen in my own reflection a short while ago.

I changed clothes in a bathroom and dried my gun with the hand dryer. I came out to find Burrell in the hallway. She led me outside the building to the smoking area. It was free of smokers, but she still spoke in a whisper.

"Listen, Jack," she said. "I spoke to a couple of older detectives who work in Homicide. Evidence in murder cases just doesn't disappear. If Cheeks destroyed those slippers and sleeping medication, other detectives in the department knew about it."

"You think there was a conspiracy?" I asked.

"Call it an agreement to look the other way."

"Why?"

"Maybe they wanted to make sure Abb Grimes got the death penalty. Didn't you?"

I would have been lying if I'd said that I hadn't wanted Abb to be put to death for the crimes he'd committed. But wanting an evil person to die, and destroying evidence that proved he was crazy, were two entirely different things.

"Not that badly," I said.

We went inside and headed to the basement. While one of the interrogation rooms was being outfitted with a phone, Burrell and I sat in the adjacent room along with the chief, and watched through the two-way mirror as a technician ran a line into the room, then stapled the line to the carpet in the floor.

"Here he comes," Burrell said.

Jed entered the interrogation room wearing a pale blue jumpsuit. His handcuffs and leg irons were connected to a chain that was padlocked to a metal belly band encircling his waist. Seeing the mirror, he shook his handcuffs defiantly.

"Crummy cops!" he shouted.

His escorts were two muscular guards. One pushed him into a chair.

"Sit down, and shut up," the guard said.

The guard looked at the mirror and raised his eyebrows. The chief pulled a piece of paper out of his pocket, and handed it to me. Typed on it was a phone number.

"That's the number for the phone in the room," the chief explained.

I took out my cell phone, and called Father Kelly at his parish. This time, he answered on the first ring.

"Jed is sitting in an interrogation room at police headquarters," I said. "I'm going to give you a number for a phone in that room. I want you to call Jed, and see if you can get him to talk."

"I'll do my best," Father Kelly said.

I gave him the number and hung up. Ten seconds later, the phone in the interrogation room rang. A guard put the call on speaker phone, and Father Kelly's voice came out of the speaker.

"Hello, Jed? This is Father Kelly calling."

Jed twitched like he'd been hit by a cattle prod. Bending his body at the waist, he brought his mouth down closer to the phone.

"Hey, Father Kelly," he whispered.

"I need to talk to you, Jed," the priest said.

"Okay," he replied.

■ ■ ■ ■

Jed knew we were eavesdropping.

Each time Father Kelly asked him a question, Jed dropped his voice, and mumbled a one-syllable response, while his eyes shifted suspiciously around the interrogation room. I had known hardened criminals who were not as distrustful of the police as he was.

Father Kelly didn't give up. The questions kept coming, and little by little, I saw Jed's chin drop, and the steely look in his eyes begin to fade. Father Kelly was playing on his conscience, and gradually wearing him down.

"You love Heather and your son, don't you?" Father Kelly asked.

"Yeah," Jed mumbled.

"Love them with all your heart, and all your soul?"

"Yeah."

"They're in trouble, you realize that?"

"Uh-huh."

"We have to help them. You must talk to the police."

"No."

"Why won't you talk to the police, Jed?"

"Because the police *lie.*"

It was the first time he'd uttered a real

sentence.

"You must work with the police," Father Kelly said emphatically. "They need to eliminate you as a suspect, so they can find the person who's behind this. I know this is hard to believe, but the police are your friends."

Jed jumped up from his chair. "Why don't you tell that to my daddy, Father Kelly? Tell him what great friends the police are when they stick a needle in his arm tomorrow morning. I'm sure he'd love to hear that."

I rose from my chair. Jed's hatred for the police was too great for him to willingly help us. But that didn't mean I couldn't get to the truth. I quietly left the room.

Burrell and the chief must have thought I was going to the bathroom, because they didn't follow me. I went next door, and entered the interrogation room. Both guards looked at me, and assuming I was a detective, let me enter.

I stood in front of Jed's chair. "Remember me?"

Jed stared at me with hatred in his eyes. "Yeah."

"I want to help you," I said.

"That's another lie," Jed said.

"I know about your father's slippers and

the sleeping medication he was taking," I said. "Detective Cheeks told me that he destroyed them. I'm going to make sure a judge knows about it, too. That's a promise, son."

Jed reeled back in his chair, and I saw a glimmer of hope in his eyes.

"You mean that?" he asked.

"Yes," I said. "Your daddy was insane when he murdered those women. You've known it for years, but Detective Cheeks made sure that no one would listen to you. Then, when your son was abducted, Cheeks pointed the finger at you so he could get you out of the way."

Jed was shaking. "That's right."

"You didn't kidnap your son, or murder your father's lawyer, or kill any of those women the police found at the landfill. You didn't do any of those things, did you?"

"No, sir."

"If I asked you to swear on a stack of Bibles, *and* take a polygraph test, you'd do that to show the police they're wrong, wouldn't you?"

"Yes, sir."

I had broken through. Kneeling, I placed my hand on his arm. "Tell me about your conversation with Heather this morning. Where did she go?"

441

Jed shrank in his chair, his voice a whisper. "I don't know."

"She offered to get something for you to eat. What was it?"

He hesitated, thinking back. "I told Heather that all I'd been eating was potato chips and sodas, and she offered to get me something."

"Was she going to a restaurant?"

"She said she was going to surprise me."

"What are your favorite restaurants?"

"You know, the usual places."

"Tell me."

"McDonald's, Wendy's, Burger King. I also like Steak and Shake."

"Are all of those restaurants within walking distance to your mother's house?"

"Yeah," Jed said.

I patted his arm and rose from the floor. Our killer worked in a restaurant somewhere in LeAnn Grimes's neighborhood. *He was right under our noses.*

"You going to find Heather and Sampson?" Jed asked.

Before I could reply, the door to the interrogation room banged open, and I saw the chief standing in the hall.

"Get the hell out here!" the chief roared.

CHAPTER
FIFTY-SIX

The chief pulled me into the hall and slammed the door. His eyes were on fire, his body tensed like a clenched fist. He jabbed me in the chest so hard it made me wince.

"You crummy bastard," the chief said.

"What did I do?" I asked.

"Don't play games with me. You know the interrogation room is wired, and your conversation was being recorded."

"So?"

"The district attorney will listen to those tapes when he prepares his case, and hear you say that Cheeks destroyed evidence. He'll want to start an inquiry. You just opened Pandora's box, and there is not a goddamn way I can close it."

I stood my ground. I wasn't going to hide the truth. The chief jabbed me again.

"Say something for yourself, Carpenter," he said.

"I was trying to get Jed to open up."

"It didn't work."

"Yes, it did. Jed told us that Heather went to buy food in his mother's neighborhood. That should help us find her, and her son."

"You *believed* him?"

"Yes. Strap Jed into a polygraph if you think he's lying."

"The kid's a sociopath. Polygraphs don't work on sociopaths."

I started to argue, but the chief cut me off. "I gave you a get-out-of-jail-free card earlier, and now I'm taking it back," he said. "I'm giving you two days to prove that Ron Cheeks purposely destroyed evidence in Abb Grimes's case. If you can't, I'm going to charge you with assaulting a police officer, and throw your ass in the county lockup."

My mouth had gotten me into more trouble than anything I'd ever done. Without thinking I said, "Two whole days? That's awfully generous of you."

He gave me another jab in the chest.

"Make that one day," the chief said.

He stormed into the stairwell. For the first time, I noticed Burrell standing at the end of the hall. She was slouched against the wall, and staring dejectedly at the floor.

"What did he do to you?" I asked.

444

"He's putting me on paid leave," she said. "Why?"

"He thinks we're in this together."

I didn't know what to say, and we walked up the stairs in silence. The first floor was a whirlwind of activity, and Burrell pulled me to one side, and lowered her voice. There was an intensity to her eyes that I didn't remember seeing before.

"We need to prove our case," she said.

"I'm with you," I said.

"I'm having the detectives in Missing Persons call every restaurant in LeAnn's neighborhood, and collect the names of each employee, along with their Social Security numbers," she said. "I'm going to run background checks on them, and see who has a criminal record. I'll e-mail you the ones I think might be our killer."

I'd always been good at making creeps, and I said, "You want me to see if I can pick him out?"

"Yes."

Burrell was directly violating the chief's orders, an act that could lead to her being fired. She could have been content to let things play themselves out, only that wasn't who she was. I said, "Call me once you have something."

She nodded stiffly and went to the elevators.

I was blinded by the afternoon sunshine as I walked through the front doors of the station house. There was a reason I was no longer a cop, and I got reminded of it every time I came here. I started across the lot toward the pickup truck, which the cops who'd arrested me had driven to the station and, at my suggestion, left the keys beneath the floor mat.

"Hey, Jack! Hold on a minute."

Chuck Cobb, the smart-mouthed detective everyone thought was my brother, was smoking a cigarette by the front door. He came over and whacked my arm good-naturedly.

"Just the man I was looking for," Cobb said. "I need you to review the Piper Stone murder report."

It was common practice during homicide investigations to have witnesses reread their own accounts of murder scenes. This allowed the detectives working the case to iron out inconsistencies, while letting witnesses get their facts straight.

"Sure," I said.

"The report's in my computer. Do you mind coming upstairs so I can print it out?"

"I don't think that's such a good idea," I said. "I'm on the chief's shit list."

"Whoops. Well, how about I print it out, and bring it to you?"

"I can wait," I said.

Cobb went inside, and a motorcycle cop came outside.

"Are you Carpenter?" the motorcycle cop asked.

"Yes," I said.

"I'm your escort," the motorcycle cop said.

"I don't need an escort," I replied.

"The chief thinks you do."

I felt like I'd been kicked in the teeth. The chief had assigned a cop to watch me, and make sure I didn't stick my nose where it didn't belong. I glanced up at the building, and found the chief's office on the top floor. Something told me he was up there, watching this.

I drove to the Sunset with Cobb's murder report lying on the passenger seat and the motorcycle cop riding my bumper. I pulled into the lot, and the motorcycle cop parked beside me. He lowered the visor on his helmet, and eyed me suspiciously. As I started to get out, my cell phone rang. It was Rose. I rolled up my window before answering.

"Do you still need me to bail you out of jail?" my wife asked.

"Not today," I replied.

"Are you still in trouble?"

"Yes."

"There must be something I can do."

I hesitated. I didn't like pulling my family into cases, but there *was* something that Rose could do. She could help prove that Cheeks destroyed evidence, while I spent my time looking for the killer, and hopefully finding Sampson.

"There is," I said. "A serial killer named Abb Grimes was given an experimental sleeping drug in the mid-1990s by a clinic in Broward, which later shut down. The drug begins with the letter Z, and made him hallucinate. I need you to find those records."

"That shouldn't be too hard."

"No?"

"Not when you know how to use the Internet."

I heard my wife's fingers typing on a keyboard.

"I'm on one of the pharmaceutical websites," Rose said. "I'll look at the popular drugs beginning with Z first. Okay. It's not Zantac, or Zaroxolyn, or Zestril, or Ziac.

Wait a minute. How about zolpidem tartrate?"

"What's that?"

"It's a sleeping drug to treat insomnia. According to the site, it was tested in the United States in the mid-1990s, then issued a patent, and is now being sold as Ambien. The site says that some patients exhibit odd behavior, including delusions and sleepwalking. How was Abb Grimes acting when he took it?"

"His wife said the drug made him crazy."

"Sounds like a match. I'll ask our records department to find out which clinics in Broward were involved in the trials, and do a trace on where they keep their records."

"You should have been a detective," I said.

"I did the next best thing," my wife said.

"What's that?"

"I married one."

I told Rose that I loved her, and then she was gone.

I found Buster sleeping on the floor as I entered the Sunset. I scratched behind his ears, and his eyes popped open, and his tiny tail began to wag.

"I think he's feeling better," Sonny said from behind the bar.

"How can you tell?" I asked.

"He growled at the postman. You want a beer?"

"Espresso if you have it."

"What does this look like? A fern bar?"

"Give me a pot of coffee, then."

Sonny served me a pot of coffee, and I asked him if I could use his computer.

"I'm sure not using it," Sonny said.

I headed into the back room, which contained a small desk with a computer, and cartons of Budweiser stacked to the ceiling. The Internet access was dial-up, and I sucked down two cups of coffee while waiting for it to connect. Soon I was online, and I called Burrell's cell phone.

"I was just punching in your number," Burrell said. "You wouldn't believe how many restaurant employees in LeAnn's neighborhood have broken the law. I've pulled out records of thirty of the really bad ones."

"Can you e-mail them to me?" I asked.

"I'll send them right now. Give me your e-mail address."

The bar's e-mail address was taped to the frame of the computer. I read off the address, and a minute later, the records appeared as an attachment to an e-mail. I clicked on the attachment with the mouse, and they appeared on the screen.

I have a nose for sniffing out creeps that's been developed from dealing with the worst scum that society has to offer. I used that instinct as I pored through the records. Each contained the suspect's name, last-known address, mug shot, and criminal history. It was a true rogue's gallery, with crimes that included rape, murder, aggravated assault, and kidnapping. Looking at each record, I asked myself if this was our killer.

Thirty minutes later, I was done.

I had eliminated twenty-eight of the suspects for reasons ranging from being too young, to living in another state until a few years ago. The remaining two suspects were better fits. Both were in their mid-thirties, and had done time in prison for kidnapping and violent sexual assault. Each man had been given a psychological evaluation in prison, and deemed sociopathic. Both were also Broward natives. I called Burrell on my cell.

"I'm down to two," I told her.

"Which ones?"

"Johnnie Lee Edwards and Thaddaeus Prosper. You need to have both pulled in for questioning. I'd also have their homes searched."

"Anything else?"

I stared at each man's mug shot. "Can I be there when you question them?"

"I can't get you into the building, Jack. Hell, I'm not even supposed to be here."

"Can I listen in? I just want to hear how they answer the questions."

"That's doable. Don't turn your cell phone off."

"I wouldn't dream of it," I said.

CHAPTER
FIFTY-SEVEN

I took Buster for a walk on the beach with my cell phone clutched in my hand. I was tired and my head hurt, and I put both of those things out of my mind.

The motorcycle cop stayed ten yards behind me. He'd put his helmet on his bike, and walked while talking into a cell phone. I caught snippets of conversation, and heard him talking to his wife about an upcoming vacation to the Keys. It was obvious he wasn't taking his assignment too seriously.

On my way back, I retrieved Chuck Cobb's homicide report from my car. I needed something to do while waiting for Burrell to call me, and reviewing Cobb's report was a good way to pass the time.

I went inside. It was Happy Hour, and the Dwarfs noisily lined the bar. I took my usual table by the window, put my cell phone in front of me, and started to read.

"You want a beer?" Sonny called to me.

"Another pot of coffee," I replied.

"Boo," the Dwarfs said.

The report was fifteen pages long. A lot had happened the day I'd discovered Piper Stone's body in the Dumpster, and I found myself stopping every few paragraphs to dredge my memory. Sonny served me a fresh pot along with a frosty mug of beer.

"What's this?" I asked.

"They made me," he said.

I glanced at the bar, and saw the Dwarfs raise their glasses.

By the time I had finished the report, it was pitch black outside. I sipped my coffee, which had gotten cold but still tasted good. On the cover page of the report was Cobb's work number and cell number. I tried both, and Cobb answered his work line.

"This is Jack Carpenter," I said. "I just finished reading your report on Piper Stone's murder. There's an error in it."

Cobb groaned. "Damn, I'm never going home tonight."

"Sorry. It's nothing huge."

"Lay it on me."

"On page five, you say that Vorbe, the grocery store manager, told me he saw Jed Grimes hanging around the Dumpsters, and called the police. That wasn't what Vorbe told me. He said an employee had seen Jed, and alerted him."

"You know, I saw that discrepancy as well," Cobb said.

"You did?"

"Yeah. The store manager's version of who saw Jed differed from yours. I called him, and we talked about it."

"What did he say?"

"He said you must have heard him wrong."

The coffee was a few inches from my lips. I put it back down on the table.

"Is that what he told you?"

"Yes."

"Were there any other discrepancies in our stories?"

"No, just that one. I didn't think it was a big deal. Do you?"

I stared out the window at the ocean, and thought about it. Most police reports contained errors, or what cops liked to call misstated facts. But this wasn't an error. Vorbe had told me one thing, and he'd told Cobb another.

"He changed his story," I said.

"If it makes you feel any better, I talked to the employees at the store, and the manager's version checked out," Cobb said. "None of the employees saw Jed hanging around the Dumpsters. It was the manager, and he called the police."

"So why did Vorbe change his story?"

"He didn't, Jack. You heard him wrong. Everything else he said checks out with what you said. Haven't you ever heard someone wrong before?"

I started to reply, then shut my mouth. There was no use arguing with Cobb. He'd already talked to the store manager, and the manager had convinced him that I was wrong. That bothered me even more than the lie he'd told.

"There's my other line," Cobb said. "I'll call you back when I'm done, and we can talk about this some more."

I folded my phone. Jed had told me that Heather had gone to get food, and was going to surprise him. I'd assumed that meant she was going to a restaurant, but it could have been the local grocery store. I went to the bar. The Dwarfs were slugging whiskey and feeling no pain. I pulled out a twenty-dollar bill, and waved it in their faces.

"Who's up for a game of chicken?" I asked.

"I am," a Dwarf named Shorty said. Shorty stood six-feet-four and got his nickname because he was always short on cash.

"How fast are you?" I asked.

"Depends who's chasing me," Shorty said.

I gave Shorty the money and told him the rules.

"Piece of cake," he said.

Shorty walked outside the bar. I went to the window, and watched him approach the motorcycle cop. Shorty was acting drunker than he was, his body swaying from side to side. The cop ignored him, and continued to talk on his cell phone.

Shorty lifted the cop's helmet off the motorcycle's bars, and went running down the beach as fast as his legs would carry him. The cop jumped off his bike and gave chase.

I headed for the door, and felt something by my leg. It was Buster, and his tail was wagging.

"You're on," I told him.

Chapter Fifty-Eight

I drove to the Smart Buy in LeAnn Grimes's neighborhood well over the speed limit. Rush-hour traffic was going in the opposite direction, and a snaking line of headlights stretched as far as I could see.

I called Burrell, got voice mail, and left a message. The grocery store manager had changed his story about Piper Stone's killing, then lied about it. Witnesses in murder cases often got facts wrong, but this was different. The store manager had lied about something that didn't need to be lied about. It said he wasn't a credible witness, and that nothing that he'd told me, or the police, could be deemed truthful.

I pulled into the Smart Buy and parked by the entrance. The parking lot was filled with water, and looked like a swamp. I waited for Burrell to call me back.

The minutes ticked by. Buster sat on the passenger seat, and I rolled down his window so he could stick his head out. I'd given him a pain pill, and he was acting fine.

I called my voice mail. Sometimes people called me, and my cell phone didn't ring, and the caller ended up leaving a message. I was hoping that was what had happened now.

There were no messages.

I stared at the front of the grocery. More shoppers were coming out than going in. Most were women, and I guessed they were grabbing food to take home for dinner. Soon there was no one coming out.

I weighed what my next step should be. Part of me wanted to go inside and grill the store manager, only my recent arrest told me this wasn't a smart idea. I needed to take the proper channels with this, or risk getting myself in more trouble.

Buster let out a menacing growl. A woman pushing a shopping cart had come out of the store, and was heading straight toward us. She was yakking on her cell phone while talking to a small infant riding in the cart. There was absolutely nothing threatening about her.

Buster started barking.

A loud tapping on my window made me jump. I jerked my head sideways. There was a man standing next to my car. It was Jean-

Baptiste Vorbe, the store manager.

"Hello," Vorbe said through the glass.

I quieted Buster down, and lowered my window. Vorbe was carrying his cane, which he leaned against.

"You scared my dog," I said.

"I am sorry," Vorbe said. "I came out to my car to get some papers, and I saw you sitting here. Is something wrong?"

I shook my head. I hadn't seen Vorbe come through the front doors, and guessed he'd come through the back, and walked around the side of the building. Had Vorbe seen me sitting in my car through one of the store's surveillance cameras, and decided to check up on me? Something told me that he had.

"If you will excuse me, I must get back to work," Vorbe said.

"Have a nice night," I said.

"You, too," he said.

I watched him limp inside. A person's walk can be as telling as his voice. His was animated, and had a bounce to it, despite his infirmity. My gut told me he was going to make a run for it. I leashed Buster and followed him inside.

The store was dead. The checkout lines were empty, and several cashiers were chatting. Through the aisles, I caught a glimpse

460

of Vorbe heading for the back of the store. He was still moving fast. I hurried after him.

I saw Vorbe push open a swinging door next to the meat section. I was ten steps behind him, and as I reached the door, a big man wearing a bloodied apron blocked me from going any further. A plastic name tag identified him as the store's meat manager.

"Dogs aren't allowed in the store," the meat manager said.

Vorbe was running away. I said the first thing that came to mind.

"I'm legally blind."

"And I'm Mother Teresa. Get the dog out of here."

I kept moving forward. The meat manager spread his arms like a linebacker. There was no room around him, and I nudged Buster with my foot. My dog showed his teeth, and the meat manager sprang back.

"You're asking for trouble," the meat manager said.

"Go back to your station," I said.

"Who the hell do you think —"

"Just do as I say."

The meat manager got out of my way, and I hit the swinging door with my shoulder. Vorbe's office was in the rear of the store, and I spied a light shining through the open door. I went to the office, and stuck my head in. Vorbe sat at his desk, wiping his sweaty face with a hanky. He looked at me in alarm.

"Can I help you?" Vorbe asked.

I entered, and sat down across from him. "You lied to me."

Vorbe started to protest. I held up my hand like I was directing traffic.

"You told me a store employee saw Jed Grimes hanging around the Dumpsters the morning Piper Stone was murdered," I said. "But you told Detective Cobb that *you* saw Jed. Why did you change your story?"

Vorbe gave me a scolding look. "I think you misheard me."

"My ears are fine. You changed your story because you were afraid Detective Cobb would want to speak to that employee, and confirm what you'd said. Only there was no employee to speak to."

Vorbe shook his head from side to side. The gesture was condescending, and reminded me of a parent scolding a child.

"Sir, you are simply wrong," he said.

"I am?"

"Yes."

"You didn't tell me one story, and Detective Cobb another?"

"Absolutely not," he said.

462

"So I misheard you."

"Yes."

"Here's what I think. You're hiding something. Let's take a trip to police headquarters, and take a polygraph test. Then we'll see who's telling the truth."

Vorbe drummed his fingers on his desk. "I would like you to leave now."

"Did you kill Piper Stone?"

"Of course not."

"How about the rest of the women we found in the Pompano Beach landfill? Something tells me they all got there through your Dumpsters."

A bead of sweat ran down his nose and hit his desk. *Busted.*

"I think you did," I said.

Vorbe rose from his chair without the use of his cane. In one easy motion, he lifted his desk clean off the floor, and tossed it onto me. It was heavy, and I struggled to push it away. Tangled in my legs, Buster yelped in pain.

Vorbe pressed the desk against my body. The expression on his face had gone from polite to murderous in the blink of an eye. I tried to draw my Colt, but couldn't get my fingers free enough to reach into my pants pocket. The meat manager appeared in the open doorway.

"Hey, boss. Is this guy giving you trouble?"

"Yes, Joe," Vorbe said. "Did you bring your gun?"

"Left it home today."

"That is too bad. Hold the desk while I call the police."

"You bet," the meat manager said.

The meat manager took Vorbe's place. In horror I watched Vorbe draw a curved knife from his pocket, and grab the meat manager's head with his free arm. Pulling him close, Vorbe slit the meat manager's throat the way a farmer slits a chicken's throat, quick and clean and ruthlessly efficient. The meat manager emitted a choking sound, and I watched blood from his wound join the blood on his apron.

Vorbe let the meat manager drop to the floor, then placed his hands on the desk. The evil lurking below the surface was now visible.

I was next.

With every ounce of strength in my body, I pushed the desk a few inches, and drew my Colt. I pressed the barrel to the desk and squeezed the trigger. The gun barked, and the bullet passed through the wood, and flew past Vorbe's head.

Before I could fire again, Vorbe ran out of the office.

CHAPTER
FIFTY-NINE

I pushed the desk away, freeing myself and my dog. Running to the open door, I looked across the back of the supermarket. The rear door was wide open, and I could hear Vorbe's footsteps as he ran away.

"Help me," the meat manager gasped.

I slipped my gun into my pocket and crouched down beside him. His eyes were glued to the ceiling, his life slipping away. He clasped my hand.

"Why?" he asked.

It was a question I'd asked myself a hundred times as a cop. Why did people kill? What purpose did it serve, except to destroy lives and wreck families? I didn't know the answer, and probably never would.

I called 911 on my cell. An automated operator put me on hold. While I waited for an operator to pick up, the meat manager closed his eyes. As he drew his last breath, I said a prayer, and watched him die.

I rose to my feet with my cell phone pressed to my ear. Buster was standing by the closet, pawing at the door. I pulled the door open and looked inside. The closet was empty. Something about it didn't feel right. The interior looked cramped.

I pressed my hand against the back wall, and it came down. Behind the closet was a hidden area about five feet tall, and a few feet deep. Hanging from the wall was a pair of handcuffs attached to a metal chain. Beneath the handcuffs, an air tank.

I had found Vorbe's holding area.

"Broward County Sheriff's Department," a police operator said.

"I need to report a murder."

"Where are you calling from?" the operator asked.

I gave the operator the details while searching Vorbe's desk. In one of the drawers I found a brown paper bag. It contained a bottle of clear liquid, a white cloth, and a pair of night vision goggles. I twisted the top off the bottle, and sniffed its contents.

Chloroform.

I had found Vorbe's kill kit.

"There's a cruiser on the way," the operator said.

I took the paper bag off the desk, and went outside to meet it.

By the back doors I found a male employee of the store lying on the floor. He'd been stabbed in the shoulder, and was holding his hand against the bloody wound. He seemed more bewildered than hurt.

"What happened?" I asked.

"The boss attacked me in the parking lot," the employee explained. "He tried to go through my pockets, so I kicked him in the nuts."

"What does his car look like?"

"His car is in the shop. He's been walking to work."

"Does he live nearby?"

"He lives in the development behind the store."

I went to the open back door and stuck my head out. It faced the Dumpsters, the sight of so much death and misery. I couldn't see Vorbe, but I could hear him stumbling through the woods, his feet dragging across the ground.

I removed the handcuffs from the paper bag, and slipped them into my pocket. Then I fitted on the night goggles, and chased after him.

■ ■ ■ ■

The night goggles turned the world a sickly green, and made me feel like I was a character in a low-budget horror movie. Buster had picked up Vorbe's scent, and was racing down a path littered with cans and broken bottles. I struggled to keep up with him.

Vorbe appeared a hundred yards ahead of me. He was running while clutching his groin. I saw him hop over an embankment and disappear. My legs picked up speed.

I came over the embankment running almost as fast as my dog. The woods had ended, and a housing development begun, with six-foot picket fences lining the back-yards of cookie-cutter tract houses. Vorbe was gone.

I stood at the top of the embankment, and let my eyes scan the fences for an opening. There were none.

"Find the man," I said to my dog.

Buster ran along the fence, bumping it with his shoulder. A gate popped open, and my dog went in. I drew my Colt and followed him.

The property had a plastic swimming pool and lawn furniture. Reaching the back of the house, I stopped at a pair of glass sliders. Inside I spotted the figure of a man lurking in the darkened living room. It was Vorbe, holding a single-barrel shotgun in one hand, a box of bullets in the other. If he got the shotgun loaded, I was history. I aimed my Colt at the slider and fired.

The sound of my gun ripped through the still night air. I watched the slider turn into a spiderweb, then disintegrate. I kicked out the remaining shards and went inside. Vorbe stood in the living room, trying to load the shotgun. The bullets I'd fired had penetrated the wall behind him. He acted oblivious to them, and to me.

"Put down the shotgun," I said.

Vorbe kept trying to load. The box slipped out of his fingers, and the bullets scattered across the floor. He dove to his knees.

"Did you hear me?" I asked.

His breathing was loud and frantic.

"Put the gun down," I ordered him.

He didn't respond. There was a name for this behavior: kill or be killed. I had never experienced it before, and it was scaring the hell out of me.

"Now!" I said.

I didn't want to shoot him, so I kicked him instead. Vorbe fell on his side, still clutching the shotgun. Then he let out a scream. Buster had grabbed his leg, and was giving it a good gnaw.

"Do it now, or my dog will eat you."

I had once read that the death people were most afraid of was being eaten alive. The shotgun slipped from his fingers. I grabbed its barrel and tossed it onto a couch.

"Your dog is hurting me," Vorbe said.

"Not enough," I said.

I made Buster back off, then told Vorbe to stand. He rose on rubbery legs, and I made him touch the ceiling. He hesitated, then obeyed my command.

"Where's your knife?" I asked.

"I dropped it in the woods," Vorbe said.

I made him go into the kitchen. It was small, with a breakfast table and a pile of dirty dishes in the sink. I removed the handcuffs from my pocket, and tossed them to him. I pointed at the refrigerator.

"Handcuff yourself to the door," I said.

Again Vorbe hesitated. Buster was beside me, and I nudged him with my foot. My dog snarled, and Vorbe jumped.

"Keep him away from me!" Vorbe said.

"Only if you start doing what I tell you," I said.

Vorbe handcuffed himself to the refrigerator door. I made him put his other hand on the door, and frisked him. From his pocket I removed the curved knife and tossed it to

470

the table. It was still covered with the meat manager's blood.

"Guess you didn't lose your knife," I said.

I grabbed Vorbe's handcuffed wrist, and squeezed the cuff. Then I checked the cuff locked to the door. He wasn't going any-where.

But I was.

CHAPTER SIXTY

There was a prize for the work that I did. I got to see things first.

I quickly searched the interior of Vorbe's house. Like most houses in south Florida, it did not have a basement, or an attic, and the rooms were relatively small.

The living room and dining room, which were connected, held nothing of significance. In the back were two bedrooms. The first contained an unmade single bed, a chest of drawers, and a picture of the Virgin Mary hanging above the bed's headboard. I banged on the closet door, but did not find any hidden spaces.

The second bedroom had been converted into a photographer's studio. The windows were covered by blinds, the walls by black backdrops, which made the space unusually dark. A tripod and camera sat in the room's center, and photographer lights were mounted on the walls and the ceiling.

I searched the den last. A wide-screen TV consumed one wall, a bookcase the other. The bookcase's shelves were lined with cheap knickknacks. I tried to pick one up, and discovered it was glued down. So were the others. Grabbing the bookcase with both hands, I pulled it away from the wall.

There was a hidden door behind the bookcase, and it was deadbolted. Buster stuck his nose to the sill, and let out a whine. I took the door down with a kick.

Buster started to go in. I hooked him by the collar, and pulled him back. I didn't want him contaminating whatever was inside the room.

I pulled the broken door out of the way, then cautiously entered. The room's interior was black, and I scratched the wall for a light switch. Finding none, I took another step forward, then heard a static-filled voice.

I listened hard. It was a police operator talking to a cop in a cruiser. Vorbe had been using a scanner to monitor patrol cars in the area.

I moved forward, the darkness as frightening as any imagined monster. Something touched the tip of my nose, and I nearly jumped out of my skin.

I reached out, and grabbed the thing that had touched me. It was a beaded metal cord that hung from the ceiling. I tugged on it, and a fluorescent light flickered to life.

It took a moment for my eyes to adjust. When they did, I found myself standing in a two-car garage. The garage door had been replaced by a brick wall, while the other three walls had been lined with cork, sound-proofing the interior.

I did a slow one-eighty. On the other side of the garage was a long wooden table with a young woman lying across it, her arms and legs bound by leather straps. Her skin was pale and white, and her eyes were tightly shut.

It was Heather Rinker.

I crossed the room and stood beside her. My hand gently touched her forehead. Her skin was ice cold, her body lifeless. The memory of Heather playing one-on-one with Jessie in the driveway of my old house flashed through my mind.

Buster jumped up on the table. Before I could pull him down, he began to lick Heather's face. Her eyes snapped open, and she stared up at me.

"Oh, my God, Mr. Carpenter," she whispered.

I swallowed the lump in my throat. My fingers undid the straps holding her prisoner. Heather tried to sit up, only to fall back on the table.

"Take it easy," I said.

"Where is Mr. Vorbe?" she asked.

"In the other room."

"Did you shoot him?"

"He's not going anywhere. Tell me what happened."

"I went to the grocery to buy some food, and he invited me back to his office for coffee. The next thing I remembered was waking up here."

"Where's Sampson?"

"In the closet. Sampson wouldn't stop fighting with him, so Mr. Vorbe tied him up. He tried to save me, Mr. Carpenter. My baby tried to save me."

Going to the closet, I opened the door. Sampson sat on a chair inside the closet, his arms and legs tied down with twine. A piece of duct tape covered his mouth. I had seen people die this way, and I choked back the rage building inside me.

"Hi, Sampson. My name is Jack," I said.

Sampson looked at me, blinking tears. I put away my gun so as not to scare him any further, and gently pulled away the duct tape. Buster appeared by my side.

"This is my dog. His name is Buster. Do you like dogs?"

Sampson nodded. Buster entered the

closet, and licked Sampson's face.

"Where's my mommy?" he asked.

"She's right here. I'm going to take you to her."

"Mommy!"

"I'm here, honey," Heather called back. "Everything's okay."

I undid the twine while looking into his perfect little face. Every stupid thing I'd said and done in the last several days now seemed worthwhile. Sampson crawled into my arms, and I carried him across the garage to his mother. It was a perfect ending, until I heard Vorbe scream from the other side of the house.

CHAPTER
SIXTY-ONE

"Please don't leave us, Mr. Carpenter," Heather begged me.

I heard a second scream, louder, more intense. I had to find out what he was doing. I snapped my fingers, and Buster lay dutifully on the floor.

"My dog will protect you and your son," I said.

I ran back into the house. Passing through the living room, I saw dots of blood on the tiled floor that hadn't been there before. The shotgun was missing from the couch, as was the box of bullets.

My eyes followed the bloody trail. It went through the living room to the broken slider, and out to the backyard. I nearly let out a yell. I'd handcuffed Vorbe to the refrigerator, something I'd done with countless suspects. He couldn't have freed himself.

I entered the kitchen clutching my Colt

with both hands. The handcuffs were still attached to the handle on the refrigerator door. Lying on the floor beneath them was Vorbe's blood-soaked hand, along with the butcher knife he'd used to cut it off.

I made it into the living room before I threw up. Through the broken slider I could hear the shrill cry of police sirens carrying through the warm night air. They were too far away to bring me any comfort.

I took several deep breaths, and tried to get my strength back. My eyes fell upon a photo album lying on the coffee table. There had been no examples of Vorbe's work hanging in the studio, and I flipped the album open to the first page. A young woman stared back at me. Her eyes were shut tight, her mouth wide open. She was dead.

I riffled through the album. It was filled with head shots of other dead women, their poses identical to the woman on the first page. There appeared to be two dozen photos in all, although there could have been more.

I went outside, and tried to determine where Vorbe had gone. I didn't think he'd gone back to the supermarket, and I went around the side of the house to the front yard.

Standing on the curb, I gazed up and down the street. It was lit up by streetlights, and I saw a gang of long-haired kids trying to break their necks on skateboards and a few older couples walking dogs. Then it hit me what Vorbe was going to do.

He was going to steal a car.

With a car, he could hit the highways and disappear in rush-hour traffic. Florida had thousands of miles of back roads, and most criminals knew how to navigate them. I was going to lose him if I didn't act fast.

I looked in the street for blood. I found a few drops and followed them to an intersection at the block's end, where I saw a mob of men in shorts and T-shirts standing in a driveway, beating the daylights out of someone. As I ran toward them, my cell phone rang. It was Burrell.

"I got your message. What's going on?" she asked.

"I found our killer. It's the grocery store manager."

"Where are you?"

I looked over my shoulder, and read the names off the signs on the corner.

"I'll be right there," Burrell said.

The men had surrounded Vorbe, and were trying to capture him. Two of the men were

479

pointing handguns at him, the rest throwing punches and kicks. Vorbe was fighting back using a Brazilian form of martial arts called capoeira, his body spinning like a top. His bloody stump was wrapped in a towel, the wrist tied with an electrical cord in a makeshift tourniquet. It didn't seem to be slowing him down.

I edged into the crowd. These guys didn't know me, nor I them.

"Where's his shotgun?" I asked.

A blond guy chugging a beer nodded toward the grass. "Son-of-a-bitch knocked my wife down as she was getting out of her car with the groceries. I came out, and took his gun away. Then the fun started."

I watched Vorbe take his punishment. He continued to swirl around the mob, using his one good hand and his feet to fight back. For each blow he delivered, he got three in return. It was suicide.

Then I realized what Vorbe was trying to do. Each time he got near one of the men with a handgun, his hand darted out. He was trying to steal a weapon, and each time he tried, he got a little closer to succeeding.

I couldn't let him get a gun. Or kill someone.

Or escape.

Everything happened for a reason. Mine

was to be here and stop Vorbe.

I aimed my Colt at his legs and fired.

The mob jumped back in unison. Vorbe stopped spinning and stared at the blood gushing out of his right thigh. He screamed and grabbed his leg.

I tackled Vorbe to the pavement and held him down. The wound in his leg was flowing freely. He struggled, making it worse.

"Take it easy," I told him.

He stopped fighting back. I tore off a piece of my shirt, folded it into a square, and pressed it against the wound. Then I looked into his eyes. I have stared at evil before, and it's always the same. Cold, hard, unfeeling.

"I want you to talk to me," I said.

Vorbe was trying to fight back the pain, and didn't reply.

"I want you to tell me about the women in the album in your living room," I said.

Still no reply.

"The police will be here soon. I want you to tell me about them."

He laughed under his breath, taunting me.

I could hear sirens circling the neighborhood. Soon the cruisers were going to find us. I knew what would happen next. The police would arrest Vorbe, and he'd lawyer up, and never say another word to anyone again. It was how evil men tortured those who hunted them. I'd come too far to let that happen.

"Last chance," I said.

Vorbe stared at me, not understanding.

I lifted the compress from his wound. Blood gushed out like a geyser and flowed freely down the driveway. Fear flowed through his eyes.

"My leg," Vorbe gasped.

"First tell me about the women in the album," I said.

I held the bloody compress in front of his face. It was the only thing that was going to stop the bleeding, and keep him alive. I wasn't going to let him die, just like I hadn't let Cheeks die, only Vorbe didn't know that. It was my last card, and I was going to play it.

"Tell me about the women, or I'm walking away," I said.

"But I'll die," he gasped.

"Shit happens."

Vorbe blinked, and then he blinked again.

I used my cell phone to tape Vorbe's confession. The phone let me record Vorbe while filming him at the same time. It was hard to believe what Vorbe was saying, and I didn't think I would have believed it, had I not been inside his house, and seen his garage and photo album with my own eyes.

Burrell pulled up in her Mustang. An ambulance soon followed. I waited until the medics were wheeling Vorbe into the back of the ambulance before I pulled Burrell aside, and played Vorbe's confession for her. When it was done, she shook her head.

"But this can't be true," she said.

"You think he's lying?" I said.

"He has to be."

I took Burrell back to Vorbe's house, and showed her what I'd found.

CHAPTER
SIXTY-TWO

I awoke early the next morning, and drove
to Starke Prison with a headache that no
amount of Advil seemed to shake. I could
have stayed home, and let the prison of-
ficials do what needed to be done. But my
conscience wouldn't let me, so I made the
trip.

At a few minutes past noon, a prison
escort led me down a long hallway in death
row, and slid back a cell door. I entered to
find two men waiting for me. One was tall
and trim, and wore a starched white shirt,
gray slacks, and a black necktie. The other
was small and round, and wore a dark suit
with a turned white collar. Hanging from
his shoulder was a sash with the faces of
black, white, and yellow children.

"You must be Father Kelly," I said.

Father Kelly pumped my hand. "Good
job, Jack."

The taller man also shook my hand. "I'm

Warden Jackson. Yes, a fine job."

"Where's Abb?" I asked.

"He's being brought from the infirmary," the warden explained. "I'm afraid he's not handling this very well."

"Did you tell him what happened?" I asked.

"I tried to have a conversation with him last night," the warden said. "When I told him that the governor had stayed his execution, he collapsed."

"Where's his wife?" I asked.

"I spoke with LeAnn this morning," Father Kelly said. "Her car broke down during the trip here, and she's stranded in some small town."

I folded my arms, and went to the door to wait for Abb. Father Kelly and the warden took a bench, and began to discuss the best way to explain to Abb what had happened. I cleared my throat, and they stopped talking.

"I want to tell him," I said.

"That's not a good idea," the warden said. "Abb may get emotional, even violent."

"He's my client," I said. "He should hear this from me."

The warden looked at the priest. "Tom? What do you think?"

"Jack's right. He knows the details better

than you or I," Father Kelly said.

The warden exhaled deeply. "Very well."

Footsteps rang down the hallway, and I pressed my face to the bars. Abb was being marched down the hall by two guards, and wore a white bathrobe, slippers, and handcuffs. He looked drugged, and moved in slow-motion. The guards led him in, and made him sit on the opposing bench.

I stood in front of him. "Remember me?"

His eyes flickered in recognition.

"I found your grandson," I said.

"Good," he said hoarsely.

"I also found something else." From my shirt pocket I removed a mug shot of Jean-Baptiste Vorbe, and showed it to him. "Remember him?"

Abb glanced at the mug shot, and shook his head.

"His name is Jean-Baptiste Vorbe. He ran a grocery store in your neighborhood."

Abb looked back at me with his dead eyes.

"He was arrested last night. I want you to see what I found in his house." Taking out my cell phone, I held it up to Abb's face and hit the play button. I had made a film of the photographs I'd found in the album in Vorbe's living room. The dead women's faces were barely discernible on my phone's tiny screen, and Abb squinted as they flashed by.

"Those are photographs of the eighteen women you were accused of killing," I said. "I found them in Vorbe's living room."

Abb twitched like he'd been jabbed with a pin.

"Vorbe is a serial killer," I went on. "He killed women in Haiti twenty years ago, then took a boat ride to Florida, and started killing here. He targeted homeless women and runaways who came into his grocery. He offered them jobs, and when they came to his office, he knocked them out, and took them home. After he had his way with them, he put their bodies in the Dumpsters. Then one night, you appeared behind the grocery."

Abb's eyes went wide.

"You don't remember any of this because you were taking a drug called Ambien," I said. "Ambien is a hypnotic, and can have bad side effects. That night behind the grocery you were sleepwalking. Vorbe's victim was lying on the ground. You picked her up, carried her around the parking lot, then put her down, and left."

Abb jerked his head, and looked directly at Father Kelly. The priest nodded confirmation.

"Vorbe decided to frame you," I said. "He

487

followed you home, and put a box of his victims' underwear in your garage. The next morning, he got the police, and showed them a surveillance video taken by a grocery store camera. You know what happens after that."

Abb looked back at me, his face filled with anger.

"The police should have figured this out the day you were arrested," I said. "You didn't have a criminal record, and there were plenty of holes in Vorbe's story. But it didn't work out that way. I want you to hear why."

I held up my phone, and again hit play. A film of Jean-Baptiste Vorbe lying in a bed in the emergency ward at the hospital appeared. Pumped up with drugs, he had continued his confession when I'd arrived, and I had filmed it as well.

"When I called the police that morning, I asked for Detective Cheeks," Vorbe said in his beautiful lilting voice. "At the store we gave free doughnuts to the police, and Cheeks often came in. He was bitter about being passed over for a promotion. I felt certain that he would take this case, and use it to make himself look good."

"Tell me why you kidnapped Sampson," I said in the background.

"I had to silence Abb," Vorbe said matter-of-factly. "I delivered groceries to his wife's house, and LeAnn and I were friends. When LeAnn told me Abb was going to let the FBI hypnotize him, I decided to kidnap his grandson."

"You contacted a group of pedophiles on-line," I said. "Why?"

"I knew Sampson, and what a problem he could be," Vorbe said. "I needed help taking him from his bedroom, so I reached out to those men."

"Did you plan to kill Piper Stone?" I asked.

"No. She came to my office, and asked a few questions. I saw her stiffen, and realized I had tripped up. So I strangled her, and threw her in the trash."

"Is that when you decided to frame Jed?"

"Yes. It seemed an excellent time," Vorbe said.

I folded my cell phone. The cell fell silent. Abb stared at me with his dead eyes. It was like he was there, only he wasn't there. Father Kelly rose from the bench.

"Abb, do you understand what this means?" the priest asked.

"I was sleepwalking when I killed those women," Abb said.

Father Kelly put his hands on Abb's shoulders. "No, no, my son! You didn't kill anyone. You were framed. You're innocent."

"What do you mean?" Abb said.

"The grocery store manager is the real Night Stalker, not you," the priest said. "This has all been a terrible, terrible mistake."

Abb swallowed hard. Then he looked at the warden.

"You still going to execute me?" Abb asked.

He doesn't believe it, I thought. Not a single damn word. I guessed that was what happened when you robbed a man of his freedom. He stopped believing in the truth.

Warden Jackson rose, and put his hand on Abb's shoulder. "On the contrary, Abb. We're going to release you."

"Release me?" Abb said.

"Yes," the warden said. "I spoke to the governor earlier. He believes a terrible miscarriage of justice has taken place, and plans to sign the papers granting you your freedom once they reach his desk."

"I'm going to go free?" Abb asked.

"Yes, Abb," the warden said.

Abb closed his eyes, and for a moment I thought he was going to weep. Instead, he

490

dropped to his knees, and went into a fetal curl on the concrete floor.

CHAPTER SIXTY-THREE

They didn't release Abb from prison right away. Too much had happened in the world during his twelve-year incarceration that Abb didn't know about, and throwing him back into society was not in his best interests. Instead, the state moved him to a minimum security facility a few miles outside of Starke, and had counselors and psychologists work with him, and bring him up to speed. One day I read in the newspaper that he was finally going home.

Not long after, Jessie came to Fort Lauderdale for a basketball game, and decided to see Heather. She asked me to join her. I normally didn't stay in touch with my clients after a case was closed, but the Grimes family was different, and I wanted to see how they were doing. I said yes, and Jessie and I drove over together.

The Grimes house looked different from the last time I'd seen it. The blinds were gone from the windows, and the "No Tres-passing" signs removed from the lawn. I knocked on the front door, and Abb opened it. He'd put on a few pounds, and his hair was shorn and neatly parted. I shed the bag to show him the beer I'd brought, and his eyes lit up.

"Doesn't that look good," he said.

Abb led us inside, where we found Heather and Jed sitting on the living room floor playing with Sampson. Jessie got on the floor, and soon I couldn't tell who was screaming the loudest, Sampson or my nineteen-year-old daughter.

"That beer's getting warm," I heard Abb say.

I followed him outside, where we stood in the front yard and drank beer and talked. Mostly about what had happened to him, but also about fishing and college football and all the things that people in this neck of the world tended to talk about. Abb had heard about Buster, and I got my dog out of my car, and coaxed him into letting Abb pet him.

LeAnn came outside and joined us on the lawn. She wore a simple red dress and a touch of makeup, and had a red bow tied in her hair. Her face had lost its anguish, and in her eyes I saw a spark that had not been there before.

"What's going to happen to Detective Cheeks?" she asked.

Cheeks had been indicted, and I'd heard that the district attorney was going to make an example of him.

"He's going to jail for a long time," I replied.

My answer seemed to satisfy her. From the pocket of her dress, LeAnn removed a small white envelope, and handed it to me. I started to put the envelope into my pocket, and she asked me to open it.

I tore the envelope open. Inside was a color photograph of Abb, Sampson, and Jed sitting on Abb's motorcycle. Their physical resemblance was uncanny, right down to their toothy grins. I slipped it into my shirt pocket.

"That's a keeper," I said.

LeAnn kissed me on the cheek. I wasn't expecting that, or the long hug that came with it. She went back inside without another word.

Abb and I finished drinking the beers. Then, in a quiet voice, he told me how the state was planning to compensate him for the years he'd spent in prison, and pay him for every day he'd been behind bars, adjusted for inflation. He told me the sum, which was over a million dollars, and laughed under his breath.

"One day I'm sitting on death row, the next I win the lottery," he said.

There was no restitution for lost time. But the money was better than nothing. I slapped him on the shoulder, and told him that I hoped he enjoyed the rest of his life.

"I'm sure going to try," Abb said. "There's something I was meaning to ask you."

"What's that?"

"Those Jane Does I was accused of killing. Were the police able to identify them?"

The question hit me hard, and it took a moment for me to realize why. Abb still cared about those women. He'd *always* cared, even when he was sitting on death row, awaiting the executioner's song. He was a good man, and it was a crying shame that no one had seen it before.

"The police found their identification in Vorbe's bedroom," I said. "Their families have been contacted and given the news."

"So it's all finished and done with," Abb said.

I nodded. The case was closed, the files put to bed.

"Good," he said.

Jessie came outside. Her basketball game was in a few hours, and she needed to get back to her hotel. I said good-bye to Abb, and fetched Buster from the bushes. Abb waved to us from the curb as we pulled away.

"Did you have fun?" I asked.

Jessie smiled. I removed LeAnn's photograph from my pocket, and showed it to her. She said, "Oh, wow," under her breath, and didn't speak again until we were sitting in bumper-to-bumper traffic on the interstate.

"Is this why you do it?" my daughter asked.

She was still holding the photo in her hand.

I pulled my eyes away from the road. "What do you mean?"

"You didn't just save Sampson. You saved all of them, Daddy. Is that why you take the chances you take?"

Traffic began to move, and I put my foot on the accelerator. I did not see myself as a savior, or a saint. I just found missing kids. But if my work also brought families back together, and revealed long-hidden truths, then that was fine by me.

"Yes, honey," I said. "That's why I do it."

ACKNOWLEDGMENTS

Without the following people's help, this book could not have been written. A big thank-you to Lisa Buchholz and Richard Theis, who didn't mind when I called them at odd hours with questions, and to my rooting section at Ballantine Books — Dana Issacson, Gina Centrello, the incredible Linda Marrow, and Libby McGuire.

Special thanks to Andrew Vita, Team Adam Consultant with the National Center for Missing and Exploited Children and former Associate Director/Enforcement for the Bureau of Alcohol, Tobacco, and Firearms. His help again proved invaluable in writing this book.

And, finally, I owe a long ovation to my wife, Laura, who can look at anything I write, and always find the story.

ABOUT THE AUTHOR

James Swain is the author of eight bestselling novels. In 2006, he was awarded the Prix Calibre 36 for Best American Crime Fiction. He lives in Florida with his wife, Laura.